D0937614

One Man Advantage

KELLY JAMIESON

DISCARD

This book is a work of fiction. The names, characters, places, and incidents are products of the writer's imagination or have been used fictitiously and are not to be construed as real. Any resemblance to persons, living or dead, actual events, locale or organizations is entirely coincidental.

One Man Advantage
Copyright © 2015 by Kelly Jamieson

ISBN: 978-0-9947491-1-6

All Rights Are Reserved. No part of this book may be used or reproduced in any manner whatsoever without written permission, except in the case of brief quotations embodied in critical articles and reviews

Cover Design and Interior format by The Killion Group
http://thekilliongroupinc.com

R0451042766

PRAISE FOR ONE MAN ADVANTAGE

"*One Man Advantage* is a sweet and sinfully decadent treat for the reader to savor and enjoy page after page. Author Kelly Jamieson creates a wonderfully addictive romance that readers will adore while craving more. Readers will thrill to the detailing that Ms. Jamieson puts into her story and the attention she pays to the game of hockey and the Minneapolis Caribou featured in this story. The characters are portrayed realistically making it very easy to get to know and like Nicole, Logan and the rest of the charming secondary characters that turns this story into a delightful read." ~ *The Romance Studio*

"The attraction between the two is obvious right from the start and you can almost feel the steam radiating from the pages. There is a very light amount of BDSM included in this story but it plays only a minor role. Not only did this story generate a lot of heat but we also got to see a lot of feeling and emotions from both Logan and Nicole. This includes the insecurities both of them have dealt with and tried to overcome since they both felt overshadowed growing up with famous family members." ~ *Romancing the Book*

PRAISE FOR THE NOVELS OF KELLY JAMIESON

"Kelly Jamieson delivers a blazing passionate read that tugs at the heartstrings!" **Carly Phillips,** *New York Times* **Bestselling Author**

"seductive and bewitching from the very start ... Softly romantic and wickedly provocative" *RT Book Reviews* **on Rule of Three**

"Kelly Jamieson now has a permanent place on my keeper shelf and I can't wait to see what she writes next." **Joyfully Reviewed**

"Ms. Jamieson once again gives the reader a richly detailed story that is brimming over with sexual tension, intoxicating desires and intriguing carnal needs that is edgy and psychologically intense..." **The Romance Studio**

"...I love Kelly Jamieson's books and the way that she depicts her characters..." **Sizzling Hot Book Reviews**

CHAPTER ONE

"I guess she's working her way through the team one by one. It'd be faster just to have a gang bang." Cody Burrell, defenseman for the Minneapolis Caribou, smirked at the ESPN reporter who'd just asked him how he'd felt about his ex-girlfriend dating one of his team mates.

His ex-girlfriend being *her*.

Nicole Lambert stared at the television, her mouth hanging open. It felt like the world slowed to a stop for a moment.

He did not just say that on national television! About her!

Maybe she'd heard that wrong. The newscast had gone back to the studio with the announcer moving along with highlights from the hockey game the night before. Which the Caribou had lost. Worse than lost. They'd been handed their asses by the Philadelphia Flyers with a final score of nine to one.

He *had* said it. Nicole blinked as heat slid from her chest up her throat and into her face, and her stomach twisted into painful knots.

Tabarnac de câlisse! Bâtard!

She pressed her hands to her hot cheeks and sat back into her couch, tuning out the rest of the sportscast. Her stomach heaved. Was she going to actually throw up?

A gang bang! Just because she'd dated a few hockey players! A shaft of pain stabbed through her heart. That hurt. That really hurt. The corners of her eyes stung and she blinked rapidly.

Then red-hot anger ripped through her. *Merde*, he was an asshole! Another string of profanities against the church ran through her mind.

Her cell phone buzzed. She lifted her head and stared at it blankly where it sat on the coffee table in front of her. It buzzed again and she reached for it. Taylor Berezowsky, her best friend. Had she just seen that? Nicole pressed the talk button. "Hi."

"Nicole. Hi. Are you watching…did you see…?"

Nicole groaned and fell back into the cushions. "I saw it. What the fuck, Taylor? Tell me I misheard that."

"You didn't." Taylor's voice held an edge of grimness. "Jesus, Nic. Fedor is freaking out here. He's on the phone with Scott right now." Taylor's husband played for the Caribou too, and Scott was their coach.

"*Sacrament*," Nicole breathed.

"I know things are bad when you're swearing in French."

"My god, Taylor. How could he say something like that? In front of the entire freakin' country! The world!"

"I know, I know. Fedor says you should be calling your lawyer and suing his ass."

"*Mon dieu*." She reverted again to French, covering her eyes with her free hand. "Sue him?"

Her miniature Schnauzer lying on the carpet lifted her black and silver head and gave a little whine, obviously picking up on Nicole's agitation. Absently, Nicole reached a hand down to rub Silvia's head.

"Yes," Taylor said. "What is it when you insult someone like that? Defamation? Slander? I don't know, but he can't say things like that. What the hell did you do to the guy, Nic? He's got a hate on for you."

"All I did was break up with him."

"I know that." Nicole could picture her friend's eye roll. "Did you cut his balls off while you were doing it?"

Nicole choked on a laugh. "Maybe figuratively. He wasn't impressed when I dumped him."

"Because he's full of himself. God's gift to hockey and women." She snorted.

Nicole's land line rang. Great. Just effing great. She glanced at the call display on the cordless phone. She didn't recognize the number. "Hold on." She punched the button on the cordless phone. "Hello?"

"Nicole Lambert?"

"Yes?"

"It's Jack Chambers."

She frowned. Jack Chambers... "From the Daily Mail?" she asked. She knew him, he was a sports reporter for the newspaper.

"Yes. I don't know if you saw tonight's Sports Rap on ESPN, but I was hoping to get your reaction to Cody Burrell's comments about..."

Her mouth dropped open again and her condo started a slow spin around her. "You have got to be kidding me!"

"No, I just—"

She clicked the phone off and stared at it as if it was covered with dog poop. She flung it down with a clatter, startling Silvia, whose head lifted again. Nicole spoke into her cell phone. "Holy Virgin Mary," she said to Taylor. "That was a newspaper reporter. Oh my god, Taylor."

"I heard. Oh, Nic. This sucks!"

"I know!" She rubbed her forehead. Her phone rang again. "Not answering," she said through clenched teeth. Silvia stood, stretched, then leaped onto the couch and stared at her.

"No, don't answer it! Want me to come over?"

"No. That's okay." She shook her head, her mind buzzing. "I still can't believe he said that." She sat back and let Silvia climb onto her lap, automatically wrapping one arm around her warm furry body.

"He's a douchebag," Taylor said. "I told you that before. Why'd you ever go out with him?"

"I'm asking myself that right now too."Actually she knew why she'd gone out with him. He had that edge, that dangerous vibe she thought meant he might be into the same kinds of things she liked. The reality was, he wasn't edgy, he was just a jerk. "But *câlisse*, I sure as hell know why I broke up with him. Douchebag is right." Silvia licked her chin and Nicole squeezed her tighter.

"When did you go out with Tyler? I did not know about this."

She sighed. "Saturday night. I wonder if he saw that."

"Well, if he didn't, he's probably going to hear about it. If reporters are already calling you about it, it's not going to go away. Hold on, Fedor's off the phone."

Nicole could hear her best friend's husband talking in the background with his deep, Russian accented voice.

"Scott's furious," Taylor reported.

Nicole sighed. "They always defend him. No matter what stupid thing he says or does."

"Huh. I know. But this is really bad."

"I'm nobody compared to him. I'm just a lowly Communications and Publications Assistant for the team. He's a superstar NHL player."

"He's a superstar tool. This is the height of douchbaggery."

Nicole choked on a laugh. "True. But I mean, the team is hardly going to stand up for me over him."

Taylor was silent. "Nic, I know you don't make a big deal out of it, but everyone knows who your dad is. And your brother. You're not just a lowly assistant. But whatevs, no matter who you are, you don't have to take that crap from him."

"Oh hon. I don't want to make this into a bigger thing than it is. If I just ignore it, maybe it'll go away."

Famous last words. Nicole's phones didn't stop ringing, buzzing and pinging with calls and text messages from friends and reporters for the rest of the evening. And the story ran over and over on the sports channels and on the late news too. By bed time, Nicole wanted to crawl into a hole and never come out. Reporters had dragged out her entire dating history, which yes, had included a few hockey players. She clutched a cushion and chewed on her bottom lip as she watched the television, mesmerized like it was some kind of horrific train wreck that she couldn't look away from.

Nobody came right out and said it, but they might as well have called her a hockey whore. Probably the only thing stopping them was the fact that her father, Jacques Lambert, was a hockey legend, one of the best hockey players of all time and now a co-owner of the new Montreal Saints.

Her phone buzzed once more and she checked the call display. She sighed and clicked the talk button yet again. "*Bonjour, Papa.*"

"*Nicole. Qu'est-ce que tu as fait maintenant?*"

What have you done now? How was she supposed to answer that? "I didn't do anything, Papa," she said in French, which was easier for him.

"Then why is the entire world talking about you and embarrassing us?"

Sure. This was her fault. Of course it was. And he was embarrassed. "Papa. I didn't start it. It was Cody."

She heard his muttered imprecation. She knew what he thought about Cody Burrell. "I've been trying to get hold of Jeff," he said. The Commissioner of the National Hockey League. Fanfuckingtastic.

"Papaaaaa." She closed her eyes. "Don't make this bigger than it has to be. Please stay out of this."

"I think it's too late for that. Christ, Nicole, did you have get tangled up with someone like that?" He gave a long-suffering sigh. "You should have gone into modeling like your mother wanted."

"Models date hockey players," she pointed out. "As you should know." Her mother had been a super successful model when she'd met her dad. And Papa also ignored the fact that Nicole wasn't exactly model material, much to her mother's disappointment and which she had reminded Nicole of many times.

"That's different," he snapped. "And you're missing my point."

"What is your point, Papa?"

"My point is, you don't belong in the hockey world. You're a girl. It can only lead to trouble."

She pursed her lips. After hearing that her whole life, you wouldn't think it would hurt so much, but it still did. The corners of her eyes stung, and when she dragged her fingertips across them, they came away damp. "I just want this to go away," she whispered. "But please, Papa, don't get involved. That'll just make it worse."

"Here, talk to your mother," he said, handing the phone over.

Nicole switched to English to speak to her mother, who wasn't any more sympathetic than her father had been. "What did you do to him to make him say such things?" she asked.

"Mom. He's an asshole."

"Nicole!"

She ended the call before she burst into tears. Her phone immediately buzzed again. With a groan, she saw her brother's name and reluctantly answered, this time in English. "Hey, Julien."

"Nic. What the fuck?"

"I know, I know."

"Are you okay?"

She closed her eyes. The one question her parents hadn't asked. "Not really."

"That fucking shithead," Julien snarled. "Just wait until the game on Thursday." Julien played for the Vancouver Canucks, who were scheduled to take on the Caribou later this week.

"No! Don't do anything." *Tabarnac*, she did not want to see her big brother start some kind of brawl on the ice with Cody. "He's so not worth it. Please don't." Much as she was fantasizing about cutting Cody Burrell's balls off, this time literally, she didn't want a fight, didn't want to see her brother getting hurt.

"Oh, he's worth pounding, all right," Julien snapped. "Hell, I wish I was there." His voice softened. "What do you need from me, Nic? What can I do?"

"Nothing." Her throat tightened. "Thanks, though. I'll just have to deal with this." They talked for a few more minutes, and once again she tossed the phone down. Then she picked it up again and powered it off. She did not need to talk to anyone else about this tonight.

Humiliating. That was the word. She heaved herself off her couch, her body incredibly weary, her limbs stiff and heavy. How was she supposed to go to work tomorrow and face everyone there? *Merde*.

"Time for bed," she said to Silvia, who immediately jumped off the couch and trotted into the bedroom, then sat on the bed and watched Nicole change into her pajamas. Nicole scooped up her little dog and cuddled her against her, pressing her face into Silvia's soft fur. "Oh Silvia." She sighed. "I love you." No matter how bad things were, Silvia loved her too.

Nicole's sleep wasn't exactly restful, her mind whirling. She cycled between burning humiliation and spitting rage, and by morning, she'd worried herself into a tightly wound knot of panic, convinced she was going to be summarily fired the moment she set foot into the offices of the Minneapolis Caribou where she worked.

When she turned her phone on, she found missed calls, and when she walked out of her townhouse condo, she met reporters hanging around outside. She paused, staring at them. Media attention wasn't entirely unfamiliar to her, being the daughter of a hockey legend and having dated a few hockey players, but that was never attention for *her*. Now she worked in Communications with the Caribou, she dealt with the media all the time. She knew those guys, for god's sake. She'd even thought some of them were friends. She eyed them with hostility.

"Guys," she said. "What are you doing here?"

"C'mon, Nicole, talk to us. What did you think about Cody's comments last night?"

For several long painful seconds she considered turning around and bolting back into the safety of her condo. Then she slid her sunglasses onto her nose, lifted her chin and strode toward her car. "*Va te faire foutre*," she muttered under her breath, resolutely ignoring them and their requests for comments.

This was nuts.

She gripped her steering wheel for a moment and swallowed. If she saw Cody today she was going to…she gritted her teeth. Slap him. Punch him. Kick him. Yeah, right. Impotent fury bubbled inside her, a feeling of hot pressure. As she left the parking lot, she stepped on the gas a little too heavily and tossed some gravel out from under her tires in a satisfying spray at the reporters. Then she bit her lip and glanced in her rear view mirror to make sure she hadn't actually hit anyone.

More reporters were hanging around outside the Halstead Center, the arena that was home to the Caribou and their offices. For fuck's sake! Nicole set her jaw, once again ignoring them as she entered the building. She shot a grateful smile at Albert, the security guy who let her in and kept the media out. For now.

Her stomach bottomed out as she once again anticipated how pleased management was going to be about this development and what they were going to do about it.

Behind the reception desk, she dropped her purse into a bottom drawer and sank onto her chair to boot up her computer. She was usually one of the first ones at the office every morning, but voices talking drifted from offices down the hall. Someone was already there and she could just guess what they were talking about. Sure enough, moments later her boss, Breck Travers, Director of Communications for the team, walked into the reception area, followed by Scott Kitchell, the team's coach, General Manager Matt Hay and Joe Thorley, one of the owners of the team.

"Ah, Nicole, you're here," Breck said.

"Good morning." She set her hands on her lap and waited for the shit to hit the fan.

"We were just on a conference call with Jeff in New York," Breck said. "I tried to get hold of you late last night, but you weren't answering."

She pressed her lips together.

"Guess I don't blame you," Breck said, his dark eyes somber. "You okay, Nic?"

His concern made her throat constrict. She nodded. "I'm okay."

"This is shitty," Joe said.

"I gather you know what's going on," Scott added.

She nodded. "Kind of hard not to." She twisted her fingers together.

"So," Joe said. "The league is suspending Cody."

She blinked. Her gaze shot from Joe to Scott to Breck. He nodded. "Yup."

"Really? Suspending him?"

"Jeff's pissed right off." Scott rubbed his face.

Her father must have called him. She closed her eyes, a wave of hot embarrassment sweeping over her.

"If he didn't suspend him, we would have," Joe added. "What Cody said was completely inappropriate. Totally disrespectful. That's just not acceptable. We won't tolerate that."

"Like we don't have enough problems." Scott now pressed his fingers between his eyebrows.

The team had been playing like crap since the season started a little over a month ago.

"I know," Matt said. "Christ. I couldn't decide if I wanted to manage a hockey team or join the circus. Now I'm doing both."

His humor cut through the tension as everyone laughed.

"We're just working out the communications strategy," Breck said. "We'll meet with the media this morning. Cody will apologize."

"He will?"

"He will," he said grimly.

"Great," she said. "Then hopefully the media will leave me alone."

"Are they hounding you?"

"They were outside my condo this morning and they're hanging around outside here too."

"Yeah, I saw them this morning." Breck nodded. "We'll deal with them." He paused. "Nicole, we think you should take some time off."

"What?" She gazed back at him. "Take time off?"

"Yeah." He grimaced. "You know. Just to let this die down."

"Are you firing me?" she asked slowly.

"No! Of course not. We just thought, for your own sake…"

"Things are really busy right now."

"Yeah. Things are always busy, though."

Damn. They wanted her out of the way and she couldn't blame them. She was letting down everyone. Her heart clenched. "So you're paying for my trip to Hawaii?" They all burst out laughing and she gave a crooked smile. "I guess that's a no."

"You know," Matt said. "If we could finish that trade deal and announce it, that would take a lot of the attention off this."

Trade? They were making a trade? "Are you trading Cody?" she asked eagerly.

They all frowned. "Uh. No," Scott said. He rolled his eyes and she knew he wanted to say more. "We need more offensive power. This is all hush hush," he added and she nodded. She knew better than to repeat anything she heard, whether to players, the media or her friends. Sometimes that was hard, since her best friend happened to be married to one of the players.

"Go home," Joe said. "Take a week. This'll all have died down by next week."

It was tempting. The thought of facing the players made her insides burn. Not only Cody, but Tyler, who she'd gone out with once and probably was never going to again. And the rest of the players. She'd only dated one other player on the team— the other guys she'd had relationships with played for other teams—but she counted some of those guys as friends. Facing any of them was going to be embarrassing after what Cody'd said. And with a sinking feeling, she realized it was going to be embarrassing facing anyone who'd seen that little comment by Cody, and that was going to be a lot of people. Sure, she could take off and go into hiding. But she was going to have to face people some time.

"I think they're suspending him for his own protection," Scott said wryly. "His own team mates are pissed at him. Your brother plays here this week. Some of the other guys you've..." His voice trailed off.

Nicole kept her chin lifted and met his eyes. She knew he'd been about to mention the other guys she'd dated who might come to her defense and try to retaliate against Cody on the ice the next time they played the Caribou. The organization had to be annoyed at being put in this position and it was all because of her and her dating history. "I'm sorry," she said, her heart heavy.

"Don't apologize," Breck said. "Cody's the one who crossed the line."

Their support meant a lot to her, but even so, she knew she'd brought this on herself. This was hurting not only her, it was hurting the team and the whole league. And probably her father, who apparently cared more about image than he did about her. *Merde.*

"I feel like the team slut."

That evening, she and Taylor lounged in the great room of Taylor and Fedor's gorgeous Calhoun Parkway home.

"You're not a slut," Taylor said. "More wine?"

"Yes, please."

Taylor plucked her glass from her hand and glided over to the bar where a wine bottle sat in a bucket. The pot lights above the bar illuminated her long blonde hair into gleaming waves of gold down her back. "Are you going to take them up on their offer of some time off?"

"I don't think I have a choice." She accepted the very large, very full glass of Sauvignon Blanc from her friend with a grimace. "I hate running away, but I think they want to get rid of me."

"Oh surely not." Taylor picked up her own glass as she sat gracefully on the red leather couch and tucked her long legs under her.

"Can you blame them?" Nicole rubbed one eyebrow. "I'm causing them a whole lot of grief."

"You didn't do it! It was that asshole Cody! Stop blaming yourself."

Nicole looked down at her wine, a feeling of pressure behind her cheekbones. She sucked briefly on her bottom lip. "I think..." She stopped, her throat closing up, and sipped her wine.

"What, Nic?"

"I think I have to quit my job."

"Whaaat!" Taylor swung her legs to the floor and sat up straight. "Don't be ridiculous!"

Nicole met her eyes. "I'm serious. This is just an embarrassment to the team. They want me to go away for a week, but they're probably too nice to say they want me gone for good."

Taylor snorted. "Or too afraid of a suit for wrongful dismissal. That's crazy, Nic. They love you."

Nicole shrugged.

"And you love your job!"

She did. So, so much. She hadn't been allowed to go as far in hockey as her brother had. No surprise there, since her brother pooped gold and peed champagne, in their parents' eyes. But she'd loved the sport with all her heart. She'd refused to try to follow in her mother's footsteps and go into modeling, like Papa had wanted, instead going to college and getting a degree in Communications. She'd had her eye on jobs in the NHL and had landed this job right out of college. It had meant moving to Minneapolis from Montreal, where she'd gone to university, but as long as she was involved with hockey somehow, it was all good.

"I have some experience now," she said, her voice a little choked. "I'm sure I could get a job somewhere else."

Sure she could. Somewhere else in Minneapolis, big companies like maybe Xcel Energy or Target. Or she could leave Minneapolis and try for a job with a different NHL team. She didn't know of any openings, but she could put out some feelers. But maybe no one else would hire her after this. She sighed.

"What about Tyler?" Taylor tipped her head to one side. "I didn't know you went out with him."

Nicole grimaced. That was what had started this whole shit storm. "I like him. But not enough that I'm going to see him again and put him through hell." She closed her eyes and leaned her head back. "I never should have gone out with him, dammit. I had no idea Cody was going to be such a jerk about it."

"Again, this is not your fault, hon."

"Yes, it is."

"It is not."

"I feel horrible. This has gone viral on all the internet sites, it's all over TV. I feel like I've let everyone down." Nicole sipped her wine. "The one thing I'm not going to do is go out with any more hockey players. Ever."

"Oh, Nic. Take the week off," Taylor said. "Let things die down. Then you can think about this with a clearer head."

Nicole let out a breath. "Okay. I'm going to take that vacation." She smiled at her friend. "Have I told you I love you lately?"

"I know you do."

"And I swear to the blessed Virgin Mary, I'll never get involved with another hockey player."

CHAPTER TWO

Logan Heller was making a ham sandwich when the call from his agent came on his phone. He licked mustard off his thumb as he answered. "Hey, Alvin. 'Sup, dude?"

Alvin didn't snort like he usually did at his greeting. "Logan. Where are you?"

"At home. Grabbing lunch."

"You need to sit down."

"Why?" He popped a piece of ham into his mouth.

"There's a good chance you're going to be traded today."

Logan choked on the ham. He bent over the counter, coughing. He gasped for air, and when he could speak, he said, "Say what? It sounded like you said I'm being traded."

"That is what I said. Apparently there's a deal with the Caribou."

"What? Minneapolis?"

Jesus Christ. He hadn't heard a whisper about this. What was going on?

"I'm gonna find out more," Alvin said. "I'll call you back ASAP. Just wanted to give you the heads up."

Heads up? Logan stared at his phone as he dropped it to the counter. Traded? What the fuck?

It couldn't be true. He couldn't even process it, but it wasn't long before his phone was blowing up. He stared at the screen, lit up with Twitter mentions, Facebook messages and texts. Jesus Christ. He'd barely started trying to scroll through them when his phone rang again.

"Yeah," Alvin said, his voice heavy. "It's a done deal."

"No fucking way!"

"Yeah. Sorry, man. You've been traded to the Caribou for Sly Sorren and Mike Enrick and a second round draft pick."

"You're fucking kidding me."

"I'm not kidding."

Logan rested his elbows on the granite counter of the kitchen in his beach house. He closed his eyes, his gut knotting. "I don't get it," he said slowly. "There've been no rumors. This is right out of the fucking blue."

"I know. But the team has salary cap issues and Minneapolis desperately needs some offensive power. And some leadership. They need you."

"Shit! This is all about money."

"Can't deny that," Alvin said wearily. "It is a business after all. But seriously, the Caribou made a well thought out choice, you will be a benefit to them."

"I don't want to move to Minneapolis! I like it here in California!"

"Minneapolis isn't so bad."

"I know exactly what it's like! I grew up six hundred kilometers from there. Their winters are the same as ours were."

"Your brother's back in Winnipeg. Didn't hear him complaining about the weather."

"That's different. The Jets being back in Winnipeg was huge. Of course he was happy to go back there. But hell, Alvin. It's not just that it's Minneapolis. Moving is a huge pain in the ass. I have a life here."

"It's part of the gig," Alvin said. "That's why you get paid the big bucks."

Logan snorted. But okay, yeah, he did get paid big bucks and he was determined to never take that for granted and act like some prima donna asshole who expected everything he wanted handed to him on a silver platter.

"They want you there next week."

"Christ." He looked around his beautiful house, then out through the sliding glass doors onto the deck and the blue haze of the Pacific Ocean. Kiss that baby good bye. He shook his head. "This sucks big time."

"I know. Listen, though, Logan. You can't have that kind of attitude in front of the media. The Caribou need help on offense, we all know that. They need leadership. They need you. You're going to be happy to go there and give the team all you can, yadda, yadda, yadda."

"Yeah, yeah, I know." Logan sighed. "This doesn't have anything to do with that asshole Burrell, does it?"

"I don't think so. They didn't trade him."

"Shit. That means I have to play with him. Jesus." The Caribou and Burrell's big mouth had been all over the news for the last two days after he'd opened his trap and pissed off the entire hockey world by insulting the daughter of hockey legend Jacques Lambert.

"Go ahead, vent to me," Alvin said. "Get it all out of your system."

"I don't need to vent." Punch someone maybe, but not vent. "I guess I better call my parents before they hear it on the news."

"There's a press conference scheduled for this afternoon at three. Emery's going to call you right away."

Emery Goldberg, the GM of the Condors.

Logan ended the call and stared at his phone for a moment. He'd lived in California for nearly eight years, played for the California Condors his entire pro career. Of course, it was stupid to think he'd play for the same team forever, even though he'd be perfectly happy doing that. But he'd had no inkling that this was in the works. Not a fucking clue.

When his phone rang a moment later, it was no surprise to see Emery's name. He sucked in air and answered the phone.

"Well, this is a really hard call to make," Emery said, his voice sounding tight. "I guess you've heard from Alvin."

"Yeah." Logan stared at the pattern of the granite, the swirls of black and flecks of gold.

"So yeah. Today we made a deal with the Minneapolis Caribou to trade you."

"This is quite a surprise."

"Yep." Emery's voice shook just a little. "Like I said, this is really tough, Logan. I think the world of you, you know that. This was a really hard decision."

Logan rubbed his chest. They'd thought enough of him to sign him to a fucking ten year deal only a year ago. The contract had included a no-movement clause, but it didn't kick in until next year.

"We had to do the best thing for the team, though. We had some salary cap issues."

What the fuck?

Logan rubbed the back of his neck. "There's been no talk about a trade," he said, trying to keep his voice low and steady.

"It happened pretty fast."

Logan nodded. "Yeah, I guess it did."

He strove to control his galloping emotions. He'd always gotten along well with Emery. Which made this even harder. "Well," he said, his voice a little thick. "I've enjoyed playing for the team. Thank you for giving me the opportunity to be a Condor and live in Santa Monica." His throat tightened up even more.

He shoved away the ham and the bread, his appetite gone, and stumbled over to the laptop on the desk. The Caribou had announced it. He was reading their comments when another call came through. He didn't know the number, but he answered it.

"Logan Heller," he said.

"Logan. This is Matt Hay in Minneapolis."

His new boss. He nodded. "Hi."

"Emery let us know he'd talked to you. I just wanted to call and welcome you to the team."

"Thanks. I gotta say, I'm a little in shock here."

"No doubt. This all happened really fast."

"So I heard." He bit his lip at the bitterness that edged his voice. He had to be cool.

"We'll talk more, of course, but I just wanted to let you know how thrilled we were to make this deal. To get a player of your caliber. We need you here, Logan."

"Um. Yeah. Thanks. I'm...ah...looking forward to it." Inspiration struck. "A new challenge. I like a challenge."

That wasn't a lie, exactly.

They chatted for a few more minutes, then Logan thumbed through his contacts to find his dad's cell phone number and called him. If it was already all over the internet, his dad would be getting wind of this soon.

"Hey, Dad." He pinched the bridge of his nose. "Where are you? At the store?" His father owned a couple of big sporting goods stores in Winnipeg.

"Yeah. What's up?"

Logan leaned his head back. "Just got word that I'm being traded."

"Traded? Really?"

Logan filled him in on the details.

"You don't sound very happy."

Logan sighed. "Not really. But I have to put on my game face for this press conference this afternoon. Will you tell Mom and Tag?"

"Yeah. I'll tell Tag to call you later. He'll want to talk to you."

"Yeah. Okay. I'll call Jase now."

"You'll be close to home," Dad said, his voice lightening. "And to Jase. Wow, with Matt at UND, our four boys will all be within what…a thousand miles?"

Logan couldn't help the reluctant smile at his father's happiness. "Yeah."

"Maybe we'll all get together more often. Your mom will be ecstatic."

"Hey, our schedules will still be as crazy," Logan reminded him. "Don't get her all excited for nothing."

"We can drive to Minneapolis to watch you play. She'll be happy about that."

Logan's chest warmed inside. "True. Okay, tell Mom I love her and I'll talk to her soon."

His next call was to his brother Jase. When Jase answered, a blasting whine of what sounded like a power saw almost took his eardrum out and he held the phone away. "What the fuck, man?" he shouted into the phone. "What are you doing?"

"Kitchen renovations," Jase answered. "Hold on, I'm going into the other room."

"You're doing renovations?" Logan asked.

"Supervising." Logan sensed Jase's grin.

"Ah. That's better. At Remi's place?"

"My place," Jase corrected. "Where I am still living, sadly, all alone." Logan smiled at the touch of bitterness in his brother's voice.

"I don't get why she's not living there," Logan said. "It was her house. Why'd she move out when you bought it?"

"She wants to live on her own for a while," Jase said. "Hey, I know it sounds crazy. Much as I don't like it, I do get it. She spent so many years looking after her brother and sister, she wants to be independent. And she wants them to learn to stand on their own feet too. That part I totally agree with. Those kids had her wound around their little fingers. It's kind of funny now, seeing them scrambling and begging Remi to bail them out and she's not here." He laughed. "Her little sister wanted to move back into the house, which is now mine. I told her she could come live with me, but she'd have to pay me rent. She had a little meltdown with Remi about it." Then he sighed. "It was hard for Remi to not jump in. But she did it."

"She'll move in there with you one day, though, right?"

"Remi? Or her sister?"

Logan choked on a laugh despite his ill humor. "Remi, asshole."

"Yeah. She will."

"How's Brianne?" Logan almost hated to ask the question. His brother's ex-girlfriend had gotten knocked up right around the time they'd broken up and Jase was apparently the father. This was a sensitive issue for Jase and his current girlfriend.

"Good. I haven't seen her much. Only about four more weeks till the baby's due."

Jesus. Logan felt like a shit for complaining about being traded when Jase had so much bigger issues to deal with. A baby. With a woman he didn't love and didn't want anything to do with. He was going to be a father. Holy crap.

"Did you talk to Brianne about that paternity test?"

Jase cursed. "You guys bugged me about that all summer."

Yeah, Logan and the rest of the family had been on him about that when they'd all been home in the summer. Strangely, Jase had been kind of resistant to the idea, saying he didn't want to be an asshole; he just wanted to live up to his obligations and take responsibility.

"You know I don't want to do that."

"You *have* to do it. You know you do. I get that you want to man up and take responsibility and all that crap. Admirable. Seriously. Especially for you." Jase had spent most of his life avoiding responsibility. Nah, that wasn't true. When it came to hockey, he was serious and mature. But he did like to have fun.

"Fuck you too," Jase said mildly.

"Come on, this wouldn't be the first time a girl trapped a rich guy by getting pregnant."

"I'm not being trapped. Remi and I are together and nothing's going to change that. Even if Brianne had some twisted idea that I was going to marry her because of this, I've made sure she knows that's not going to happen."

"She's still going to get money out of you, though."

"Yeah. I'll do what I have to do for the baby."

"And you're sure it's yours."

"Yeah."

"You can't be a hundred per cent sure," Logan reminded him. "Unless you get that test done."

"Yeah." Jase sighed. "I know."

Weirdly, Logan was kind of jealous of Jase. Not the mess with the ex-girlfriend and the baby, but...well, he was going to be a dad and he had Remi.

This past summer, Logan had spent time at home, at the lake with his family and their friends the MacIntoshes. Scott MacIntosh, who was his older brother Tag's age, was married and had two little kids. Now Jase had Remi, and a baby on the way, and when Tag had started dating Kyla MacIntosh, who'd grown up into quite a sexy babe, Logan had felt kind of...left out. Lots of his buddies were married now too. Somehow, puck bunnies who hung around the arena didn't excite him anymore.

He sighed. "Good. Well, I have some news."

He proceeded to update Jase, who was as flabbergasted as he'd been. "Christ! Not even a rumor! What the hell, man?"

"I know."

"It is closer," Jase said. "And you'll be in our division, which means we'll play each other more often too." He gave an evil laugh and Logan remembered the last time they'd played against each other and the hit Jase had leveled him with at center ice.

Logan shook his head, smiling, as they ended the call. His smile faded though as he looked around the house on the beach that had been home for the last few years. Dammit. Starting all over in a new city wasn't exactly what he'd had planned for this year.

His game had been going well so far this season. He already had ten goals and eight assists. The fans liked him there in Santa Monica. He never would have imagined this was coming.

He started scrolling through Twitter. One corner of his mouth lifted in a wry smile at some of the invectives against the management of the Condors. "Goldberg's lost his mind!" one person declared. "He just royally screwed the Condors!" another Tweeted. People were pissed off that he'd been traded. Well, good. He wasn't alone then. Except he couldn't go on Twitter and tell the world how he felt.

Then he saw the other comments—suggestions that he was being traded because he was screwing around with the coach's wife. That he wasn't getting along with the coach. That he and Lamppinen, one of the other centers, had been in a power struggle.

He leaned back in his chair. Jesus Christ. What a fucking nightmare. People were nuts!

The press conference. He'd set things straight there. There'd been no goddamn affair with Dave's wife. He and Dave got along great. Sure they had differences of opinion sometimes, who didn't? As for Lamppinen—yeah, he annoyed Logan at times, but that was just crap.

He fucking hated that this could happen to him without having any say in it whatsoever. But that was the game. This was how it went. It happened to other players, all the time. It was a reality they had to deal with.

But it still sucked donkey balls.

Later that afternoon, he faced the media. After eight years in the NHL, he was used to this. Being one of the Heller brothers, one of the few families to ever have three siblings playing in the NHL at the same time, had attracted a lot of attention. Plus he and his brothers were all damn good players. If he did say so himself. He was often interviewed by media during and after games. He'd had to put on a game face many times, after crushing losses where he had to come up with something positive to say, once after one of his team mates had been hauled off the ice on a stretcher with life-threatening injuries. But this...this was pretty hard.

It was hard to hide his dismay at being traded, but as usual, he never liked to let on he was anything but happy and nonchalant. So he kept his answers brief and smiled a lot.

"So were you surprised by this deal, Logan?" one reporter asked.

"Yeah, I was." He looked around the room in the Santa Monica Coliseum where media events were held, lights glaring on him, the room full of television cameras, photographers shooting still images, reporters sitting there with smart phones and recorders thrust toward him. "I got the call earlier this afternoon from my agent, giving me a heads up, and that was the first I'd heard of any trade plan. So yeah, it was a bit of a shocker."

"Emery Goldberg seemed a little shaken up about this too when he announced the deal. How'd that phone call with him go?"

"It was a bit tough," Logan said honestly. He started to say more and got a little lost. His smile felt more like a grimace. "Yeah, it was tough."

"The Caribou are obviously making some big changes and trying to take their game up a notch. What are your thoughts on the team and how you'll fit in there?"

"Well, I haven't had much time to give that a lot of thought. They've got a good team there, though, great goaltending, good defense. I'm hoping I can contribute on the offense." He shrugged. "I'll just play the game I've always played. I'm looking forward to it."

"Assistant coach Brad Laasch was your coach in Dartmouth. What'll it be like playing for him again?"

"Really looking forward to that." And that was true. "Brad taught me a lot back then and I've always considered him a great mentor. It'll be awesome working with him again."

"Had you really heard no trade rumors at all?"

"Not a sniff." The reporters laughed and Logan gave them a crooked grin, lifting his hands in the air. "Seriously."

"You just signed a ten year deal with the Condors last year," another reporter asked. "How do you feel about that now?"

"Well, honestly, when I signed that deal, I intended to play here in California for the duration of that contract. Nobody likes to be traded, but...sh...er...stuff happens." Another murmur of laughter swept the group. "I feel fortunate to be going to a hockey club that has such a great reputation for being well managed, good people to work for, and I'm looking forward to contributing there."

"How do you feel about playing with Cody Burrell?" a reporter asked with a smirk.

The room went silent other than a clicking camera and Logan kept his face carefully neutral. "Cody's a talented hockey player."

Finally it was over. As Emery stepped up to the microphone to say a few more words, Logan headed to the side of the room. Some of his team mates had showed up and gave him solid slaps on the back and shoulder. He smiled and nodded, emotion rising in his chest.

"Beers after this," Kevin said in his ear. "We're buying."

"Damn right you are."

CHAPTER THREE

Hawaii wasn't in the budget, but Nicole didn't want to hang around in Minneapolis with reporters camped outside her condo. At a bit of a loss as to where to go and what to do, she debated heading to Montreal to visit her parents or her old college roommate who still lived there, but *merde*, the media in Montreal would be even more rabid about this story. Any Canadian city was out of the question—this was hitting the news way more up there than it was here. Hockey wasn't nearly as important to American sports fans as the current NFL season.

She would've gone to Vancouver to visit Julien, but dammit, his team was on a road trip and he was going to be in Minneapolis. So she spent the week in New York City, lost and unnoticed—and a little lonely—among the millions of people there. She went on a shopping spree that was intended to be retail therapy, but didn't really make her feel much better. Though she did now have some lovely new clothes and boots. She did some sightseeing in the chilly November weather— museums, Central Park, the Statue of Liberty. She even got her hair cut and highlighted, and a French manicure. She wasn't one to spend a lot of time on feminine frivolities, in fact she didn't think she'd had a manicure since she'd left home to go to university. Her mom had always taken her for manicures and pedicures and facials, maybe hoping that some day her ugly duckling tomboy daughter would turn in to swan. So much for that hope. But maybe looking her best would give her bruised and battered confidence a little boost.

And she thought a lot. The hurt and humiliation from Cody's remarks faded, although she still felt a little stab whenever she thought of them. Although his words had been cruel, she forced herself to examine them for truth. He wouldn't have said them if she hadn't had relationships with hockey players in the past. So she *had* brought this on herself.

Then she thought more about her job and whether it was really a good idea for her to work with a hockey team. If she was going to hold herself to that vow to never ever get involved with a hockey player again, she was not exactly avoiding temptation by going to work every day for the Minneapolis Caribou.

Her heart contracted though, thinking about giving up her job, about having to take a job in some other business. She loved hockey with a passion and loved this way of being involved with it. Sure, her position wasn't high level, but she'd only been out of college five years. She had every intention of learning the business part of the sport as well as she knew the game itself and working her way up. There was no reason a woman couldn't do that.

But she also had to think about the team and whether having her there was going to be detrimental to them after this. Which really, really sucked ass.

It was on the flight home that she finally made her decision. She'd run away to New York with her tail between her legs, but maybe it had been good to have some time and distance to think about things. To let things settle inside her. She loved her job and she shouldn't have to give it up because of one asshole's stupid remarks on national television. She wasn't going to run away again. She was going to walk into the office tomorrow with her head held high and anyone who wanted to mess with her could go screw themselves. She'd ignore all the crap and just focus on doing her job, keeping her career goals in sight. But the one thing she was not going to do was get involved with another hockey player. That vow she'd made to Taylor still held.

So when the man sitting beside her on the flight home Sunday afternoon started talking to her, she smiled and listened. He was a computer programmer at General Mills.

Kind of cute, even with the glasses. What the heck, he wasn't a hockey player, and he didn't seem to have a clue who she was. So she ended up with a date with him for the following week. She might as well go out with someone outside the business. In the terminal, they exchanged cell phone numbers and a plan to meet for drinks Thursday evening, then she drove to Taylor's house to pick up Silvia. She rang the bell, found the front door unlocked and walked in with easy familiarity. "Hello! Anyone home?"

Of course they were home, with the door unlocked, but who knew where they were in the ginormous mansion. Maybe she should have reminded Taylor what time she was coming home. *Merde*, they were probably in bed playing sheet shinny.

She made a face, dropped her purse on a table and wandered in to the great room. Empty. Hmmm. And where was Silvia? She should have come running to greet her with ecstatic joy. Well. Should she check the bedroom?

"Hey," she called, moving down the hall. "You guys home?"

She smacked right into a wall of naked man chest which emerged from a bedroom. "Oomph!"

He grabbed hold of her upper arms. "Whoa there. Who the hell are you?"

She gazed up at him, every sense taking him in, her eyes wide, her mouth open, the scent of spicy male shower gel and humid warmth enveloping her. *Tabarnac,* what a man. His grip on her arms was powerful and yet surprisingly careful. He glared down at her with a knee-weakeningly authoritative stare. Tall. At least several inches over six feet tall, since she was five nine and her new boots had three inch heels. Broad enough to take up the entire width of the hall. Drops of water beaded on wide muscular shoulders and a few trickled down over sculpted pecs and a—*mon dieu de câlisse*—eight pack abs and then lower still into a thatch of dark hair at his groin and...she gulped and tried to pull away from him, up close and personal with his nakedness. He released her and whipped a towel from around his neck to wrap it around his hips, but not before she got a glimpse of his package. Wow. Impressive.

She blinked and opened her mouth, her heart thudding. "Who am I? Who are *you*?"

He scowled at her. "I'm a friend of Fedor's."

"Well, I'm a friend of Taylor's. Where are they?" She frowned. A shiver worked its way over her flesh beneath his fixed stare, his narrowed eyes and the dark scruff of beard on his square jaw giving him a dangerous air. Had this guy murdered them or something? But then why would he be taking a shower in one of their bathrooms?

"They took some mutt for a walk."

"Mutt!" Her fingers curled into her palms. "Silvia is no mutt! She's a purebred Miniature Schnauzer!"

"Oh." He tilted his head slightly. "Ah...it's yours?"

"Yes. They've been looking after her while I was out of town." She folded her arms across the chest of her brand new Jones New York pea coat, her new leopard print scarf wrapped around her throat, and tapped the pointy toe of her new boots. "And once again...you are...?"

"Logan Heller."

She blinked. *Câlisse!* She should have recognized him, but with his damp hair all darkly slicked back and...well, naked, she'd been a little distracted. She frowned. "Er...what are you doing here?" She didn't recall the Condors being in town until late December.

"Staying with Fedor. Till I find a place of my own." His towel slipped low on his hips and Nicole's eyes were drawn to the way his sculpted obliques arrowed down to his groin, his hip bones square and strong looking. *Tabarnac de câlisse*, she wanted to lean over and lick every one of those drips of water off that incredible body. Or maybe fall to her knees and...

When she looked up, she saw he was smiling knowingly and checking her out in pretty much the same way. She swallowed. "Maybe you should get dressed before we continue this confusing conversation."

"What's confusing about it?" He shrugged and ran a hand through short wet hair, obviously unconcerned about being naked. Hockey players wandered around the locker room naked all the time. She'd accidentally run into a naked hockey player more than once when she'd been down near the dressing room after a game.

"Why are you here?"

He regarded her with pursed lips, a shadow flickering across his brown eyes. "Not into hockey, are you?"

Her eyes widened. He didn't know who she was. She couldn't help but grin. "A little," she lied. She tossed her newly highlighted hair behind her shoulders. "Why?"

He shrugged, and the towel slipped again. This time he reached for it and adjusted it on his hips, drawing her eyes yet again. Heat built inside her, starting low down between her legs and spreading through her body. "If you followed hockey, you'd know I was just traded to the Caribou."

Her jaw went slack again. "Traded?"

"Yeah." His eyes narrowed. "What?"

"*Mon dieu*," she whispered, lifting her hands to her mouth. "So they did it." She'd carefully avoided watching television or reading newspapers while she'd been in New York. "Who'd they trade?"

His eyes narrowed. "Sly Sorren and Mike Enrick. And a second round draft pick. Why?"

She sank her teeth into her bottom lip. So it wasn't Cody. They'd said they weren't trading him, but she couldn't help but have that faint hope. Oh well. "Oh. Um. I was hoping it wasn't Fedor."

"Oh yeah, you said you're a friend of Taylor."

"Um. Yeah."

His eyes warmed as he studied her, gaze again tracking over her body. The way he looked at her made her bones melt, made her feel like he knew every kinky thing she liked to do in bed. Heat flashed beneath her skin at his sexy perusal.

"You almost look like her sister."

Nicole blinked. She'd never heard that before. Yes, they were both blonde and similar height, but Taylor was elegant and feminine, where Nicole was athletic and still felt like the tomboy she'd been as a kid. Huh. Must be the new highlights and clothes. "We're not sisters." Once again her gaze dropped to his remarkable chest and abs.

"I told you who I am." He gave her a slow smile. "You gonna tell me your name?"

"Oh." She bit her lip. "Do I have to?" Damn, that was the wrong thing to say.

He grinned and leaned one shoulder against the wall. "No. But it'd be nice to know what to call you. Other than...hot."

Every nerve ending in her body went on high alert and her nipples hardened. *Sacrament*! This was just cruel!

Merde, she *was* a hockey whore. She closed her eyes against the wave of intense attraction she felt for this guy. She didn't even know him. All she knew was he was a hockey player, for god's sake, and she wanted to lick him.

"You okay?"

She opened her eyes and saw his lifted eyebrow. "Fine." She took in a deep breath and let it out. "I'm Nicole Lambert." She pronounced it the French way, with the long *i* in Nicole, the soft *a* and the rolled *r* in Lambert, not the flat English way.

"Hi, Nicole." Then recognition flashed in his eyes. "Nicole Lambert."

She wanted to drop her eyes, imagining what he was thinking. But instead she lifted her chin and met his eyes.

Holy shit.

Logan had met her dad a number of times, but he'd never met her and hadn't recognized her. She kept a pretty low profile usually, but last week she'd been all over the news after that asshole Burrell's stupid remarks.

She was hockey royalty, the daughter of Jacques Lambert. Apparently she also worked for the Caribou, he'd gathered from the news stories.

He slowly straightened, flashing her another smile. "Hey. Nice to meet you."

She gave a tight smile in return, her cheeks pinking up. "Likewise."

"Uh..." He felt he should offer some kind of sympathy for what had gone down, but had no clue what to say. Maybe it was better to just ignore it and pretend it had never happened. "I should get dressed," he finished lamely.

"Good idea." But just as he turned away to go back into the bedroom Fedor and Taylor had offered him, he caught the way her eyes dropped to his butt in the towel. He caught the flash of interest on her face and his cock instantly hardened. Holy hell. Girls checked out his ass all the time, but the way she looked at it…Christ, never mind. What was he thinking?

He hung the towel in the attached bathroom, ran a comb through his wet hair, then grabbed a pair of jeans and a long-sleeved T-shirt lying over the arm of a chair in the room. When he emerged, he found her in the living room looking out the front window.

"I'm not sure where they got to," he said and she jumped and whirled around. "Fedor and Taylor, I mean. And your dog. They probably went to the park."

"It's getting dark."

"Are you worried about them?"

She frowned. "No." She'd unbuttoned her jacket, but still wore it, her hands shoved into the pockets making her shoulders hunch a little.

"Take your coat off and stay awhile." He might as well play host while Fedor was AWOL. "Can I get you a drink? Coffee?"

"No thanks. I just want to get Silvia and get home."

"You were out of town?" He sat on the leather couch.

"Yeah. New York. I had to…get away for a while." The way her gaze caught his, then skittered away, told him she was wondering if he knew about what had happened.

"I don't blame you." He leaned back and lifted one leg to cross his ankle over his knee. "That was quite a shit storm."

There, it was out there. She nodded slowly, moving closer. She perched on the edge of a chair. "Yeah. I'm hoping things have died down now."

"I think they have. Now they're all talking about me."

She smiled, and it was fucking stunning. His breath left his lungs all at once.

She was one of those women who looked like nothing special, until you looked closer and saw the perfect bone structure, the creamy skin, the glow of health. Or until she smiled and her face lit up. Her big eyes weren't accentuated with a bunch of shadow and mascara, and her full lips wore only a light sheen of gloss. He'd dated a model who'd been like that. With no makeup and her hair not done, she'd been the girl next door. But in photographs, with the full hair, makeup and clothes deal, she'd turned into a glamazon. He could see Nicole being like that. Hell, just a smile turned her into a goddess.

Wasn't her mother some kind of supermodel back in the day? He seemed to remember Jacques Lambert being married to a gorgeous model.

"Yeah, I guess Logan Heller being traded is pretty big news."

She knew who he was. His chest warmed.

"Unfortunately," he said, unable to stop the bitter word from leaving his lips. Then he pasted his smile back on.

"You're not happy about it." She said it as a fact.

"Nobody likes to be traded."

She nodded. "True. But it's a really good organization to play with."

"Riiiight. With an injured list as long as my arm, a jerkoff mouthpiece defenseman who got himself suspended and a record of two, nine and one, I'm sure it is." Shit. *Shut the fuck up, man.* He knew better than to let uncensored remarks out to anyone he talked to. Especially someone who worked for the Caribou.

"Okay, well, we have some challenges. I gather we lost to B.C. the other night?"

"Oh yeah."

She made a face. "I was trying to avoid the news while I was gone." She sat back a little in her chair. "So I didn't hear about the game. Or the trade."

"You work for the Caribou."

She nodded. "I'm their Communications and Publications Assistant."

He nodded. "Cool."

"For now."

He tilted his head. "For now?"

She sighed. "As long as they don't fire me."

His chin jerked down. "Why would they do that?"

"Do you even have to ask?" She rolled her eyes. "I've caused the team all kinds of embarrassment. They don't need that."

"You didn't do anything," he said slowly.

"Whatever." She waved a hand. "It's going to be awkward. I wouldn't blame them if they wanted to get rid of me. I know what people think of me." She bowed her head, her long, shiny fall of gold hair obscuring her face. Then she looked up, her chin once again in the air.

"Um...what do you mean? What do people think of you?"

"You tell me," she challenged him, blue eyes flashing. "What do you think of me?"

CHAPTER FOUR

Logan grinned. "I already told you. I think you're hot."

She scowled. "Yeah, see, that really doesn't help."

His smile faded. "Um. You lost me, gorgeous."

She blinked at him.

At that moment the front door opened, the alarm pinging softly, and the scrabble of paws on hardwood floors filled the air. They both turned toward the foyer and the mutt he'd met earlier hurtled into the room and threw itself at Nicole. She opened her arms and let the dog jump onto her lap, gathering it up in a wriggling, licking embrace.

"Silvia! My baby! I missed you so much!"

He sat back and watched with amusement as she lavished love and affection on the dog.

"You're here!" Taylor rushed in, unwinding a thick scarf from around her neck, her cheeks flushed from the cool November air. "Sorry, Nic! Oh wow! Look at you." She paused and studied Nicole. "You look great! Love the hair. When did you get in?"

"Not long ago."

"So you met Logan." She looked back and forth between them.

"Yep," Logan said, not mentioning how they'd met. "We were just chatting while Nicole waited for you."

"Good, good. Sorry we weren't here." Taylor tossed her jacket onto an ottoman and sank down on the couch. "We took her for a walk and it was so nice we just kept going." She looked up at her husband, who'd followed her in. "I think we need to get a dog."

Fedor groaned. "Oh no."

"What? You liked having her around. Last night you were playing with her."

Fedor grinned. He was an ugly son of a bitch, but had a heart of gold. People might wonder how the hell he'd landed a hot babe like Taylor for his wife, with his crooked nose, missing teeth (albeit not noticeable at the moment wearing perfect dentures) and scarred forehead and chin, but obviously Taylor had fallen in love with the man inside the battered body. "Yes," he admitted in his still slightly accented voice. "She is fun."

Taylor gave a satisfied smile. "It will be good practice for us."

"Practice?" Logan asked.

"For when we have kids."

Fedor choked and Logan laughed.

"I should go." Nicole stood, the dog still in her arms.

"Oh don't rush off!" Taylor stood too. "Stay for a drink or something. Dinner."

"I shouldn't. I have to get home and unpack and…I have to work in the morning."

"Oh just one drink! I want to hear about New York and what you did all week. And I haven't packed up Silvia's stuff yet."

Silvia's stuff? This *was* like having a kid, apparently.

"Okay." Nicole sat and lowered Silvia to the floor. She slipped her jacket off.

"I'll get some wine," Taylor said. "Fedor, can you find Silvia's bag? I think some of her toys are in the den and her dishes are in the kitchen."

Taylor and Fedor both disappeared, leaving him alone with Nicole again.

"So you're staying here." She crossed her long legs. She wore black trousers and his eyes dropped to her feet in pointy toed, high heeled boots. Just the kind he liked. Naked, with those sexy boots…favorite fantasy. Well, one of several. His gaze tracked back up, over the teal blue turtle-neck sweater that hugged her body. She was slender, but with strong shoulders, still feminine, especially those nice breasts outlined by the soft sweater.

"Yeah. Fedor was nice enough to offer a place to stay since I was shipped out on such short notice."

"How do you know him?"

"He used to play for the Condors. Till he got traded about three years ago."

"Oh that's right. That's when I met Taylor and we got to be friends."

Taylor returned with a glass of wine which she handed to Nicole, then turned to Logan. "Logan, what would you like? Probably a beer?"

"Yeah. But I can get it."

Nicole watched him stand, his big feet bare on the plush carpet. Her gaze moved back up over long legs and powerful thighs in those faded jeans, then over the long-sleeved navy blue T-shirt that hugged his chest and shoulders. When he turned to walk away, she couldn't help but watch his tightly-muscled butt. Her pussy gave a warm squeeze.

Oh, he was just delicious.

He disappeared and she looked at Taylor, who watched her with one eyebrow lifted.

"What?"

Taylor shook her head. "Nothing. How are you? Really?"

"I'm okay." She straightened her shoulders and smiled at her friend. "You know."

"Did you see Cody's apology?"

Nicole blinked. "Noooo. I didn't."

Taylor made a face. "I'm sure the league made him do it, but he sounded sincere."

Nicole pursed her lips. "He should have been flogged."

"Oh, you and your kinky toys," Taylor said with a laugh.

Nicole couldn't help but smile. "I don't have a flogger."

"No, you just like guys who do. Seriously, though, it was good that he did it. You can probably find it on the internet somewhere."

"Yeah. Maybe some day. So. You have a house guest."

"Yep." Taylor smiled. "He's a good guy. Not all that happy to be here right now. Fedor's really happy, though, he thinks Logan will be good for the team. Things have been really tense."

Guilt stabbed Nicole in the gut. "Have they?"

"Not just because of Cody. The trade kind of shook everyone up. Which might be a good thing. They lost again the other night."

"Yeah, Logan mentioned that."

"Your brother got two goals."

Nicole smiled. "Good for him."

"The team needs something," Taylor continued. "Hopefully Logan is it."

"That's a lot of pressure to put on one man," Nicole said slowly.

"Hmm. Yeah."

That one man walked back into the room carrying a beer, followed by Taylor's husband. Nicole's breath caught a little in her throat. She watched Logan sit on the couch again, leaning back casually, legs spread wide, and once again she couldn't seem to stop herself from looking at him, her gaze going to the bulge at his crotch. And once again all her girl parts drew up into a squeeze.

When she looked up, he was watching her too, amusement tipping the corners of his mouth up. *Ostie.* She tugged at the turtleneck of her sweater.

"Did Silvia behave herself?" she asked Taylor.

"She was a perfect angel." Taylor stroked Silvia's head with a smile. "I really do want a dog of my own."

"Dogs are special," Nicole agreed. Awareness of Logan watching her made every nerve ending in her body tingle.

"So tell us about New York," Taylor said brightly. "What did you do?"

Taylor convinced Nicole to stay for dinner. They all ended up in Taylor and Fedor's huge kitchen, sitting at the big island drinking wine and cooking. Logan wasn't much of a cook, but Fedor jumped right in to help peel shrimp while Nicole chopped vegetables. Taylor directed everyone and Logan found himself slicing a crusty loaf of bread and spreading it with the garlic butter Taylor had whipped up.

After hearing about Nicole's trip to New York, talk turned to hockey.

"Jacoby's just started skating again," Fedor said, going through the injuries the team had recently had. "He had a broken foot. Dewey missed nine games because of a broken thumb. Now Cody's suspended. Not that he was doing a lot for the team anyway." He shook his head as he tossed another shrimp into a colander.

"Burney got off to a bad start this season too," Nicole added, referring to the goaltender. "He has some personal stuff going on that hasn't helped him."

Logan looked at her, sitting there deftly chopping tomatoes.

"We have some good players," she continued, unaware of his scrutiny. "Things just aren't clicking."

"Distractions don't help either," Fedor said. Then he realized what he'd said and shot a glance at Nicole. "I...uh...didn't mean you."

Nicole looked up at him and shot him a smile. "I know. The team was in trouble before that even happened."

"I think Coach should put you on a line with Dewey and Tyler," Fedor said to Logan.

"I don't know." Nicole shook her head and set down her knife. "Dewey's been struggling too since his injury."

"Playing with Logan might help," Fedor said.

"Maybe. With all the new guys brought up, it's been hard to find good match-ups. Scott's been juggling the forward lines so much, trying to find some chemistry, but it hasn't been working."

Logan realized he had stopped spreading butter and was staring at Nicole, his jaw a little slack.

"I'm thinking Logan would work well on a line with Adam and Danny," she continued. "Danny's got almost twenty assists this year. I can see him feeding Logan the puck really well."

She shrugged. "Of course, they'll have to see you guys skate together. Chemistry's a hard thing to predict."

Jesus Christ. He was in love.

He blinked at Nicole as she picked up the cutting board and carried it to the stove where Taylor stood stirring some chopped garlic in sizzling olive oil. He'd thought she was attractive when they'd first bumped into each other in the hall. Now...he was in love. Seriously.

She had to have been reading his fucking mind, because he'd already been thinking about who the coach was going to put him with, examining the possibilities and thinking that, yeah, Danny Mohan and Tyler Gladstone and him would make a pretty powerful offensive combination. But she was right. Sometimes you couldn't predict chemistry. Huh.

"Talbot's line has been doing a pretty good job," she continued. "They're pretty strong defensively, but they do create some good offensive chances."

Something expanded in Logan's chest, big and warm, as he listened to her. They talked more hockey, Nicole participating in the discussion with such confidence and knowledge that he felt himself sliding deeper and deeper into...something. Okay, maybe it was crazy to think he was in love with someone he'd just met, but he was definitely in lust with her, and holy crap, it wasn't just wanting to get her naked and wrap that long hair around his hands, it was...attraction. Serious attraction. To more than just her hot body and pretty face. Jesus. This was kind of crazy.

Why the hell had she been dating a loser like Cody Burrell? Logan didn't know him well personally, but on the ice, the guy was a loudmouth who liked to take cheap shots, and apparently he was just like that off the ice too, judging by his treatment of Nicole.

"If only we were the ones making the decisions," Nicole said with a grin. She met his eyes and he smiled back at her. She blinked a little and looked away.

"Yeah," he agreed. "But I think Scott has a good head on his shoulders."

"I respect him," Fedor said. "He's been frustrated like the rest of us."

Finally Taylor made them change the subject and talk about something else. Logan listened politely as they tried to sell him on the city, although he couldn't help but think regretfully of his beachside home in California. In some ways it was shitty, but it was the reality of his life and he was going to have to make the best of it. And maybe having Nicole Lambert there might make it a little easier to adjust.

The next morning, Nicole arrived at the Halstead Center and this time no media swarms greeted her. She kept her chin up and a smile in place as she greeted other Caribou staff, even though she was hyperaware of their looks and hearty smiles, and the glances they exchanged as she settled in at her desk. She took a deep breath, her skin hot and itchy. The atmosphere in the office was thick with undercurrents. But she could do this.

After a week away, she had a ton of emails to go through, many of which led to items being added to her to do list—research, proofreading, office supplies to order, photography requests to deal with. It was good to be busy.

"Welcome back!" Breck greeted her when he came in. "How was your holiday?"

She forced a smile. "It was fine. I went to New York."

"You look great. Like the hair. Come on into my office, we have a ton of stuff to go over. I just need coffee."

"I'll bring it for you." She poured him a cup and added the milk and sugar he liked, then carried it into his office, along with a notepad and pen.

"Thanks. Did you hear about the trade when you were away?"

"Um. Yeah."

"There's a lot to do." Breck threw himself into the chair behind his desk. He grabbed the coffee she'd set there and took a big gulp. "A lot. As you know, Logan Heller is joining the team as of today."

"I met him last night."

He lifted one eyebrow.

"He's staying with Fedor and Taylor," she hastened to explain. "Taylor was looking after my dog, so I, um…ran into him…" Her cheeks heated. "When I went to pick her up last night." She was probably being way oversensitive, imagining that he was thinking something else of her.

"Ah. So. We need to arrange for photographs for him. He needs security access, we need his photo added to the website, Faceoff, you know all the stuff." He waved a hand. She nodded. "Other things on the website need to be updated with the changes. There are a ton of media requests we need to deal with that piled up while you were away."

She scribbled notes on her notepad.

"We'll want to hold a press conference ASAP to introduce Logan to the Minneapolis media. We want new team photos done. Also we want to add him to the billboard campaign, so we need another photograph to match the ones of Burney and Mohan. You can set that up with Ryan." Ryan Sender, the team photographer.

"Okay."

They went over some other things that needed to be done, and then he said, "And you can help Logan find a place to live."

She blinked. "A place to live? Me?"

"Yeah. You know the city. See what he wants to do—rent, buy, whatever—scope out some good places and take him to have a look. We need to get him settled in."

"That'd be 'other duties as assigned'?" she asked dryly.

He laughed. "Exactly. Okay. Logan's meeting with us at ten. I'll let you know if there's anything else he needs after that. You look after him, okay? We want to make this transition for him as seamless as possible. He doesn't need a lot of hassles to take his mind off his game."

Oh yeah, she'd like to look after him, all right.

Tabarnac, she had to stop thinking things like that!

She was typing up an article for Faceoff, the game day publication for the Caribou, when Logan Heller arrived for his ten o'clock meeting with Matt and Scott. After the meeting, he'd be skating with the team for his first practice with them. First game would be Wednesday night, at home. In fact, their next five games were at home, which was probably good for him and would give them time to look for a new home.

She looked up when he walked in and her belly did a flip. God, he looked good, wearing jeans with a black leather jacket and grey striped scarf. When their eyes met, she struggled to keep her composure and gave him a warm and professional smile. "Hi," she said. "Welcome!"

"Thanks."

"You're here to see Matt and Scott. I'll show you to Matt's office. Come on this way." She led the way down a hall, acutely aware of him following right behind her. She rapped on Matt's open door and stepped inside. "Logan's here," she announced.

Logan followed her in.

"Come see me when you're done," she said to him, all polite and professional as she moved out of the office. "We have a lot of things to go over."

He gave her a hot stare and her tummy did another flip flop. "You bet."

Oh-oh.

She sat back down in front of her computer and stared blankly at it. There were a lot of sparks zapping between her and Logan Heller and now she was going to have to spend time with him, getting him all set up with the team and helping him find a place to live. This could be dangerous.

Maybe she should rethink quitting her job. She pressed a hand to her stomach where butterflies swooped. No. She was not quitting her job. She was a strong, professional woman. She could totally do this. It would be fine.

She determinedly focused on work until the men emerged from Matt's office nearly an hour later. Logan carried his jacket now, the loose blue and white shirt he wore untucked over the jeans.

"I'll leave you with Nicole," Scott said. "Nicole, can you bring him over when you're done?"

She smiled again. "Of course. Have a seat." She nodded at a chair in front of her desk and reached for some papers she'd printed out. She began going over the business items she needed to review with him. "And Breck wants to do a press conference tomorrow," she finally said. "We'll schedule it before practice. It will be here in the media room. And that's about it. Other than somewhere to live." She beamed another fake smile. "They asked me to help you find a place, since I know the city."

"Um. Yeah. Thanks." He didn't even look a little overwhelmed with all the information she'd just laid on him. "I do need to find a place."

"I assume you want to rent something."

He shrugged. "I guess that makes sense. I need to sell my place in California. I don't want to rush into buying something here."

"Are you thinking you won't be here that long?" She nearly closed her eyes. Why had she said that?

He rubbed his forehead. "It just doesn't all seem real yet."

Sympathy tugged something inside her. It did suck having your whole life uprooted and moved across the country in the space of a few days. "Well, I'll try to make it as easy for you as I can. Any thoughts about where you want to live? Apartment? House? Townhouse?"

"No. Jesus." Their eyes met again and Nicole felt that snap of attraction again. He had beautiful eyes, dark brown with long thick eyelashes. She wanted to reach out and rub her fingers over the scruff of whiskers on his square jaw. She felt almost as if she was leaning forward in her chair, drawn toward him. She gripped one arm of the chair. "I don't know," he continued. "I had a condo on the beach in California. I guess there's no beach in Minneapolis."

She smiled. "Well, not ocean beach, for sure. But there are a lot of lakes."

"Where do you live?"

She sat back a little. "Uh...I have a little townhouse condo not too far from here. But I'm sure you can afford something much nicer." His multi-million dollar contract was no secret

"Yeah." He grinned, clearly unconcerned about money. She'd been like that once. "That neighborhood Fedor lives in seems nice."

"Very nice." They talked about prices and things he liked.

"A hot tub," he said. "I'd really like a hot tub."

"Um. Yeah. You could always get one put in though."

"Not if I'm renting."

"True." She'd gone all warm inside thinking about him in a hot tub. And he was looking at her as if he was thinking the same thing about her. Her skin tingled all over under his hot gaze. "I'll do some research and come up with some options. We can talk more tomorrow either before or after the press conference."

"Okay."

"I guess that's it for now."

"Well." He set his hands on his knees. "Um. Matt said you'd show me around. I'm supposed to find Scott in the dressing room."

"Oh. Of course." Yeah, she knew that, but damn, she did not want to leave her office. She still felt acutely aware of everyone's attention. If only she could hide in the office for a while longer. Over in the arena she'd have to face the coaching and training staff and possibly some of the players. *Merde.* "Hold on one sec. I just have to send out this weekly schedule advisory to the media." She finished off the email and sent it to sports editors and media reps. "Okay, let's go."

She did a couple of quick clicks on her computer to lock it, then stood. "We can get to the arena through the tunnel. It runs under Bismarck Avenue." Once again, she was conscious of his bulk behind her as she led the way out of the offices and into the elevator.

"That was fun last night," he said as they walked through the short tunnel. "I didn't expect...that...my first night in town. Figured I'd be sitting in a hotel room all alone."

"It's nice of Fedor and Taylor to let you stay with them."

"Yeah. I appreciate it. Fedor's a good guy. I don't want to impose on them too long, though."

"You could live in that house with them for a year and never see them, it's so huge."

He laughed. "True that." After a short pause, he said, "You know a lot about hockey."

She slanted him a look as they walked. "You sound surprised."

"I guess I've never met a girl who knows that much. I mean, there are girls who like hockey, but…"

"I played hockey. In high school. I was pretty good, but my parents didn't think it was a worthwhile career choice. For a girl."

"Women's hockey hasn't quite reached the same level as men's."

She bristled. "That doesn't mean we should just give up on it."

"I never said that." He shot her a look.

She sighed. "Yeah. I just mean…well, never mind. I still love the game."

"That's why you work for the Caribou?"

"Yes."

"What did your parents think you should do for a living?"

"My dad thought I should be a model." She rolled her eyes.

"You could be."

"Oh yeah. Sure. Or maybe an astronaut. That's just as realistic."

He blinked with surprise.

Wait, what? Had he been serious with that comment? She'd thought he was just sucking up with gratuitous flattery.

"My mom pointed out often that I wasn't ever going to be a model, pretty much as often as my dad pointed out I was never going to have a hockey career. Actually, I don't think he really cared what I did. He was pretty focused on my brother and his career. He didn't have much time for a girl, even if she did play hockey." She made a face. "Sorry, that sounds like I'm whining. I'm not."

"You didn't sound like you were whining."

They walked into the bowl of the arena right near the loading docks. Huge trucks were parked there, unloading boxes, some containing merchandise for the Caribou store up on the concourse level, others with food for the commissary. The faint smell of exhaust fumes lingered in the cool air and the rumble of the HVAC and ice making equipment forced her to speak louder. "Dressing room is this way." She turned left and used her access pass to open the doors. The noise faded as the doors closed behind them.

"Hi, Travis." She greeted the assistant equipment manager, who avoided her eyes. She cringed inwardly, but kept a smile in place. "Have you met Logan?" She made introductions and they shook hands.

"Got your gear all ready for you," Travis said.

"I've been in this arena before," Logan reminded her as they moved on. "As a visitor, of course."

The visitor's dressing room was farther down the hall.

"Yes."

"Hey, Nicole." Logan stopped again and touched her arm.

She stopped too and turned to face him. "Yes?"

"Would you like to have dinner with me tonight?"

Her stomach twisted into knots as she stared at him.

He'd just asked her out.

And *tabarnac de câlisse,* she *so* wanted to say yes.

There was no denying the attraction between them. It had been there last night when they'd met. It had sizzled back and forth all evening. Every time their eyes met, she'd felt a jolt like a small electrical shock, a sudden burst of heat in her lower belly. Beneath the easy, lazy smile and the deceptively uncaring way he shrugged those big shoulders, he had an intense way of looking at her that made her just want to give into it, just surrender to him and do whatever he wanted.

But she couldn't.

Tempted as she was, standing there in the depths of the arena surrounded by rumbling ventilation equipment and guys pushing dollies loaded with boxes, however much she just wanted to throw herself into his arms and let him kiss her into next week, she could not do that again

She became aware her mouth was hanging open. She snapped it shut and glared at him. "Oh my god. You did not just say that."

CHAPTER FIVE

She looked like she wanted to punch him. Her hands curled into fists at her sides. Today she wore a pair of grey tweed trousers and a black turtleneck. Plain and simple, but she made it look elegant and sexy, especially the rear view he'd noticed in the office, the way her pants hugged her hot little ass.

"What?"

"I...I..." She just glared at him, eyes shooting sparks. "I'm just going to pretend I didn't hear that."

"Uh..." Now it was his turn to be at a loss for words. Women didn't turn him down very often. Or, well...ever. "What's the problem?"

Her eyes widened. She muttered something under her breath that he didn't understand, then lifted her chin. "I think we should keep this strictly business."

"Oh." Disappointment flooded him. He was a social guy, liked going out and having friends. Like he'd said, last night had been fun with Fedor and his wife and Nicole. He'd felt as if maybe it wouldn't be so bad, if he had friends there in Minneapolis. Yeah, he was hugely attracted to Nicole, but that was a pretty normal thing to happen between a guy and a girl, right? No? What had he done wrong?

"Hey, you're here!" Scott emerged from the dressing room and greeted him. "You two done for now?"

"We are," Nicole confirmed with a taut smile for the coach. "I'm going back to the office to start researching some places for Logan to live and getting some things set up for him."

"Great, thanks, Nicole. Logan, c'mon back into my office."

With one last glance at Nicole, during which their eyes met and the connection briefly sizzled, he followed Scott through the home dressing room for the Minneapolis Caribou, which was pristine, the carpet with the Caribou logo on it meticulously vacuumed, all the players' gear—including his own, now—hung perfect and neat in their cubbies.

He had to put Nicole and his strange fascination for her, as well as his letdown at her reaction to his invitation, out of his head and focus on hockey. On his career. Which was the most important thing.

He and Scott had a good talk. He'd always liked and respected Scott, from what little he knew of him. It wasn't as if he didn't want to play for him, but it was always an adjustment to get used to a new coach with a different style. Scott was pretty frank about the problem on the team and his frustrations, and also what he expected of Logan.

"You have a good work ethic," Scott said. "We need someone like that. We need some leadership."

Logan nodded. "Yeah." Christ they were looking to *him* for leadership? He wasn't like Tag, who'd been team captain for years, or even Jase, who'd just been named assistant captain of the Wolves. And this team already had a captain. He mentioned that to Scott.

"Yeah." Scott rubbed his face. "You know Ron's been struggling with some injuries this year. It's been tough for him. He's got a lot of good qualities. I'm not putting this on him, not at all. And yeah, he's the captain. But there's leadership that comes from the role you're given—from the C on your chest—or leadership that comes from within. I'm just saying, you have some natural qualities that we need here."

Logan nodded. No pressure at all. Huh.

As they talked, some of the other players began arriving for the practice, and Logan joined them when he and Scott were done. He greeted all his new team mates, trying for easy and friendly and happy to be there, even though he felt like a total outsider and truthfully still wasn't all that thrilled to be there. On the ice, though, under Scott's direction, he relaxed and focused on the game he knew and loved—the feel of the ice beneath his blades, the speed and power of skating, the sweetness of handling the puck on his stick.

He loved working his body hard, pushing himself to his limits and beyond, and even though mentally this change was tough, he knew from experience that by getting into it physically, his head would follow. He could shut everything else out and just be himself, trusting his muscles, trusting his skills, trusting his intuition. His body knew how to move. He had agility, speed, strength and flexibility, able to race from end to end of the ice, move side to side, turn in sweeping circles or tight circles, change direction in an instant and burst from a dead stop. He could cup the puck on his stick and maneuver it with finesse. His instincts and experience helped him know what angle to shoot from and how hard, where the puck was, where his team mates were. Christ, if someone in the crowd got up to go for beer, he knew it.

He was determined to show them his best in this first practice.

By the end of the practice, sweaty and on a pretty good adrenaline high, he remained on the ice after the others had left. He skated in a slow circle, on one foot, then the other, stick handling the puck just for the fun of it, and gazed up into the rafters of the cavernous arena, the banks of lights blazing down on him, the dark rows of seats empty. He breathed in the chilled air, the scent of the ice and sweat.

This was it. This was going to be his home from now on. For how long, who knew. He'd thought he was a Condor for the long haul, but that wasn't the case. He wasn't likely to be traded again tomorrow, but you never knew. Whatever. This was where he was now and he had to make the best of it.

He lined up, drew his stick back and aimed a perfect slapshot at the net. The crack of his stick on the frozen puck vibrated around him and the puck shot into the net, damn near going right through it. He smiled.

As he walked into the dressing room, he heard the song Pumped Up Kicks playing on the sound system. He couldn't help but move to the catchy beat and did a little dance over to his cubby.

Fedor laughed at him.

"You'd better run, better run, outrun my gun," Logan sang, grinning, and the other guys laughed too. "Turn it up, it's a good song."

Tyler Gladstone moved to the music too as he yanked his practice jersey over his head and some of the other guys boogied a little too.

After he'd showered and dressed, then joked around a little with the other guys, he found his way back to the office where Nicole sat at her desk, sipping from a giant cup of coffee as she clicked with a mouse, her eyes on her computer screen.

Damn.

He'd never been one to give up easily when he wanted something, but he must be crazy. He'd just arrived in town and was ready to jump pretty much the first girl he'd met. Maybe he should just heed what she'd said and keep it business, while he went out and hit the hotspots in Minneapolis and met girls who'd be more interested in him than Nicole was.

But he got the feeling she *was* interested. Things had sparked between them last night, and not just because he'd been naked. He was pretty sure she'd felt the same heated awareness, the way she'd checked him out, the way their eyes kept meeting while they were making dinner, then eating. So hey, that was enough to encourage him not to give up. He grinned as he approached her desk.

She looked up and he didn't miss the flicker in her eyes when she saw him. Yeah, there was something there.

"Hey." He leaned on her desk. "How's it going?"

"Good." She pushed her chair back so she wasn't looking way up at him. She picked up a piece of paper from her printer and handed it to him. "Here. These are the things I've got lined up so far. A couple of photo shoots. Press conference. Interviews."

He looked it over and nodded. He was going to be busy the next few days. He had other things to do too, like lease a car. Find a place to live.

"Find any houses for me yet?"

She frowned. "I haven't had much time," she said, her voice a little testy. "I've just gotten back from a week's vacation and I have a ton of work to do. Besides looking after you."

Ooh. She was still pissed.

"There are all kinds of media requests for interviews with you. There's a game tomorrow night and a million things to get done to be ready for it. I'm trying to prioritize things and I think the game being tomorrow takes precedence over your housing situation, since you do in fact have a bed to sleep in tonight and are not homeless."

He lifted his eyebrows, wishing she hadn't mentioned sleeping and his bed. Because his mind went straight there, wanting her in his bed. And not sleeping. Preferably with those sexy boots on. "I understand," he said mildly. "I wasn't trying to pressure you. Just asking."

She licked her bottom lip and dropped her gaze, which was so profoundly sexy, blood rushed to his groin. "I'm sorry. I don't mean to be bitchy."

He laughed. "You're not a bitch, gorgeous. But you're obviously stressed. What can I do?"

She lifted those pretty blue eyes and his entire body went hot and tight. "Nothing, of course. I apologize. I'm supposed to be making things easy for you, not complaining to you. What do you think about lofts?"

He blinked. "Lofts?" What the hell?

"There aren't a lot of upscale homes for rent in Minneapolis. I thought you might be interested in some of the loft condos. There are some really nice ones and some aren't that far from here. You'd be close to work."

"Huh. Yeah. I guess." It wasn't oceanside, but whatever. He had to let go of that.

"Okay. I'll do some more checking and set up times to go see them. I know your schedule."

"Okay." He didn't move off her desk.

She gave him a look, with raised eyebrows. "Is there something else?"

Reluctantly he stood. "No." He glanced at the paper in his hand, then lifted it. "I guess I'll see you tomorrow."

She gave a cool professional smile. "Yes, I'll be there."

"Great."

Okay. Much as he wasn't used to having to convince a woman to date him, he knew when to back off. He headed out.

He'd go buy himself a new car. Something nice. Maybe an SUV for dealing with Minneapolis winters, something he was well familiar with, having grown up not far away in Winnipeg.

Which reminded him that he should call his parents again and update them on how things were going.

He used the GPS map on his cell phone to locate a Jeep dealership and studied the directions, then called his Mom.

"Do you want me to fly down to California?" she asked, his Bluetooth in place as he drove. "I can pack up the things in your house and have them shipped. Get the place ready to sell."

"You don't have to do that."

"Who else is going to do it? You don't have a wife to look after you."

He frowned. A wife to look after him? Jesus. He sighed. "No, I don't. But that's a lot of work for you, Mom." And dammit, did he want his mother packing up all his stuff? Christ, he just hoped she'd think the steel suspension bar was for working out. At least he'd brought the cuffs with him.

"I can handle it. I don't mind a little trip somewhere warm. But I want to go now, because Jase's baby is due in a few weeks and I'll want to go to Chicago when the baby's born to see him or her and help."

Logan frowned. "Really?"

"Of course. It'll be our first grandchild. The MacIntoshes have two already, and if things keep going the way they have been with Tag and Kyla, they'll have more."

"What!"

"Kyla's not pregnant," Mom hastened to assure him. "But they've been spending a lot of time together. He's practically living with her, with how much time he spends there."

"I thought he was going to buy a house."

"Well, he looked around a bit, but he didn't want to rush into things, and then he started spending so much time with Kyla...I think he's given up on that idea. For now."

"Huh."

"It's so nice." Mom's voice warmed. "I don't know if I've ever seen him this happy. And it's Kyla!"

Logan rolled his eyes. Okay, Kyla was already like part of the family, having grown up with them as one of the kids of his parents' best friends, but geez, you'd think his mom had always wanted a daughter or something.

"It's just so exciting and romantic," she added. "And Remi and Jase too..." She sighed. "And a baby. It's just too bad how that happened."

As usual, Logan couldn't live up to his two older brothers, who'd led the way with their hockey talent and now were thrilling their mom with their girlfriends and babies. "Not to put a damper on your excitement," Logan said dryly. "But Jase won't have full custody of the baby. And we're still not certain it's his. Don't get too excited about it, Mom."

After a short pause, she said, "I suppose you're right."

Damn. Now she sounded sad. He sighed. "I just don't want you to be all disappointed and heartbroken if it turns out to be not even his baby."

"He's pretty sure it is."

"I know, but...never mind."

"Okay. Back to me going to California. I'll check into some flights and see what I can arrange."

"Thanks, Mom. I'll pay for the flight."

"Of course you will." She laughed.

It would take a huge load off his mind to have all that stuff looked after. How else was he going to do it? They had a steady schedule for the next few weeks. "Okay, I gotta go. I'm at the Jeep dealership."

Nicole was running around the arena Wednesday night during the game, attending to various things—ensuring there was enough food for the media up in the press box and for staff downstairs, making sure Ryan had the list of game shots required by both the team and the NHL, making sure everything was set up for the post-game media scrum—so she didn't have time to watch a lot of the game. But she did stop a few times to watch. There was a feeling that this was a pivotal game for the team after the trade, Logan's first game. She found herself looking for him on the ice and on the bench.

Too bad they were losing.

It *was* against the defending Stanley Cup champions, but it wasn't a great start for Logan. Although he himself was playing well. From the press box, she watched him take a face off in the neutral zone, control the puck and race the length of the ice to beat the Pittsburgh goaltender on the glove side, sending the crowd into a frenzy. She smiled.

The next time she looked, he was being checked hard into the boards by a Pittsburgh player, and she winced.

Obviously one player wasn't going to turn things around for the team immediately, but she could see subtle differences. Some of the players who'd been lackadaisical lately seemed to have more energy, more fire. Scott had put Logan on a line with Dewey and Tyler, as Fedor had suggested. It was going okay, but she still thought it would work better with Adam instead of Tyler. But then she wasn't the coach. She was just the Communications Assistant.

Logan came *that* close to scoring again near the end of the third period, and even though the Caribou pulled their goalie in the last minutes of the game, they lost three-two. But there was reason for optimism based on some of the action, so although the game went in the loss column, it didn't feel horrible. At least to Nicole. She couldn't help but wonder how Logan was feeling after his first game. But she wasn't going to seek him out to ask. No, she was not.

The next afternoon, she watched Logan posing in front of the camera for headshots, the photographer's lights shining down on him in the photography studio. Team photographer Ryan Sender chatted with Logan as he shot, talking about—what else?—hockey. They talked about the loss last night and Logan didn't seem too broken up about it. He seemed to be a pretty easygoing guy, yet she kept getting glimpses of something beneath the surface. His nearly constant smile, easy laugh and nonchalance on the outside made him seem carefree and charming, but she sensed that he used that charming exterior to cover up something else. Obviously he had to be serious about his career, about hockey. He wasn't all about fun and games, despite the jokes and smiles. He had to have passion for the game and a determination to succeed, to get where he was. She'd seen hints of that passion and determination in his eyes, when he looked at her...okay *that* wasn't for hockey.

In the last few days, she'd spent a lot of time with both Ryan and Logan. Ryan was a good looking guy, possibly even more handsome than Logan, but she'd never felt all tingly around him like she did around Logan. It was really getting annoying.

But the important thing was, she was resisting temptation. Difficult as it was being around him, she had managed to keep things businesslike. She'd scheduled photo shoots, interviews, press conferences, all the while acting coolly professional and distant. She could totally do this.

"Okay." Ryan looked down at the screen on his digital camera. "I think we're good."

Nicole straightened from the counter she'd been leaning against to watch the shoot. "Great. When can you get me the images?"

"I'll work on them for the rest of the day. Should be able to upload them for you to look at tomorrow."

"Perfect. We want to get the billboards done as soon as we can. Thanks for doing this so quickly, Ryan. And the headshots too, for the programs and the website."

"Not a problem."

"We're off now to look at some lofts." She reached for her jacket. "Trying to find a place for Logan."

To her surprise, Logan took her jacket and held it for her to slide her arms into. He gently settled it on her shoulders, then grabbed his own black leather jacket. "Thanks." Now she tingled even more, impressed with his manners.

"Good to meet you, Ryan," Logan said.

"Yeah. Again, welcome to Minneapolis."

They took the elevator down from the third floor studio and then walked out the building lobby onto the street. A few snowflakes had started to drift down from the overcast sky, big fluffy flakes. Nicole turned her face up to them.

"Snow," Logan said. "Great."

"I guess you didn't have much snow in California."

"No. But I'm used to snow. And it's not as if I never left California."

"Yeah, there's a lot of travel involved in hockey. You grew up in Winnipeg, right?"

"Yep."

"So you're pretty close to home here."

"Yeah. My parents are thrilled." The wry smile he sent her made her heart bump a little in her chest. He flicked a button on a key fob and the lights blinked on the brand new Jeep he'd parked at the curb. Again he surprised her by opening her door for her and offering a hand to climb into the high vehicle. She didn't need help, she had long enough legs, but his manners made her chest go all warm and soft.

"Where to?" he asked, once he was in and had his seatbelt on.

"I'll give you directions." She looked down at the information she'd printed out. She had three places lined up for them to see. "The first one's not far from here."

"So yeah, I'm used to snow." He picked up the conversation again. "Where did you grow up? I guess Montreal mostly?"

"Yes. We lived there until I was sixteen and Dad got traded to New York. But I went back to Montreal to go to university."

"You speak French?"

She laughed. "Of course. Have you heard my dad's English?"

He grinned. "Yeah. But you don't have an accent at all, you speak perfect English too."

"Well, I grew up in a bilingual home. My mom's Anglophone. My brother and I went to French schools, but we mostly spoke English at home. Well, my dad tried. And then of course we had to go to an English-speaking high school in New York."

"What did you major in?"

"Communications. Hence the job in communications," she pointed out.

"Of course. I majored in Economics."

Her head whipped around to stare at him. "Economics? Seriously?"

He shot her a look, one corner of his mouth lifted in a crooked smile. "Don't sound so shocked."

"I'm not! Okay, I am."

He laughed.

"Do you have a degree?"

"Yep, from Dartmouth College."

"Oh! Did you play NCAA there?"

"I did."

"I didn't realize that." A degree in economics. Whoa. Suddenly—weirdly—he was even more attractive.

"My brothers both got into the NHL through major junior hockey. Jase wasn't much into school, so there was no way he was going to university. My parents practically killed themselves getting him to graduate from high school."

"That's good they did."

"Yeah. And Tag was smart—not that Jase isn't," he quickly added. "But he has ADD, so school was hard for him."

She nodded. "Yeah. Good for him for graduating then. Um, turn right at those lights ahead."

"Tag just wanted to play pro hockey as fast as he could." Logan did a shoulder check to change lanes. "And they wanted him as fast as they could get him, so he was playing for Phoenix when he was eighteen."

"That's really young."

"It is. But he was always mature, and he had the skills. He was ready. I wasn't."

She shifted in her seat a little to look at him. *Câlisse*, he looked good, his big hands easy on the steering wheel. In profile, the small bump on his nose was more evident. No doubt broken at some point in his hockey career. She wanted to know more about him. "No?"

"I mean, I wanted it. I just wasn't as mature as Tag was at that age. I was bigger than him, though." He grinned. "And I liked the idea of getting an education too. In case the hockey thing didn't work out."

"Was there ever any doubt about that?" With the talent in his family, it seemed crazy that he might have thought he might not make it as a pro hockey player.

He huffed a laugh. "You never know."

"Was there a lot of pressure on you to make it?" she asked slowly, thinking again about those two older brothers in the NHL.

His face tightened, barely noticeably, but she caught it. Her interest was piqued even more. Not that she should be interested in him. "My parents never pushed it. They tried to be encouraging. I mean, they *were* encouraging. But even so, yeah, I felt pressure."

She nodded. "I guess I can relate to that," she said slowly. "Sort of. My brother Julien was definitely a lot to live up to." As were both her parents.

"He's a good player."

"He is." She couldn't deny that, and she loved her brother and was proud of him. "But all my parents' focus was on him and his hockey career."

He stopped as the light turned red and glanced at her. Their eyes met. "Yeah. I know the feeling," he said quietly and the connection between them stretched out warm and palpable. She swallowed, unable to break eye contact with him.

CHAPTER SIX

Logan looked away, checking to his left for traffic, then made the right turn.

"It's a few blocks down," she said, a little breathless. "I'll watch for the sign." *Merde*, it was happening again, that crazy feeling of being drawn to him. She'd been fighting it all week, but now it had roared back to life, just talking to him about mundane things like college and family.

"Okay. I guess I was lucky that my parents encouraged me. That sucks that your parents wouldn't encourage you to do what you wanted."

"Yeah. But whatever." She waved a hand. "I'm happy doing what I do now. Mostly." She couldn't stop from adding that little disclaimer after what had happened last week.

"I can tell. You seem very efficient and you know the business."

She grimaced although she was touched. "Thanks." After a short pause, she said, "Too bad about the loss last night."

He shrugged. "You win some, you lose some."

"Very original."

He smiled, still looking ahead through the windshield as he drove. "I can speak in sports clichés with the best of them. We didn't play a full sixty minutes. We have to find a way to put the puck in the net. Generate some offense. Everyone needs to give a hundred and ten per cent. At the end of the day, it is what it is, going forward."

Nicole burst out laughing. Oh man! "Seriously," she gasped once she'd stopped laughing. "How did you feel last night?"

"I felt good."

"Really?"

"No." He slanted her a glance. "I'm trying to be positive. It wasn't bad. Just different. It's going to take a while for me to get used to things—new coach, new team mates, new building."

"Yeah, I'm sure it will. You played well, though. That goal was pretty."

"Thanks."

"You and Scott get along?"

"Yeah. So far. He's great."

"Don't sound so enthusiastic."

He glanced at her again. "Apparently I'm not doing a good job of acting happy about this."

She tipped her head to one side. He *was* doing a good job of it, any time she saw him with other people, but the few times they'd talked about it, she'd sensed his frustration. This must be hard for him. She'd been all wrapped up in her own problems and embarrassment, but he was going through a major life change. She knew how important it was that a player have a good relationship with his coach and how long it could take to adapt to a new coaching style, a new personality. Plus, there was getting to know all the other players and finding his place on the team. And then all the personal stuff, like finding somewhere to live. And buying this mondo spiffy vehicle he'd driven them to the photo shoot in. She swallowed a sigh.

"What?"

"Nothing. I know this is hard for you."

His lips pursed briefly. "Nah. It's all good."

She didn't believe him. "Oh, right there." She pointed. "Turn right into this parking lot."

She studied the converted warehouse adjacent to World Market Square, all old brick and arched windows.

"Looks nice," he commented, pulling into a parking spot.

"It does. There's a gym across the street and a park just behind the building. And of course you're close to World Market Square, which is quite a neat market."

"Price?"

She bit her lip. "There are only a couple of units available. One is eight hundred thousand, the other is one point two million."

"Which are we looking at?"

"I thought the one point two million one."

He nodded without even flinching at the numbers. "Okay."

Inside the building they were met with the realtor, who took them up to the seventh floor out of eight. They walked into the loft, the ten foot ceilings giving an open feel. Dark wood floors gleamed in the sunshine that streamed in floor to ceiling windows. The two walls of windows met in one corner of the living room, giving an incredible view of the city. A door in the wall of windows led to a balcony, which was where Logan headed first.

Nicole followed, looking around. It wasn't going to be her place, but she studied it anyway, taking in the modern black fireplace set into old brick, halogen lights on tracks suspended from the ceiling, matte taupe walls with pristine white baseboards.

"There's a powder room here." The realtor, Mary, showed them. "And the bedroom and bathroom are through there." She indicated an opening in the wall beside the fireplace. Logan wandered in there, and Nicole hesitated. Did she really need to see the bedroom?

No, she did not.

So she hung around in the main open area, a kitchen, living and dining room combination.

"Hey, Nicole," Logan called. "Come see."

She bit her lip and walked to the bedroom. It too was spacious and full of light.

"Lots of room for a king size bed," he said. "Which I need."

Of course he did.

"And it would be so easy to hang a swing from those beams."

Her heart missed a beat and she gaped at him. "Whaat?"

He laughed. "You should see the look on your face!" He slapped his thigh, still chuckling.

Why had he said that? Was he joking? Or did he know something…how could he?

"And the bathroom's great." He moved away. "Check it out."

Disoriented, she peeked in and did have to give a little sigh of pleasure. This place put her little condo to shame. Ceramic tiles in shades of latte, cream and mocha covered floor and walls, including a huge glassed in shower and a big soaker tub.

"Let's see the kitchen." Logan turned around and left. Again, she trailed along behind.

The kitchen featured maple cabinets, dark granite countertops and stainless appliances.

"Looks good," Logan said.

"Closets? Do you want to know about laundry? Storage?"

He grinned. "Oh yeah. I guess I should."

The realtor spent some time showing them more features, and then they left. "I like the windows of that one," he said when they were back in his Jeep. "Lots of light. I should just take it."

"You need to look at more than one!"

"Why? I know I like it."

She stared at him, shaking her head. "But you haven't seen anything else! What if they're better?"

"Oh, all right. Let's go."

Must be a man thing. She shook her head.

They spent the rest of the afternoon looking at the others she'd picked out to see, also lovely, one in a much newer building, the other in another historic building in the Midtown Exchange that had a similar feel to the first one.

"Yeah, I like that first one," Logan said. "Let's go back."

"I'll call the realtor. You'll need to meet with her."

"Oh. Okay."

"Are you sure you don't want to look at more? It's a big decision. You might want to check out other neighborhoods…"

"I'm hardly ever home. We're on the road a lot. In the summer I go home. It doesn't really matter where I live."

"As long as the ceiling will support a swing."

A surprised laugh popped out of him. His dancing eyes met hers. "Noooo," he said. "Don't be silly."

She lifted one eyebrow.

"I'm not really into swings. But I do need a hook for suspension bondage."

Her pussy immediately gave a warm squeeze. She kept her smile in place and her tone light. "Oh stop. You're getting me all hot and bothered."

His eyes widened. "Really?"

"No." She rolled her eyes. "I'm joking. As were you."

But some kind of intuition told her he wasn't joking. And as their eyes once again met and held, her intuition told her that he knew she knew that.

"Damn," he murmured.

Heat swept over her body, a tiny ache developing low down inside her. She gazed at him in the late afternoon dusk as they stood on the sidewalk outside the last building they'd looked at and licked her lips. "Okay! Well, enough kidding around. That makes my job easier, if you're going to decide that fast. I'll leave it up to you to contact the agent and get things started."

"Thanks for finding these. They were all great."

"It's my job," she said dryly. "Other duties as assigned."

"Okay. Would it be other duties as assigned to have dinner with me tonight?"

Her hand paused on the door handle as she went to open the door of the SUV. "What? Again? You're asking me out again?" *Tabarnac?* Not again! She closed her eyes briefly. Why was he doing this to her! She could let her imagination run wild and picture them having a romantic dinner somewhere, eating by candlelight, talking (about hockey) and laughing and then maybe going back to her place, and her belly did a little flip of lust at the thought of hot, athletic sex with him…oh holy Virgin Mary.

"No!" he said. "I'm not. Definitely not. This would totally be a business dinner."

She snorted. "Bullshit."

She caught his eye, the amusement glinting there, the tug of the corners of his lips, and she went all melty inside. But at least this time she had a built-in, ready-to-use excuse, an impermeable defense strategy against his charm. Thank god.

She really couldn't go out with him that night. "I'm sorry. I can't. I have a date tonight."

His eyes shadowed. "Oh. I'm sorry. I didn't realize you were seeing someone. I..." He shook his head. "Never mind. Okay. I'll drive you back to the arena."

They'd left her car there earlier.

The easiness that had developed between them throughout the day had disappeared, replaced with a stiff awkwardness. Nicole clasped her hands on her purse on her lap as they drove. She'd accepted that date with Paul, who she'd met on the plane, because it was time for her to move on, to date someone outside the hockey world. Nobody was ever going to insult her again because of dating a hockey player. She was sticking to her resolution on this, no matter how tempting the big, charming man beside her was. But damn, it was hard! Especially since he seemed to like her too. It was enough to make her melt like a skating rink in the spring.

"I changed my mind," he said suddenly.

Huh? She turned to him. "About what?"

"The condo. I don't want that one after all."

"Oh." She blinked. "Um, okay."

"You were right. I really need to look at more and make an informed decision."

"Yeah. Okay. I'll do more research and find some other to look at. Will you have time this weekend?" They had a game Friday night, but the weekend was mostly open.

"Yeah. This weekend would be good."

"Next weekend is Thanksgiving. That might not be a good weekend to do it."

"Thanksgiving, yeah. Apparently Taylor and Fedor are having a bunch of people for Thanksgiving dinner on Thursday."

"That's right. She does that every year. There are a lot of players who don't have family here, so she does a big dinner for anyone who wants to come."

"You'll be there?"

"Yes." She bit her lip briefly. "She invites me too since I don't have family here either."

"This American Thanksgiving is a big thing."

She smiled. "Yes, it is. It's nice to be included, I have to admit, when all you hear about everywhere is Thanksgiving this, Thanksgiving that. I'll be helping her cook, actually."

"Cool."

They arrived at the arena and he pulled into the parking lot. "Which is your car?"

"That red Mustang over there."

"Sweet."

She grinned. She loved her car. "Thanks."

He pulled up behind it in the dark, now empty parking lot. "There you go. Thanks for helping me out with this and ah...enjoy your date tonight."

She eyed him in the dimly lit vehicle. He seemed sincere. Damn, this guy confused her! "I'll try," she said honestly, although she wasn't entirely confident about that.

Nicole smiled at Paul across the table in the restaurant he'd taken her to for dinner. Nice place, if a little...staid. The steakhouse had a menu that probably had existed in the nineteen seventies. Meat. Potatoes. Garlic toast. Yum.

"I work for the Caribou," she told him in answer to his question. "In Communications."

"The Caribou?"

"The hockey team."

"Oh. Oh yeah. Cool. I'm not much into hockey." He ran a hand over his hair. He was nice looking, not geeky at all, with a lean build and decent shoulders.

"No?" Great. "How about football?"

"Nah. Not much into sports at all."

She tipped her head to one side, keeping her friendly interested smile firmly in place. "So what do you like to do when you're not at work?"

"I like gaming. Just got the newest Xbox system."

She felt one eyebrow lift even though she tried to stop it. He was how old? Thirty? "Cool. What kind of games do you like?" Probably not NHL13.

"I'm liking this new game, King of Fighters."

"Uh-huh." She had no clue what he was talking about.

"I'm kind of an amateur game designer," he said with a modest smile. "I like to play around with that."

"You're a computer programmer, right?"

"That's right."

Something else she had no clue about. She nibbled her bottom lip. What the hell were they going to talk about?

"And I play on-line games, too," he said. "Really into Death Trap right now."

"Awesome."

They managed to make some stilted conversation through dinner, but the effort exhausted her. When Paul dropped her off at home she had no intention of ever seeing him again. But when he invited her to go out again on the weekend, she thought about it. Just because he wasn't interested in hockey didn't mean he wasn't interesting. The whole world didn't watch hockey. There were other things out there. Maybe it was she who needed to broaden her horizons. So she agreed to go out again Saturday night.

"Great!" Paul said with a big smile. "I'll call you or text you on Saturday." And he leaned forward and kissed her. A quick, lips-closed smooch. Nice. Harmless. She waved as she let herself into her condo.

She could do this. There were so many other things out there she could be interested in that she'd never really given much thought. She'd find some new hobbies, take up some new activities. She worked long hours at times, especially game days, but she needed to make room in her life for other pursuits. Maybe she'd even buy an Xbox.

Logan left the ice after the practice Saturday morning, sweating, breathing hard and muscles burning, but feeling satisfied. Last night they'd pulled off a win, but their play had been uneven and Coach had kept them practicing hard, telling them they still had a lot of work to do. Coach was clearly frustrated with the losses, but made sure to spend a lot of individual time on the coaching part of it, like with Tyler

Gladstone, a guy who hadn't been playing up to his potential, working with him on getting him playing with more speed, attacking more instead of gliding and planting. Logan could see that was exactly what was wrong and why the guy hadn't been getting much ice time. COach talked to them about energy, focus, playing a north and south game and managing the neutral zone. He worked them hard on drills during practice. Logan couldn't find fault with anything he did, and when a couple of the guys in the locker room grumbled about the relentless pace, Logan spoke up.

"Hey," he said, "You in this to win or not?"

They looked back at him in surprise. One of them was Cody Burrell.

Logan had had to grit his teeth the first time he'd seen Cody. He'd never really liked the guy. He had some hockey skills, but his borderline hits and stickwork pissed people off. He liked to dive to draw calls, and infuriated players even more when he took off after his cheap shots, refusing to fight.

Now they were playing on the same team and Logan had to get his head around that.

"C'mon," Logan said. "We all need to step up. Doing what we've been doing isn't working, we need to work harder, try different things."

"We suck." Adam Corbet, a left winger, shook his head.

"Bullshit." Logan frowned. "Maybe I see things clearer, coming from outside, but I saw a lot of good things in last night's game. You guys do a great job of keeping out of Burney's way. He could see every shot that was coming at him last night."

"That's true," Burney said. "I can't stop what I can't see."

Logan watched the others shrug and nod. "You also do a really good job of hanging onto the puck in the offensive zone. What I saw that wasn't so good was sometime guys playing all by themselves. We need to play together, for the whole game. That's what we were working on this morning."

He couldn't stand guys who didn't want to work and it was going to be torture to play for a team where guys complained about a tough practice or only focused on the negative. He was going to shut that noise down right away. "That practice felt great," he added. "Feels good to work hard."

They nodded and mumbled agreement, and as Logan yanked off his practice jersey, he saw Coach give him a long look as he walked through to his office.

"What's up tonight?" Logan asked the others. Saturday night, new in town...he did not want to spend the evening alone. He'd been thinking about Nicole a lot, annoyed that she'd gone out with some other dude. For some reason, he'd never even thought there was another guy in the picture, probably because of the way she looked at him and the tensions that sizzled between them every time they got within a few feet of each other. He had every intention of trying to convince her to spend the evening with him when they'd finished their condo shopping, but if that didn't work out—like if she had another date, goddammit—he needed a plan B. He found himself arranging to meet a bunch of the guys at a downtown bar they assured him was a happening place.

After showering and dressing, he was off to pick up Nicole at her place. It had taken some convincing to get her to agree to that; she'd wanted to meet him at the places she'd lined up to look at. As he drove, he grinned.

He'd almost been stupid enough to take the first place he'd looked at, but he hadn't changed his mind about it because he thought he needed to see more before deciding on one. Truthfully, he would have been fine in that place. In fact, he probably would still go for it. But he'd suddenly realized that if he was done looking for a place, he wouldn't see nearly as much of Nicole. Heh.

She'd been amazing the last few days. Her boss, Breck Travers, the Director of Communications, was in charge, but he and Nicole had both been there for him through the fucking endless interviews, press conferences, media scrums and photo shoots. He could see how much Breck relied on her and weirdly it made him feel like he could rely on her too. She had his back and he kinda liked it.

He jumped out of his brand new Jeep, the one year lease generously given to him by the dealership in exchange for some promo work, and headed to the door of Nicole's townhouse condo. She greeted him at the door, already with dressed in her black jacket, a big purple scarf wrapped around her throat that made her face stand out, so pretty, so glowing. Her long blonde hair flowed down her back.

"Hi." She slung her purse over her shoulder. "I'm ready."

He looked over her shoulder into her home. "What, I don't get to come in?"

CHAPTER SEVEN

"No." Nicole shoved at him with both hands. "Let's go."

Logan laughed. She couldn't budge him unless he let her, and this time he did let her push him out of her condo onto the front steps. Though it was interesting that she was so determined to get him out of there.

"Mary gave me keys to the places, so we don't need to worry about meeting up with her."

"That's very trusting of her."

"We use her all the time for finding places for new players. I think she trusts me."

Once again, she directed him as he drove.

"So how was your date the other night?" Logan asked.

Silence. He glanced sideways at her and caught her faint frown. "It was fine."

"Fine? That good, huh?"

She pressed her lips together. "It was good."

"Who is this guy? Is this serious?"

"Who are you, my father?"

He grimaced. Nah, he didn't want to be fatherly. "Just interested. I didn't realize you had a boyfriend."

"I don't." A soft sigh escaped her. "It was our first date. I met him on the plane last weekend coming back from New York."

"Oh. Nice guy?"

"Yes."

He didn't want to ask, but he had to. "Going to see him again?"

"Tonight."

Shit! He resisted the urge to slam a hand on the steering wheel. Annoyance bristled inside him and heavy silence filled the vehicle as he drove.

The first place they looked at was downtown, a thirty-nine story building that he hated. "No," he said, just walking in the door. "Definitely not."

She shot him an amused look. "What's wrong with it?"

He shrugged. "Just don't like it. Let's go."

"Don't rush on my account." She locked the door behind them. One corner of his mouth reluctantly kicked up.

The next place wasn't far away and it wasn't much better.

"There's a doorman, for Chrissakes," he muttered as they headed to the elevator. "I can't live in a place with a fucking doorman."

"Why not?" She punched the button for the tenth floor and turned to him.

"I don't know. It makes me feel old. This place makes me feel old." He waved a hand. "I think old people live here."

She tried to hide her smile. "You might be right. Let's look, though."

They had a quick look around the place, which was nice, but he'd already made up his mind.

"Okay, last one." She sighed when they were back in the vehicle. "Are you sure you're in the right mood for this?"

"What's that supposed to mean?"

"You seem kind of...grouchy."

Yeah. Grouchy was a good word to describe his mood. He'd been feeling pretty good until she'd told him she had another date with...whateverhisnamewas. "I'm fine," he snapped.

She grimaced and he sighed. "I'm sorry. I am kind of grouchy."

"What's the problem? Anything I can help with?"

He stared at her, frustration mounting inside him. "Yeah, as a matter of fact. You can cancel your date tonight and go out with me instead."

Her eyes went wide and her lips parted. "Uh..."

"Never mind." He was being an idiot. "Where's the next place?"

"Um. The next one overlooks Lake Calhoun. I thought you might like that."

"Maybe." It wasn't the Pacific Ocean, but he was open to it.

"I also have the key to the one we looked at the other day, near World Market Square. The one you were going to take at first. We can go back, if you want to have another look."

"We'll see."

They wandered through the condo, brand new and sparkling clean and beautiful. "It's a long way from the arena. I didn't think that mattered at first, but I really did like that first one."

"Let's go back there then."

"You're being very patient." And he was being a jerk.

"It's my job," she said lightly.

She was doing a good job of keeping things light and distant, but every time he looked at her mouth, he got dirty thoughts. He wanted to shove his hands into her hair and kiss her crazy. He wanted…he almost groaned out loud at what he wanted. What was it about her?

He liked her. He liked how she knew hockey, how he could say stuff that she understood, not like the puck bunnies who pretended they knew hockey, but didn't, who really only liked hockey players. He liked how strong she was to keep her head up high after being publicly insulted. He liked how she'd taken her love for hockey and found a satisfying career despite her parents not encouraging her to follow her dreams.

And he was hot for her too, hot for her tight athletic body, her lush mouth, her sexy eyes. Jesus.

When he walked into the loft condo, the first one they'd looked at, something swept over him. Something easy and comfortable. Yeah, this was the one.

At first he truly hadn't cared where he was going to live. Nowhere was going to be as nice as the place he'd had in California. He liked this one. But for some reason his mind was always going to associate Nicole being there with him, laughing in the bedroom about his joke about the bondage hooks, the heightened awareness of each other, the way tension had snapped between them.

He looked out the wall of windows. The loft faced south, so the late afternoon sun to their right lit up the sides of the buildings and cast shadows that created a three dimensional effect. The view was pretty spectacular even if it wasn't the ocean.

He checked out the gas fireplace, found the switch and flicked it on. It flared to life, realistic flames that soon cast some warmth in the empty room.

"It works," Nicole said.

He took off his jacket and laid it on the floor. He looked at her as he sat on the floor, leaning against the wall opposite the windows. "Take off your jacket."

"Why?"

"Because I said so."

She snorted. "Hah." But pleasure expanded inside him as she unwound her scarf from around her neck and removed her jacket, laying it on top of his on the floor. Beneath she wore a pair of low-rise jeans that hugged her hips and legs all the way down to the beige Ugg boots. On top, a black long-sleeved T-shirt clung to her full breasts.

"Come here," he said.

She walked over and slid down the wall until she was sitting on the floor beside him.

"It's a nice view."

"Yes." She stretched her long, jeans-clad legs out in front of her and crossed her booted ankles.

Logan had always thought Ugg boot were the Uggliest thing ever invented for women to wear on their feet. Give him a pair of pointy toed stiletto boots any day. But he found himself unaccountably charmed by her chunky fleece-lined boots.

He turned his head to look at her, and she too rolled her head against the wall. Their eyes met.

Lust slammed into him like a body check.

They looked at each other. Moments accumulated. Heat built.

He dropped his gaze to her mouth, so lush and soft looking. His gaze dropped lower still and observed her breasts rising and falling with her quick, shallow breaths. She was affected by him too. There was something there.

He would never move in on another dude's girl, but she'd only dated the guy once and he'd eat a hockey puck if he was wrong about her being as attracted to him as he was to her. He leaned in closer, slowly. Her eyelids dropped, her lips parted and then he closed his own eyes as he brushed his lips over hers. Once. Twice. And then he opened his mouth on hers and kissed her deeper.

He lifted a hand and dragged his fingertips over the soft skin of her jaw, then cupped her face and held it while they kissed. And yeah, hell yeah, she kissed him back, opening for him, and when he slid his tongue into her sweet mouth, she made a soft little sound in her throat that encouraged him. Her tongue moved against his and his brain shorted out, heat sizzling over every nerve ending in his body.

"Don't do this," she murmured, shifting her mouth away from his. He kissed her cheek instead.

"Say it like you mean it," he murmured back. She groaned and triumph flared inside him. With his thumb on her chin, he tilted her head back toward him and kissed her again, longer, deeper.

"I can't do this," she whispered. "I can't."

"Why, sweetheart? It feels like you want it as much as I do." He nuzzled her hair, her ear, breathed in her scent, something fresh and clean, green and citrusy. Heat pounded through his body with every beat of his heart, building in his balls.

"I… câlisse."

"Hmm, what?" He opened his mouth on the side of her neck and sucked, so gently.

"I don't want to want you!" she cried, but her hands grabbed his arms and her fingers dug into his sweater, holding on to him, not pushing him away.

"Why?" he asked again. "What's wrong with it? Christ, Nicole, there've been sparks flying ever since we met."

She moaned.

"Right?" He was pushing, because if she really wanted him to stop, he had to stop. He wanted to be sure of what was going on.

"Right." The word sounded dragged out of her. He smiled and moved in for another kiss, another hot, mind-scrambling, sense-robbing kiss.

Nicole got lost in it. The voice in the back of her brain screeching, *No, no, don't be an idiot!* was drowned out by the pounding of her heart in her ears, and the heat and need building in her core obliterated sensible thought.

"I hate to bring this up," he murmured against her lips. "But I have to ask. Is it because of that other guy?"

"What other guy?" She tried to open her eyes, but her lids were heavy, her body pulsing with need.

He chuckled. "Never mind then." And he kissed her again.

It was like a drug, sliding through her veins all warm and blissful, making her melt from the inside out. He licked inside her mouth and bit softly at her lips. *Câlisse*, the man was a good kisser!

Her body strained toward him and, helpless to resist, she moved closer.

"Oh yeah." He hauled her onto his lap. She shifted her position so she straddled him because, oh wow, she could get things lined up, that ache intensifying between her thighs pressed right against the bulge at his crotch. Her breath left her all at once and her head went light as a fierce rush of desire for him shot through her.

He slid a hand into her hair and pulled her face down to him for more of that luscious kissing, his other hand lower on her back, bringing her closer to his body, and they rubbed together as he consumed her with that incredible mouth, endless, fierce kisses that robbed her of all good sense and resolve.

She knew she should stop. She should be wrenching herself out of his arms and running out of that empty loft as fast as she could. But she could not get her body to do that, erotically helpless against the lust rolling through her.

"So good," he sighed against her mouth. "Nicole. You taste so sweet." His hands moved over her body, up and down her back, and then one slid down into the gap where her low rise jeans had ridden even lower, finding skin. His touch sent sizzles over her entire body and she gasped. First his fingertips brushed the base of her spine, then the crease between her cheeks, then he easily pushed his hand lower and cupped one ass cheek in his big hand. *Tabarnac*, that felt good!

Her head fell back and he kissed her throat, opening his mouth on her pulse there, then dragging his tongue up the side of her neck. Her breasts thrust forward, aching, needy, her nipples tight and tingling inside her bra. And then he covered one breast with a hand and gently squeezed. Sensation exploded in her, pleasure and need, and she whimpered.

"Hot," he whispered. "You're burning hot, Nicole."

She made some kind of little noise that might have been agreement, her mind spinning uselessly. And when he found the hem of her T-shirt and gently worked it up over her breasts and tugged it over her head, she didn't stop him.

The room was warm from the fireplace, but even so she shivered, her bare skin crying out for the touch of his hands. When he put his hands on her, holding her ribcage, she gave another soft cry of pleasure.

She looked at him, saw him gazing at her breasts, plumped up by her underwire bra, her nipples visible through sheer black lace.

"Christ, you're beautiful. Jesus, Nicole."

She almost wanted to cry at his compliment, because people never told her she was beautiful, and at how helpless she felt to resist him, how angry she was going to be at herself about this. She bit her lip and met his eyes and concern shadowed them as he looked back at her.

He held her so gently, kissed her mouth softly. "It's okay, Nicole. It's okay."

And she nodded, wanting to believe him, wanting this to be okay even though she knew it wasn't.

He kissed her again, hands stroking her bare skin now, kisses that went on and on, slow and hot and wet. Eventually his fingers worked open the fastener of her bra at her back and he tugged it off her. Again he studied her, awe and lust on his face, and feminine power and satisfaction swept through her.

"Let's move," he ordered, and he lifted her off him, then reached for their jackets lying on the floor nearby. He spread them, and with dazed submission, she let him lower her there and move over her. He gazed down at her, his face tight with male dominance and sensual hunger. Then he paused to remove his sweater and the T-shirt layered beneath it, both coming off together. She took in his body with avid eyes, her tongue dragging across her bottom lip. She'd seen him before, that day in the hall at Taylor's place, but now...god he was beautiful, so big, muscles shifting beneath his smooth skin, his shoulders wide, chest strong, abs flexing. She reached out to touch, tracing his biceps, between his pecs over the dusting of hair there, smoothing over his shoulders, trailing down to where his jeans rode so low she could see the elastic of his briefs, which also sat dangerously low on his lean hips.

"Sweet Jesus, that's sexy," she muttered.

He smiled and lowered himself, half on her, half beside her, shoved his hands into her hair and held her head as they kissed more, bodies moving together, her hips lifting against him with aching need. The sensation of his naked torso against hers had pleasure sweeping through her, her chest feeling hot as if she were glowing inside. She rubbed her breasts against his chest and he let out a low groan.

"You feel so good." He nipped her bottom lip, then dragged his tongue over it. "So soft." His hands caressed her, her arms, her breasts, her waist, her hip.

She'd never been a soft girl. She'd been an athletic tomboy most of her life. Yes, she had breasts which she was quite happy with, but she didn't have a curvy figure. Her waist wasn't tiny, her hips were boyish, her shoulders strong. But Logan's admiring looks and hot touches made her feel feminine and beautiful and desirable.

And so when he undid the button of her jeans, she knew they'd reached a point of no going back. She opened her mouth to say stop, but no sound came out. She was dying with wanting him, melting into him, so much pleasure filling her body at his kisses, his touch, his whispered words, and yet she ached for so much more. She felt drugged, helpless...and so she let it happen with an overwhelming feeling of inevitability. Unstoppable. Irresistible.

If she was going to do it, she wasn't going to ruin things by continuing to protest. Why play games, even with herself? As he'd said, there was no point in protesting unless she meant it.

And if she was going to do it, she was going all in and it was going to be good.

CHAPTER EIGHT

Logan rose to his knees and moved above her, lowering the zipper of her jeans, then tugging them down her hips and knees, slowly, carefully. He pulled off her boots and let them drop to the floor with a thud, then removed her jeans the rest of the way, leaving her in black thong panties. And socks. She tried to toe them off and with a smile he reached to help her.

He lifted her bare foot to his mouth and kissed it, watching her with hot eyes, and her body turned liquid. Then his tongue blazed a hot trail up over her calf, pausing on the sensitive skin on the inside of her knee, making her quiver. He kissed her there, then lowered her leg to the floor. His attention shifted to her panties.

"Pretty." He touched the black velvet bows on each hip. When he dragged his fingers along her abdomen just above the edge of the panties, she shivered. Then he bent and kissed her stomach, just below her bellybutton and then just above. Every nerve ending tingled, every muscle tightened as his mouth moved higher and then kissed her between her breasts. "Mmm."

With fascination, she watched his face, the pleasure in his eyes before his lids slowly drifted closed, long eyelashes dark against his cheeks, his mouth so sensual. He turned his face into one breast, opened his mouth and gently sucked, then his lips sought her nipple. She shuddered with pleasure as he took it into his mouth and sucked, first gently, then harder. Her hands slid into his silky hair to hold his head there as her own eyes closed and her chin came up. Sensation shot straight to her womb at the tug of his mouth on her breast. Little pleasure noises spilled from her lips.

He moved to the other breast, cupping the first with his hand, drawing on the other nipple with delicious little pulls, then scraping it so delicately with his teeth. Her body twitched in response and she shifted her legs, her pussy squeezing. "So good," she whispered. "Oh god, so good."

"Mmhmm. So sweet." He kissed her nipple, then began kissing his way down her stomach again, his big body shifting lower. Both hands cupped her breasts as he laid a kiss on the triangle of black fabric at the apex of her thighs. Excitement spiraled through her, *câlisse*, she was burning up inside. He licked along her skin, then took the edge of the panties in his teeth and tugged them down.

She lifted her hips off the satin lining of her jacket to assist him, watching him switch to using his hands. His hands looked so big and masculine, his fingers curled around the scrap of fabric, and her tummy did another little flip of lust. He carefully removed the panties over one foot, then the other, and she blinked when he shoved them into the front pocket of his jeans.

"What are you doing?" She lifted her head and went up onto her elbows.

He grinned. "If you have to ask that, I'm doing something wrong."

"I mean..." She sank back down as his hands slid up her thighs. "I mean, what...?" But when he bent and kissed the patch of hair he'd just revealed, she lost her thought.

"Christ, you smell good." He nuzzled her there. His hands still on her thighs, he pushed them open, nudging his way between.

"Oh god." She squeezed her eyes shut as her pussy melted. "Logan..."

"Yeah?" He leaned in and his tongue dragged over her folds. She gasped, then gasped again as he licked her there. Small wails escaped her as pleasure vibrated through her body. "You're so wet, Nicole." He lapped at her sensitive flesh again. "I love that."

She squirmed, more heat cascading over her body, her clit pulsing in anticipation.

"Such a pretty pussy." He pulled back to study her. Her face burned at his words. "So pink and shiny." His fingers slid though the thick cream there, finding her entrance, pushing gently inside. "Oh yeah." He used his thumbs to part her and once more licked his way up and down, kissing her inner lips, nibbling gently on her, licking around her clit, but not on it, even his breath on her sensitive skin making her tremble.

She groaned with aching need and frustration.

"You taste incredible," he murmured. "And you like this, don't you?"

"God yes!" She reached for his head and threaded her fingers through his hair. When she let her fingernails scrape over his scalp, he growled against her pussy. "Oh yeah, feels good, Logan."

His tongue slid over her, his lips sucked gently on her, torturing her, letting the flames inside her build higher and hotter. She lifted against his mouth and he wedged himself between her thighs, lifting her feet to his shoulders. He slid his hands beneath her ass and cupped her, bringing her up to his voracious mouth, and *sacrament*, he was good with that mouth. His tongue circled her clit again and again and then finally stroked over it. Sensation rocked her body, spreading from her center out, and she cried out, gasping for breath.

"Like that?" he murmured, one long finger sliding back inside her.

Aching, she mumbled her agreement.

And then he took her clit in his mouth and sucked. She almost hit the ceiling, she was so hypersensitized, so needy, whimpering with delight, every nerve ending on fire. His tongue rubbed over the knot of nerves and pressure built, that delicious buzzing and tingling intensifying, spreading through her whole body. "Ah! Oh god, yes." She let it grow and swell inside her, taking her up, Logan's mouth on her pussy, and then she cried out when it exploded, sparks shooting through her veins, waves of pleasure pouring over her.

Logan lifted his head from Nicole's sweet pussy, out of breath, her taste on his tongue, his lips wet. Holy hell. How did this happen?

Well, it had been building between them for a while, but wow. He sucked in air and pushed up onto his knees. She lay there, blinking her dazed eyes. He leaned forward, taking his weight on his arms, and kissed her mouth.

It blew his mind, her lying there naked beneath him, still trembling from her orgasm. The orgasm he'd given her. He smiled against her lips, then straightened and reached into his back pocket for his wallet. He flipped through it and pulled out the condom, tossed the wallet aside and ripped open the package.

"Oh," Nicole breathed, watching him.

Had to get these jeans off. His dick throbbed painfully behind the zipper pressing against it. He unzipped and shoved them down to his knees, releasing his heavy cock, but then he paused. It seemed wrong to not be naked when she was, so he fell back onto his ass and wrestled his jeans all the way off, which meant the Nikes had to go too. Jesus. Urgency burned in him, he needed to be inside her, wanted to feel her still coming around him.

"I'll make you come again." He kicked the jeans aside. "Thank Christ for that fireplace. Next time'll be in a bed. "

She swiped her tongue over her bottom lip, studying him with warm eyes, and once more he leaned over her and kissed her, sliding his tongue slowly in and out of her mouth. She moaned and the sexy little sound made his dick twitch.

"Gotta glove up," he said, amazed he could think of something like that when his head was spinning with lust. He wanted to be inside her so bad.

"Thank you."

He rolled on the condom and ran his hands over her thighs again, firm and slender. She was fucking gorgeous, her hair all spread around her on the floor, her body tight and lightly muscled, but still feminine. Especially her breasts, which made him nuts, the way they filled his hands, the pretty pale pink nipples tightened into perfect suckable points.

On his knees, legs spread wide, he edged closer, pushing her thighs up and back, opening her to him. He found his dick and pressed against her wet heat. Their eyes met and they breathed in tandem, short, shallow pants as deliberately he pushed into her. Her teeth sank into her lush bottom lip on a small gasp.

"Oh baby," he whispered. "That's good. Hot and tight around me."

She blinked.

He recognized the hunger in her eyes, growing again after her first climax, and he wanted to give her what she needed. He groaned at the urge to pound into her, his head falling back as he eased into her body, her pussy muscles closing around him tight and warm. A long groan escaped him. "Nicole. Ah Christ. You have no idea…" He loved sex, probably the only thing he loved more than hockey, and he liked his sex like his hockey— fast and rough and sometimes a little dirty. This was killing him, but he didn't want this to be a quick fuck on the floor, he wanted it to be more. He wanted it to be good for her. No— better than good.

He pushed in further, deeper, his dick throbbing inside her. His blood pounded in his veins, heat sizzled up his spine, and then he reached for her waist and held her tight as he pulled out and thrust back into her. He kept it slow, but forceful, watching her eyes glaze, her breath uneven through her parted lips.

"This is crazy," she whispered.

"I know. But I like it. You like it too." He held her gaze steadily, heat building inside him, fast and hard. "Don't you."

"Yes. I like it. You inside me like that…fuck me. God, Logan!"

"You want it harder?" He narrowed his eyes at her, her hips lifting against him.

"Yes!"

"Aw fuck." He looked down at where they were joined, his cock shiny with her cream, sliding in and out of her pretty pussy, her small patch of dark gold curls damp. "I knew it…I had a feeling…" Her breasts jiggled with each stroke of his body into hers and her breathing became noisier, small gasps and pants. He stretched out over her, resting his elbows on either side of her head, held her face and kissed her, hard. Their bodies moved together, both of them strong, straining against each other, and when she wrapped her long legs around his hips, the top of his head nearly blew off.

She arched and twisted beneath him. Her arms came around him too, and he lifted his mouth and pressed his cheek against hers, eyes closed.

"Nicole," he muttered. "I wanted this so bad. Wanted you...like this."

She groaned and her hips tilted against him.

He pulled her arms from around him and clasped her hands, then pinned them to the floor on either side of her head. Their eyes met in a collision of heat and sparks, power and surrender. Understanding. He fucked her harder, faster. The clasp and pull of her body on his dick was exquisite torture. Then her body went still and taut, her fingers tightening on his, her heels against his ass. She cried out and he kept moving, thrusting as her pussy rippled around him. Sweat built on his body, fire burned beneath his skin, heating him, and his balls throbbed with the need to come. The pressure exploded inside him. Guttural noises escaped from his mouth, long low sounds of agonizing pleasure, and then he buried his face in the side of her neck, his cock pulsing inside her.

He stayed inside her for a long time after he came, partly because he didn't want to move and partly because he didn't think he *could* move. Eventually, though, his arm muscles started to protest as he tried to hold some of his weight off her and he slowly pulled out of her body, reaching down to make sure the condom stayed in place.

Now what the hell was he supposed to do? He hadn't really thought this through, this having sex on the floor in an empty loft. He climbed to his feet and headed into the bathroom, and luckily enough, there was toilet paper on the roll. He got rid of the condom and brought some tissue back for Nicole. Once again on his knees, he moved toward her.

"What are you doing?"

"Um. Just going to clean you up." He'd worn a condom, but she was really wet, that little patch of curls damp, her inner thighs slick.

She clamped her thighs together. "You don't have to do that."

"Yes. I do." Firmly, he parted her legs and gently wiped her, then returned to the bathroom to flush the tissue. When he walked naked back into the living room, she had rolled to her stomach, her face buried in the collar of the jacket she was lying on.

The long smooth curve of her back begged him to sweep his hand over it and her perfect tight little ass had his palm itching to give her a tap there. "Hey." He dropped down beside her again. He gave in to the urge to explore her with his hand, her skin satiny smooth beneath his palm as he stroked down her back, over the curve of her hip, then rested on her waist. "What's wrong?"

"Oh god. You have no idea."

He rolled her onto her back and looked into her eyes. "That was sensational," he murmured. "Maybe a little too fast, but I think we both wanted it that way. This time."

"This time," she repeated, closing her eyes.

"Sorry about the floor. This isn't the most comfortable place." He stretched out beside her and pulled her into him, wrapping her up in his arms and legs. "Are you cold?"

"No. Dammit, quit being so nice."

He paused. "Am I supposed to be an asshole?"

She sighed. "No. Of course not."

A chiming noise filled the room. He lifted his head. What the…?

"My cell phone." She rolled away from him. She crawled across the floor to where she'd dropped her purse and the view of her doing that had his dick surging to life again. Jesus Christ. She sat and pulled the phone out, reading the screen. Her lips pressed together and her eyes closed.

"What is it?"

She turned her head and looked at him. "Paul. He's texting to confirm our date tonight."

Logan's insides tightened, hell, his whole body went tense. "You're not going."

She frowned at him but didn't reply.

"Seriously, Nicole."

Her chin firmed a little as she looked down at the phone in her hand. "You don't get to tell me what to do."

Oh man. Heat flared inside him. "After *that*? Seriously? You're going to go out with some other dude?"

"I have to."

"Bullshit," he snapped. "You can cancel. Text him back and tell him you can't make it."

"You don't understand." Her face twisted as if she was in pain before she bent her head, her long hair falling over it. He didn't get it.

"You're right. I don't understand."

"This can't happen again." She started thumbing the keys on her phone.

"Nicole." His voice came out hard and sharp. "Don't do that."

She ignored him and fury welled up inside him. She sent off the text, slipped her phone back into her purse and rose to her feet. Christ, in the now nearly dark room, the light of the fireplace flickered over her skin, lighting it in shades of gold, her body long and lean and beautiful. She found her clothes and started dressing. Fuck!

Then she paused.

"My panties."

He tipped his head, grabbed his own clothes and yanked them on, ignoring her.

"Fine," she snapped. "Keep them." When they were both dressed, she turned and met his eyes again. "Please don't tell anyone about this."

His jaw dropped. "Tell anyone?" he repeated stupidly. He shook his head. "Who the hell would I tell?"

"I don't know. The guys in the dressing room."

His mouth dropped even lower. "Are you fucking kidding me? Why the fuck would I tell them about this?"

She looked away and hitched a shoulder. "I don't know. Just...you know, guys talking. Just please, don't."

His hands curled into fists and he resisted the urge to punch a hole in the wall behind him. His heart punched against his ribs, his face heated and his shoulders stiffened. "What *was* this?" he demanded, not moving. "What the fuck, Nicole? Do you think that little of me that..." Words failed him. He gave his head another shake. Somehow he'd envisioned them going back to her place, going inside with her, spending the evening, and yeah, ending up in bed again. He wasn't sure if he'd ever been more pissed outside of the rink.

She flipped her long hair out over the collar of her jacket and picked up her purse. "We should go."

CHAPTER NINE

"You're so big." The sexy brunette in the painted-on black dress squeezed his biceps. Logan smiled down at her, the music of the night club pulsing around them, the lights throbbing.

This was what he needed. A few drinks, a few hot girls coming on to him. He wasn't sure which one he'd take home tonight, but he had a feeling he could probably talk both Scarlet and Jenny into joining him.

Fuck. He didn't *have* a home to take girls to. He was fucking staying with Fedor and Taylor. Visions of a hot threesome vanished in a puff of smoke. He sighed, but kept his smile in place. Maybe Scarlet would take him back to her place.

Or maybe not.

He couldn't get Nicole out of his head, damn her. Christ, he kept thinking about them rolling around on the floor, then having her pinned there beneath him, looking up with that expression of dazed submission. And wrath flared up again when he remembered she was out with some other guy. Unbelievable!

His interest in Scarlet and Jenny and every other single available woman in the club evaporated. He needed to sit down. Somewhere quiet. Hell. He was going home. Alone.

In the taxi, he thought about the evening. At least he'd gotten together with some of the guys. Bonding always happened pretty good over a few beers, a few laughs. He'd gotten to know a few of them better and that was positive. He had to make as much effort off the ice as he did on.

Fedor and Taylor were already in bed when he got to their place, letting himself in with the security code they'd given him. The house was dark and quiet. He might as well be alone. Shit, he should've brought Scarlet there anyway.

Then one corner of his mouth kicked up as he ran a glass of water in the kitchen sink. He didn't want Scarlet. He wanted Nicole.

Nicole managed to mostly avoid Logan for the next few days, keeping busy at work and trying to avoid the arena when practices were going on. Every time she thought of him, she got that full achy feeling in her pelvis. Every time she thought about his hands on hers, pressing hers to the floor as he fucked her, her knees went weak. The way he'd looked at her, all strong and dominant male, had annihilated her resistance and the way he'd been so gentle and appreciative had destroyed her resolve.

She hated herself for being so weak. Her determination that she would never get involved with another hockey player had lasted…how long? Oh yeah, less than two weeks. Admirable, really. *Tabarnac*!

And if anyone found out…oh god. Oh god, her insides started burning and churning at what people would say about her. He'd been offended when she'd asked him not to tell anyone. She'd insulted him and she regretted that. But her fear about being the object of more scorn made her say it.

Hell, she deserved scorn. They could call her a hockey whore and how could she deny it? They'd had sex on the floor of an empty condo! Hell, she should have quit this job. She still could. She slammed her keyboard tray under her desk with a crash.

"Whoa," Karla said. "What's wrong?"

Nicole looked over at the Director of Client Services. She forced a smile. "Nothing."

"Seemed like you were angry there."

"I slept in this morning," Nicole lied. "I don't like starting the day that way."

"Oh, I know! It totally starts things off bad. I'm going over to Caribou Coffee, want something?"

"Mmm. Yeah. Large black coffee. Hey, I'll come with you." She needed fresh air and a walk.

On their trip for coffee, they got talking about what they'd done the night before. "I went to the gym and worked out," Nicole said. "How about you?"

"I was scrapbooking," Karla said. "With my friends."

"Oh you do such beautiful scrapbooks."

"You should come with me some time."

"Oh." Nicole balked. "That's not really my thing."

"But it's fun! It's a good creative outlet."

"I'm not all that creative." But hey...maybe this was something she should try. Something different than watching hockey, working with hockey, working out at the gym or hanging out with Taylor. And her hockey player husband. "But yeah, maybe I could try it some time."

"Cool. Have you started your Christmas shopping?"

"No." It wasn't even December yet! Oh right. Tomorrow was Thanksgiving. "You?"

"I've started. Got plans for Thanksgiving?"

"I'll be at Taylor and Fedor's place. She does a big dinner. I'm going to help her cook."

"Sounds fun. Your family's in Montreal, right?"

"Just my dad. My brother's in...well, I'm not sure what his schedule is right now. And it's not Thanksgiving in Canada, that was last month."

Karla chattered on about her big family get together that would be taking place, and when they got back to the office Nicole smiled. She hadn't thought about Logan for a good twenty minutes. Yay! Then she rolled her eyes.

The next afternoon she arrived at Taylor's house with a small bag carrying some dressier clothes she'd change into for dinner, several bags of groceries and two bottles of wine.

"You didn't need to bring this!" Taylor helped her with the bags. "I have so much food."

"I want to contribute. I'm going to make my *tourtière* and sugar pie."

"Yum."

"I know they're not traditional Thanksgiving dishes here, but they're good."

"That's okay. I think I might be the only American here." Taylor laughed.

"Seriously?" Nicole thought about it. "Who's coming?"

"Well, you, of course. Fedor's Russian. Logan's Canadian."

Nicole's stomach swooped. Logan. Of course. Taylor named off some other players, all Canadian. "Oh, Adam's wife is American. And I think Danny Mohan is American, too. Teppo is from Finland."

"It will be a multi-cultural Thanksgiving."

"I think it's fun," Taylor said. "Gotta check the turkey." She opened one of two built-in ovens and peered in. "You know, stuffing a turkey is really disgusting."

Nicole grinned. "I'm glad you did that before I got here."

When she'd basted the turkey and checked the ham in the other oven, Taylor said, "Let's open some wine."

"Great idea."

As Taylor poured Merlot into two generous glasses, Nicole said, "Hey, Tay?"

"Mmm?"

"Would you come to hip hop dance classes with me?"

A little wine sloshed onto the counter and Taylor choked on a laugh. "Hip hop?"

"Yeah." Nicole nodded enthusiastically. "I want to take up some new hobbies. I thought that would be fun."

Taylor handed her the wine. "Seriously?"

"Sure. It's good exercise and it's something different than going to the gym or running."

"You love going to the gym and running."

"True." She shrugged and sipped her wine. "I just thought I should try some new things. I'm going to try scrapbooking with Karla from work, too."

Now Taylor really did choke. "Scrapbooking? You?"

Nicole frowned at her friend. "Why not?"

"Um…no reason. It just…um…surprises me." She bent over laughing again.

"What is so funny?" Fedor asked, coming into the room.

"Your wife is laughing at me," Nicole complained, setting down her wine. She pulled an apron out of one of the bags she'd brought and tied it around her waist. "Just because I want to try some new things."

"Trying new things can be good." Another deep male voice spoke, this one with no accent and Nicole closed her eyes briefly as her body went on alert. He made her think of trying dirty new things. "What kind of new things?"

She turned to look at Logan. "Never mind."

He met her eyes and instead of his usual sexy warmth, he gave her a narrow-eyed, unsmiling look. She swallowed.

"Oh come on," he drawled, sauntering into the room. His faded and ripped jeans rode wickedly low on his hips, the sleeves of a long-sleeved black Henley shirt shoved up on big strong forearms. He nabbed a cracker from a plate on the counter. "Tell us. I could use a laugh."

She pursed her lips and looked down at the counter. "Um..."

"Nicole wants me to take hip hop lessons with her," Taylor said. "And she's going to start..." Another choked laugh. "Scrapbooking."

Logan's mouth twitched. "Scrapbooking, huh?" Then his eyes dropped to her apron and this time a small smile did break free. "Cute."

Nicole looked down at her apron that said, *If hockey was easy they'd call it soccer.* "My brother gave it to me."

"Julien."

"Yes." She slid her gaze away from him and began to assemble her ingredients.

"I have a T-shirt that says *kiss a hockey player, because other athletes play with balls,*" Taylor chimed in.

Logan laughed and Nicole resisted looking at him, although the urge to see his smile was powerful.

"That's one of the top ten reasons to date a hockey player," Logan said.

She bit her lip against the urge to ask, but Taylor asked for her. "What is?"

"Date a hockey player, because baseball players only know how to hit balls."

Nicole kept her head bent to hide her smile, but Taylor burst out laughing.

"Good one." Fedor grinned. He turned to his wife. "You're going to hip hop? This is dancing?"

She slid up against him and smooched his jaw. "Yes, dear. Dancing. Like this." And she stepped back and did a few fast moves with legs widespread, arms waving, hips shaking.

Fedor's mouth dropped open. "That was hot."

"Great," Nicole muttered. "Forget that idea. I'm not going to a beginner class with you."

Taylor danced up behind her and shook her body against Nicole's back, then smooched her cheek. Nicole couldn't help but grin and then she caught Logan's eye and there it was, that heat once again. She gulped.

"Yeah." He nodded and folded his arms across his chest. "I'm up for seeing you two hip hop dance together."

Taylor laughed again and danced over to him, sliding her palm across his cheek. "Oh you sick man you," she teased.

Nicole pressed her lips together, envious of Taylor's harmless, easy flirting with Logan.

"Okay now," Taylor said. "If you guys are going to be in the kitchen, you're going to help."

"I think we should watch football," Fedor said. "It will be safer."

"Good plan." They moved into the great room and Fedor turned on the big screen television.

"Potatoes." Taylor picked up a piece of paper. "Gotta peel potatoes. And make the salad dressing and trim the beans. Then set the table."

Nicole smiled at her friend's organizational skills. This wasn't her first big dinner party there, so she knew Taylor had lists and spreadsheets and timelines for everything.

With the football game playing in the background, they chatted as they worked in the kitchen, but Nicole was exquisitely aware of Logan on the far side of the big room, his long legs stretched in front of him on an ottoman. She tried to focus on her pie, but more than a few times when she glanced his way, he was looking at her too. Their eyes collided, then slid away.

"There," she said. "*Tarte au sucre*, ready for the oven. Now for the *tortière*."

"That's more of a Christmas dish, right?" Taylor asked.

"Yeah. But since my family doesn't have much of a Christmas, this is the only time I ever get to make it."

"Does your mom make it?"

"No." Nicole shook her head. "She's American. It was my *mémère*—my dad's mother—who taught me to make it."

"Cool."

A while later they moved into the dining room, a stunning room with red walls, an immense black table and black leather chairs. Nicole gazed out the big mullioned window for a moment, looking onto the spacious back yard now blanketed with fluffy white, the shrubs wearing caps of soft snow. "It's still snowing. It's so pretty."

"It is. But holy crap, that's a lot of snow." Taylor frowned. "I hope everyone can make it here okay."

"It'll be fine."

"I hope so." Taylor had already set out stacks of dishes and flatware, enough for the eighteen people who'd be there. "I decided to do buffet style this year. A sit down dinner for eighteen is crazy."

"It is a lot of food."

"Okay," Taylor said when they were done arranging everything to Taylor's satisfaction. "I'm going to change and beautify myself before people get here."

Logan appeared in the dining room doorway. "You don't need to beautify," he said to Taylor. "You're always beautiful."

Nicole turned her back and rolled her eyes. She could not believe she was jealous of her best friend. Just a little.

"Sweet talker." Taylor smiled and glanced at her watch. "Nicole, you can use the spare bedroom you've used before to change and get ready. I put your things in there."

"Thanks."

"Fedor wants to know if you picked up any chicken wings," Logan said.

"Chicken wings! Is he nuts? This is Thanksgiving."

"He says he needs Buffalo chicken wings to watch football."

"Phhht. I'll go talk to him." She hustled out of the room, leaving Nicole and Logan alone.

"Excuse me," she said trying to get past him where he blocked the door. "I need to go change."

He looked down at her, his mouth a flat line. "How was your date Saturday night?"

She smiled, her eyes narrowed up in fake cheer. "Lovely. How about you? I heard you went out with some of the guys."

"Yep."

"I heard there were girls all over you." Oh hell, did she say that out loud?

"Yep. That's why I went."

Her smile faded. Bastard.

They stood there facing each other. Nicole had to break the eye contact, she just couldn't hold his gaze without wanting to fall to her knees in front of him. "Please. Let me by."

After a brief hesitation, he stepped aside. She hurried out of the dining room and down the hall to the guest room. Closing the door behind her, she pressed her hands to hot cheeks. The attraction she felt to Logan hadn't diminished and only reinforced how extremely painful her date with Paul had been. They just had nothing in common, and much as she wanted to expand her horizons and have some kind of interests outside of hockey…he just wasn't going to do it.

She changed out of her jeans and sweater into the dress she'd brought, a sleeveless black dress that was simple, but she liked the shape of the neckline and how it fit her body. She brushed her hair and touched up mascara and lip gloss, then went out to greet the other guests who started arriving.

Taylor started music, but the guys made her turn it off until the football game was over. People filled the kitchen and great room, talking and laughing, offering to help with food. Nicole stirred gravy while Logan mashed potatoes, and she had to fight to keep her eyes off his big flexing muscles as he held the pot and plunged the masher in and out. Ergh.

"So what are the other top ten reasons to date a hockey player?" Taylor asked Logan.

He shot her a sexy smile. "Let's see how many I can remember. Um…they always wear protection."

Nicole choked. And coughed.

"You okay, hon?" Taylor asked.

"Yes," she wheezed. She could *not* look at Logan. Even so, she sensed his grin.

"They have great hands," he continued.

Oh yeah. Oh god, yeah.

"They have great stamina."

She bit her lip. Their sex on the floor hadn't required a lot of stamina; they'd both been so hot for each other, it hadn't lasted all that long. But she had no doubt he had lots and lots of stamina. Actually, so did she...

"Nic, you're whipping the gravy into a froth," Taylor said. "I think it's good."

"Oh. Yeah. Okay." She set down the whisk. And Taylor had to go and talk about whipping. "It's hot in here," she said without thinking, and then she caught Logan's smirk and her face turned scorching. "I mean, I've been standing over this hot stove...I need more wine."

She grabbed her glass and downed the rest of the contents, started to reach for the bottle, but Logan was there with it. He poured some into her glass.

"Thanks," she croaked. She met his knowing gaze, his brown eyes gleaming.

With everyone helping, the food was carried into the dining room and arranged on the glossy black sideboard. Now Taylor got her wish and started some music on the sound system that had speakers in every room. With much laughter and talking, people filled their plates with turkey and ham, *tourtière*, and all the many side dishes. Some sat at the dining room table, others moved into the great room and balanced their plates on their knees as they ate.

"No, no, you cannot sit there," Fedor said, as she went to take a chair at one corner of the dining room table.

She paused, glancing at Taylor, who shrugged. "Um. Why not?"

"Unmarried people should not sit at the corner of the table. Otherwise they will not marry. Is Russian superstition."

She grinned at her friend's husband. "I'm not superstitious."

"Sit here." With a laugh, she took the chair he offered, which was next to him, with Logan on her other side. Taylor sat across from her along with several other Caribou players and the wives of two of them.

"So what's everyone thankful for?" Taylor asked, picking up her fork.

"I'm thankful for all this food," Logan said. They all laughed. "Seriously, thanks to Taylor and Fedor for hosting this."

Everyone agreed and lifted their glasses in a toast. Taylor beamed.

"I'm also thankful for the great hockey fans here in Minneapolis," Logan added.

"You're liking it here?" Danny asked.

"Yeah. It's pretty good. Definitely more of a hockey city than in California."

Fedor snorted. "They barely know what hockey is in California."

"It's different, for sure," Logan said. He caught Nicole's eye. "In a good way," he added. "

"I'm thankful for good snow tires in this blizzard," Teppo said.

"Blizzard?" Nicole looked out the window. In the dark, snowflakes continued to fall from the sky, piling higher and higher on the ground and trees and shrubs. "This isn't a blizzard."

"True that," Logan added. "There's no wind. It can't be a blizzard."

"You Canadians are experts on that?" Danny said.

Logan and Nicole exchanged glances, which should have been with harmless amusement. But no. The sizzle was still there. She looked back down at her plate.

"Blizzards happen here too," she said.

"I'm thankful for Veil," Adam said.

Silence. "What?" Taylor asked, looking at him. "Vail? Colorado?"

He grinned and his wife Manda gave him a punch in the shoulder. "Shut up."

"Oh no," Logan said with a laugh. "What is it?"

"Veil," Adam said again. He spelled it.

"Still clueless." Nicole smiled and looked around at the others at the table who seemed equally stumped.

"It's a new product," Adam said. "Manda ordered it on the Internet. It's a flavored strip that women put on their tongue when they're, uh...you know."

Nicole blinked.

"When they're what?" Taylor asked.

"Going down. Giving head. Giving a BJ."

Nicole's eyes went wide and she choked on a laugh, as did everyone else after a few stunned seconds.

"Seriously," Adam continued. "I've never been so happy in my life since she got that stuff."

His wife groaned and covered her face. "Thanks for sharing, dude."

"I don't get it," Nicole said. Once again she couldn't help but glance at Logan and heat swept over her body as their eyes met.

"You don't know what a blow job is?" Logan asked her.

She gave him a disgusted look. "No," she said disdainfully. "I have *no* idea."

"That's too bad. Maybe I could..."

"So what is this again?" Taylor asked. Nicole shot her a grateful look. "You put it in your mouth while you're...doing it...why?"

"It's flavored," Manda answered. "It tastes good and disguises the taste of semen."

Taylor's mouth dropped open and Nicole laughed.

"Oh. Well. Hmm."

"So where did you say you get that stuff?" Fedor asked casually. More laughter ensued and Taylor gave him a reproving look. "What?" he asked. "More blow jobs cannot be bad."

"Amen," Logan said fervently. Nicole caught the wicked sparkle in his eye.

"When I said I don't get it, it's not because I don't know what fellatio is," she said. "It's because I don't understand the need to disguise the taste."

"Mmm," he murmured. "My kind of woman."

CHAPTER TEN

Nicole's hot glare at him made him want to laugh.

"Stop it," she hissed at him.

He leaned closer to her. The scent of her hair, that fresh citrusy smell, rose to his nostrils. "Stop what?"

She just scowled at him again. Then Logan looked across the table and saw Taylor watching them with a small smile. Oh-oh.

"What flavors does it come in?" Danny asked.

This whole topic was hilarious. And arousing. Especially with Nicole there beside him, looking especially hot in that little black dress and some pointy toed black shoes. Not that he had a fetish or anything, but shoes like that always turned him on, especially with her long legs, and now thinking about her going down on her knees in front of him...hell. He was getting a stiffy. He shifted in his chair.

"Mango, cherry, passionfruit."

More laughter.

"Maybe we should try it." Danny looked hopefully at his wife.

She grinned. "Maybe we should."

Okay, if they talked any more about blow jobs with Nicole sitting right there beside him, Logan was going to be in serious pain.

But it was a fun day and evening with good people, a great chance to get to know some of his new team mates better, including their wives, and a great chance to just watch Nicole as she moved around the kitchen helping Taylor, helping clear the dishes and put away food when they'd finished. Gradually people started leaving and eventually it was just the four of them. It was nearly midnight.

"Oh my god," Taylor said, kicking off her shoes and throwing herself down on the couch. "I'm exhausted."

"It was fantastic," Fedor said. "Thank you, sweetheart." He sat beside her and lifted her legs across his lap, then started massaging her feet.

Nicole dropped into a chair too. Logan sat down on a chair next to her, admiring her long legs stretched out in front of her, still wearing those hot shoes.

"I'm tired too," she said. "But you did more work than I did. I guess I should get going too."

"Oh stay a little longer. Have one more glass of wine and relax for a few minutes before you leave."

"We must finish the wine," Fedor said. "Is Russian tradition. If you have alcohol, it must all be drinked."

"Drunk," Taylor said with a grin.

"I am not drunk," Fedor said, affronted.

They all laughed, including Fedor.

"I'll get it for you." Logan rose and went to the kitchen.

"Thank you." She accepted the glass when he returned, meeting his eyes only briefly.

The four of them got talking and the next time anyone looked at the clock, it was nearly two in the morning.

"Oh man." Nicole stood and stretched, which made her short dress rise up on her thighs and stretch across her breasts. "I better go."

"I don't think you should drive," Taylor said. "You've had a lot to drink."

"Not that much. I had a few glasses of wine earlier this afternoon and just two now."

"But still. The roads are bad. In fact, I'm not sure you can even get out right now."

"It's still snowing." Logan walked to the front door and opened it. Snow swirled in on a frosty breeze. "Christ. You can barely see your car."

Nicole made a noise of distress behind him as she peered around him. "Holy crap."

"I could help you clear it off. And we'll have to shovel the driveway. Jesus, I don't know if *anyone* is going to get out tomorrow."

She bit her lip. They both knew how much work it was going to be to shovel her out and she hated to put them to the trouble that late at night.

"Just stay here," Taylor said with a yawn. "We'll shovel you out in the morning."

"This *is* a lot of snow," Nicole said. "But Silvia is all alone."

"She'll be okay for a while longer."

Nicole sighed. "Okay, fine. I'll stay."

Logan closed the door and turned around.

"Good," Taylor said. "You can sleep in that spare room. I'm going to bed, but I'll get some pajamas for you and put them in there." She turned to her husband. "C'mon, hon."

"Good night."

Taylor and Fedor turned off some lights in the living room and kitchen and disappeared down the hall, leaving Logan and Nicole alone in the dimly lit great room, the fireplace glowing on one wall.

"Well," Nicole said, avoiding his eyes. "I guess I'll go to bed too. Good night."

"Nicole."

She paused and flicked him a wary look. "What?"

"Come here." He made his tone authoritative, because she seemed to respond to that.

She looked at the floor, but didn't move.

"What's wrong?" he asked, wanting to move toward her, but wanting her to respond to him. "You're upset because of what happened at the loft."

She lifted big blue eyes to him and his chest went soft inside when he saw the anguish in them.

"It's not that bad," he said softly. "Come here."

She slowly blinked, then took two steps toward him. He set his hands on her hips and pulled her closer. "Talk to me. C'mon, let's sit down. Let's just talk for a while."

He read the doubt on her face, but led her toward the big red leather couch facing the fireplace. When she sat down, he reached for a fuzzy beige blanket draped over one arm and swept it over both of them as he sat beside her. He tucked it around her and pulled her into his arms.

At first her body was tight and tense. Then she relaxed into him and he exhaled with relief. Christ, he wanted her. It was crazy.

"Talk to me," he said again. "What's going on?"

"You know what's going on," she whispered, her face turned away from him despite being pressed against his body. "You know what happened with Cody. You know I can't do this."

Oh fuck.

"I'm not Cody," he said, voice hard. "Not even fucking close."

She sighed. "I know you're not. But…when he said that stuff about me…about the…" Her voice caught and she paused for a moment. "The gang bang…I know that's what everyone was thinking about me."

"Fuck no!"

"Yes." She fingered the soft blanket. "He said that because it's true. I've gone out with a few hockey players. And I'm not going to do that again. I'm not going to open myself up to being slammed like that again in front of the whole world."

Shit. Fucking hell. What a dipshit Cody Burrell was. If Logan hadn't been pissed at him enough before, he was now.

Logan wasn't known as a fighter on the ice, but he'd never backed down from one either. He was big and strong and knew how to throw a punch, and at that moment, he wished Cody played for another team so he could slam him into the boards, drop the gloves and punch his lights out.

"I'm not Cody," he said again. Hell, he didn't know what to say.

They sat there in silence for a few minutes, his hand rubbing up and down her back. She relaxed a little more against him.

"I guess that was a shitty thing to go through," he finally said.

"Ya think?"

His lips quirked. "Okay, just call me Captain Obvious."

He felt her smile against his shoulder. "It was humiliating. And mostly because I brought it on myself."

"Jesus, Nicole. You didn't do anything wrong. Other than get mixed up with an asshole."

"He wouldn't have said that if I hadn't dated other hockey players. My dad was right. Women shouldn't be involved in hockey."

"Well forgive me, because god knows your dad is a helluva hockey player, and he's pretty smart when it comes to hockey, but he's an idiot when it comes to his daughter."

She huffed out a little laugh. "Sure."

"Seriously, Nicole. What father wouldn't encourage his daughter to follow her dreams?" He reached for her chin and tipped her head back so he could see her face. "I mean, sometimes our dreams aren't always realistic. Yeah, if you wanted to make a living playing hockey, it'd be tough. Not many women have played in the NHL."

"Nobody really has. Manon Rhéaume played a couple of preseason games. Hayley Wickenheiser played with the Finnish men's league. Some have played in North American minor leagues."

"Even so. You could've done that. You shouldn't have had to give it up if you loved it."

She met his eyes and hers softened and warmed. "You really believe that?"

"Of course."

She gave a shaky smile. "Thanks." She dropped her gaze. "I think…maybe I was afraid to push it because I wasn't really sure if I was good enough to make it."

His heart tightened. "I bet you were. You have good hockey genes."

One corner of her mouth kicked up.

"I guess I kind of had the same fears." He snuggled her back in against him. "Two older brothers who were instant superstars. All my life I tried to live up to them and always came up short. When I was in college I was terrified I wouldn't get drafted, and terrified that I would. I knew I wouldn't be first round pick like Tag, or even a second like Jase. Or if I did

get drafted, I'd never make it through training camp without
being sent back to the minors."

"You're just as good as they are."

He laughed.

"Seriously. I mean, you play different. All three of you are
really smart, but you use your body more. You're a very
dynamic player. You have really good puck instincts and
amazing hands. I love the way you play the puck so close to
your feet, for such a big guy that's really amazing."

Warmth filled his chest. "Thank you. I didn't know you paid
that much attention to my game."

"I don't."

"Yes, you do."

"Okay, I do, but it's part of my job. I like to know the
players and what their strengths and weaknesses are. I can't
believe you worried about living up to your brothers."

"And still do to this day."

She looked up at him again. "What? Do your parents
compare you guys to each other? That's not right."

"No." He shook his head. "Not like that. I just mean, Tag
and Jase are both settling down with girlfriends, like, serious
get-married girlfriends. Jase is having a baby in a couple of
weeks and my mom's so stoked about it, it's all she talks about.
She's going to be a grandma, like her best friend Jenn
MacIntosh. Whose daughter, by the way, is Tag's girlfriend, so
Mom's all thrilled because she loves Kyla and now she'll be
like the daughter she never had or something—all thanks to
Tag."

"Ah."

He wasn't sure why he was telling her all this shit. All his
life he'd tried to be all happy and nonchalant about it all,
pretending he didn't care, but the truth was…he did care. A lot.
If he didn't make it after Tag and Jase had, he'd be a huge
loser. When Nicole had confessed her own feelings of not
being good enough, he'd immediately felt an affinity. An
understanding that had prompted him to share his own stupid
feelings. But nobody really needed to know that he felt
inadequate compared to his brothers. After being traded away
by the team he'd dedicated his career to, his self esteem had

taken another beating. He knew it wasn't personal, that decisions like that came down to dollars, but even so, it hadn't exactly been ego-boosting to be given the boot. "Please don't spread this all around.

She went still against him. "Like, to whom?"

"I don't know. You probably talk to Taylor. Don't tell her I'm a big insecure loser."

She drew back slowly. "Logan. You are hardly a loser."

He made a face. "You know what I mean."

And then she astonished him by lifting her hand to his face, laying her palm on his cheek and smiling at him, a small, soft smile.

His body went instantly hard, his blood racing hot through his veins. He pulled her against him and kissed her, hard and fast and urgent. And she kissed him back.

⁓

Nicole wanted to jump on top of him and kiss him crazy. She didn't know why, but when he'd made that comment about being a loser, her heart just melted and she lost it. God, he wasn't a loser, he was a fiercely talented NHL hockey player. His new team mates loved him. She'd seen how he was not only fitting in, but taking control of things on the ice and in the dressing room. Management was thrilled. Sure the team had a long way to go, but the mood was a lot more upbeat than it had been a few weeks ago, and it was because of Logan.

He'd asked her not to tell anyone how he felt. For a few seconds, she'd been offended, and then she remembered that she'd asked the same thing of him. And suddenly she felt badly about that, about insulting him that way, when she could see he wasn't the kind of guy to run around bragging about his sexcapades.

So when he pulled her up against his big, hard body, she went willingly, and surrendered her mouth to his as he kissed her, on and on, his tongue sliding into her mouth, his hands anchored on her body. And that aching lust swelled up inside her, so fast, so hot, her body pulsed with it and she kissed him back, desperate, pressing her body against his.

"You've been driving me nuts all day," he muttered against her cheek, panting.

"Ha," she choked out. "You've been making *me* crazy. Talking about those reasons to date a hockey player. You did that on purpose, didn't you?"

"Hell yeah. There are more, you know."

"I don't want to know them," she moaned, as he opened his mouth on her jaw.

"Hockey players have a long stick."

A laugh escaped her even as she let her head fall back so he could drag his tongue over her neck.

"They know how to use their wood."

"Stop."

She felt his smile against her skin. "Here's the one I think you really like," he said, his voice husky. She waited a couple of tingling beats and then he continued. "They know when to play rough."

And with that, he caught her hands, pinned them behind her back and had her flat on the couch. With his heavy weight on her, she gazed up at him, enthralled. Her insides went hot and achy and her muscles weak. He stared down at her with masculine satisfaction, studying her face. He knew what she wanted.

She struggled to draw air into her lungs, lips parted. He withdrew one of his hands from beneath her back, still easily holding her wrists with the other. He gently stroked some hair off her face. His erection pressed against her lower stomach and her breasts swelled and ached, her nipples tight. He rubbed his thumb over her lower lip, then trailed his fingers down her throat, over the neckline of her dress and lower to her breast. He closed his hand over it and gently squeezed and a small sound escaped her lips as pleasure poured over her, pooling low in her core.

She was helpless, trapped by his big body and his hands and his mesmerizing gaze...and she loved it.

"This is what you like, isn't it." He leaned in closer and licked over her bottom lip.

She didn't answer. Admitting it made her vulnerable.

"It's okay." He rubbed his nose along the side of hers. She closed her eyes and breathed in his warmth, the scent of his skin, zesty clean and male. His scruff of beard rasped over her jaw and she rubbed her face against his, seeking more of the sensation. "I like it too."

Oh. She felt herself melting, her body weakening, all her breath leaving her body.

"My room," he said. "Now."

He pushed up off her, releasing her hands only long enough to stand, and then he reached for them again to pull her up off the couch too. He tugged her with him, first to the fireplace where he flicked the switch to turn it off, then across the dark room, lit only by a night light in the kitchen.

She wasn't a tiny, helpless female, although he was much bigger than she, but she felt that way as he led her down the hall to the bedroom where he was staying, where she'd bumped into him that day she'd come back from New York. He quietly closed the door behind them.

Milky light from the large window filled the dark room, creating blue and silver shadows. Outside, snow still swirled and drifted down from a pale sky, low clouds reflecting the light of the city, the snow casting it back and creating an illuminated landscape outside the house almost as bright as daylight.

Logan turned and pushed her back against the door, crowding her up against it with his body, bending his knees a little to find her mouth with his. She reached for his waist and held on as her legs trembled and he pressed in closer, one hand sliding to the back of her neck, the other finding her breast again.

Once again, the only thought in her head was, damn, he was a good kisser. So sexy. So dominating and yet so tender. She couldn't get enough of it, of him, of the taste of his mouth, the feel of his lips on hers, his tongue stroking inside, his beard scraping against her skin. Her pussy clenched hard as his thigh pressed between hers and she tried to arch against him as much as she could with the door at her back and his body against her front.

His strong hand shifted to her jaw, tilting her head, and he took her mouth again in a deeper, darker kiss. His body radiated heat and power. His hand kneaded her breast, rubbed over her sensitive nipple, and she wanted her dress and her bra gone, wanted to feel his hands on her bare flesh. God, what was he doing to her? She whimpered.

"I'd love to fuck you right up against this door," he whispered in her ear, making her shiver. "But Taylor and Fedor might hear us."

"Quiet," she replied in an equally hushed tone, her entire body quivery with lust. "Have to be quiet."

"Yeah. And that's no fun at all." He nipped at her ear lobe. "Because I want to make you come until you scream."

Heat shot through her. *Tabarnac de câlisse*, he was setting her on fire.

The hand at her breast stroked down over her waist, her hip, then his fingers moved on her thigh to pull her dress up. "This is a sexy dress. And I love the shoes."

"Mmm." His fingers found skin and slipped up beneath her dress. When his palm closed over her hip, bare but for the string of her thong panties, she let out a sigh of pleasure. She burned for him, fire rippling beneath her skin, liquid gathering between her legs. And he kissed her again, holding her face and her hip, fingers pressing into her ass, his big thigh thrusting up against her pussy.

Her clit throbbed, her inner muscles tightened and she tried to grind against him, seeking pressure where she needed it.

"Hmm. Hot, aren't you, baby."

She sank her teeth into her bottom lip, unreasonably turned on by the endearment. She was far from a baby. But damn, that made her hot. His lips skimmed her throat and sucked gently there as his fingers curved around her ass cheek. Sensation shimmered over her body and anticipation tightened every nerve ending as his fingers slid further around, further down, and then gently slipped beneath her thong panties and pushed into her pussy from behind.

Her knees nearly gave out and she parted her legs a little to give him wicked access to her body there.

"Wet," he whispered, kissing her collar bone. "So wet, Nicole."

She could only moan helplessly as he found the slick, swollen folds of her pussy. He stroked deeper, searching out the sensitive opening, one finger sliding in. He stroke and rubbed there, making her need and excitement build even higher. Her veins heated, her clit ached and she struggled to breathe. Her fingers dug into his sweater, into the hard muscles beneath.

"Wet and hot." He continued to torment her both with words and his fingers between her legs. "So sexy."

Her head rolled against the door. "Bed."

"Oh yeah, we'll get there, no worries, babe. But I'm having fun here, like this. With you up against the door and me fucking you with my fingers."

More heat flashed over her. His fingers moved in her again. She could feel how wet she was by the slickness of his touch, and she shifted, trying to get him in deeper, trying to press her clit against the hard bulge of his cock. She needed to come so bad, her whole body tight and aching with need.

His other hand lowered to her thigh and lifted it against his hip. "Oh yeah," she groaned as the pressure against her pussy increased. "Oh yeah, that's good."

He rocked into her and kissed her again, his fingers buried inside her, wet and thrusting. Her pussy tried to clench around him, draw him in deeper, and he made a noise of appreciation as their bodies moved together, mouths joined. Sensation built, tightening her womb, pulsing in her clit, and she reached for it, strained toward it, let it roll over in hot, throbbing waves of pleasure. She moaned into his mouth, her pussy tightening on his hand.

"Oh yeah," he murmured. "Oh yeah, come for me, just like that."

She trembled and went limp, her body sagging between his and the door. Then she lifted a hand and gave his shoulder a half-hearted punch. "You said we couldn't do it up against the door in case we made too much noise."

He laughed and pulled back from her, wrapping his arms around her. "That was a lot quieter than it would've been if I'd really fucked you there."

Another hot spasm in her pussy.

"Now." He gave her a gentle smack on her ass that sent a jolt of heat right to her pussy. "The bed."

CHAPTER ELEVEN

Nicole was so aroused by the things he did, the things he said. Holding her down, pinning her against the door, spanking her. Calling her baby and telling her he knew she liked it rough. These were things she kept deep inside and didn't admit to every man she had sex with, because a lot of them didn't get it. And a couple of times when she'd thought they *did* get it, she'd been wrong, like with Cody Burrell. She never should have gotten involved with him.

Had she finally found a man who understood? Who knew what she wanted, but wasn't a jerk who just liked to smack women around? She was beginning to get a swelling feeling of hope inside her, along with all that heat. Logan was different.

Logan led her over to the bed in the silvery shadows and stopped beside it. His fingers searched the back of her dress for the zipper, found it and began to tug, but before he got it very far down, he turned her so her back was to him. Slowly he drew the zipper down, and she shivered at the tickle of his warm breath on her skin. The soft pressure of his mouth. The drag of his tongue, following the zipper down, over her spine. Tingles spread through her body with delicious warmth, intensifying when he arrived at the base of her spine with his mouth. The zipper stopped, and for a moment, he just kissed and licked her there. Then he reached up to slide the sleeveless dress off her shoulders, down her arms and then all the way to the floor.

She couldn't see him, but was sure he was kneeling on the floor behind her, his hands on her hips, his lips and mouth moving over her lower back and then her butt cheeks. She moaned and her head fell back, her hands clasped in front of her as sensation cascaded over her body at the whispering, feathering touches. And then he nipped her. Just a gentle closing of his teeth over her flesh, right on the sweet spot of her ass, right where a little pain could make her wet. She gave a soft cry.

"Sssh."

She bit her lip. Oh yeah. Quiet. Taylor and Fedor.

His hands molded her ass, stroked the backs of her thighs while he continued to kiss and nibble at her flesh. Heat swept from her hairline to her toes and back up, centering in her aching pussy. He eased the panties down over her hips until they dropped to the floor along with her dress, then lifted her feet one a time to move the clothes aside.

Her breath caught again as he rose to his feet behind her, flicked the clasp of her strapless bra and tossed it aside too. Now she stood there, naked other than her black patent pumps. She felt the beat of her heart in every pulse point on her body.

His arms circled her body, one hand sliding up between her breasts, the other going low, resting on her belly, his fingertips on her pubic curls and he whispered in her ear, "Keep the shoes on."

Her body responded to the commanding tone of his voice, softening, and her mind responded as well, wanting to please him, wanting to just let go and let him take control. "Okay."

His mouth teased the sensitive skin on the side of her neck as his hand cupped her breast and she turned her head to find his mouth with hers. With his arms holding her like that, she felt secure and safe and treasured, something she wasn't sure if she'd ever felt before in her life.

He lifted his mouth from hers and walked her closer to the bed, only a couple of steps. "Lie down."

She met his eyes as she turned and sat on the bed, then stretched out on her back. This was crazy, wearing shoes in bed, but if he liked it, she liked it too. She bent one knee, watching his face as he studied her. He stood there, still fully dressed, but his fingers began working the button and fly of his black pants open as his gaze roved over her. The heat and appreciation in his eyes made her feel beautiful and sexy and warm.

"Oh yeah," he murmured. "So fucking sexy with those heels. I'm gonna fuck you with those on, Nicole."

Her pussy clenched hard and grew even wetter. She dragged her tongue over her bottom lip, watching him reveal his body to her. She devoured him with greedy eyes, her gaze tracking over those big shoulders, strong chest and narrow waist and hips. The shadows sculpted his arms into bulges and dips and outlined his shape in black. And then she looked her fill at his groin, where his cock rose so aggressively from thick brown hair between solid thighs. Her breath squeezed in and out of her lungs in small bursts.

He bent over her, hands on the bed on either side of her, and slowly licked her bottom lip. Her eyes drifted closed.

"Shit."

Her eyes popped open.

"Be right back." He strode across the room, fumbled around and returned holding several small packets. He held them up and she smiled.

"You're right. You *do* always use protection."

He grinned and set one knee on the bed as he dropped the condoms on the bedside table.

"And you do have a long stick." She reached for him, his cock so fascinating and tempting.

"Yes, I do." He was enormous, and she swallowed as her hands circled him. He was hot and velvety soft, but stiff as a...yes, hockey stick, but much thicker. He groaned as she pulled gently on him. She longed to taste him and she began to shift lower on the bed to try to get him closer to her mouth.

He sensed her intent. "Whoa," he said, stopping her. "Not yet."

"Oh." She peered up at him. "But I want to."

"You don't need some of that stuff...what was it? Veil?"

Her eyes danced. "I don't know until I taste you."

"Witch." He reached for her long hair and wrapped it around his hand, holding her head in place. The tug on her scalp elicited pinpoints of fiery pleasure. "Let's save that for later. I want to fuck you."

She so wanted to feel him in her mouth, but her pussy felt empty and needy too, so she nodded and he climbed fully onto the bed and moved over her.

"Last time was fast," he muttered. "Want this time to last longer."

"Well, supposedly you have great stamina."

She felt his smile against her breast where he rubbed his stubble. "True that."

She parted her legs and let him settle between them. His mouth on her breasts had her blood surging hotly. He took one hard nipple between his teeth and bit her, so gently, and a flash of heat zinged from her breast to her pussy. She arched up into his mouth and he flicked his tongue over the nipple, then sucked it deep into his mouth. "Oh god."

He drew on it with tight, hard pulls and flames built in her womb. She lifted up against him, his skin now hot and bare against hers, his cock thick and heavy between them. Her body shuddered with exquisite delight and he moved to the other breast, laying a trail of kisses between, his beard scratching erotically on her flesh. She grabbed onto his shoulders, and when her fingernails dug in, he jerked and groaned. "Easy, babe." And he rose up, reached for her hands and once more cuffed her wrists in one big hand and held them above her head.

She loved it. Because she trusted him.

There were times she'd been in this position and she'd been scared. Now she realized that what she'd been seeking all along wasn't just size or strength or control or even just domination—it was trust. It was choice. It was power. *Her* power.

Because even as he held her down and did what he wanted to her body, she knew she had a choice. And even as he held her down and did what he wanted to her body, he was doing it for her. He was caressing her, sucking on her tender nipples, exploring her body with his mouth and hands, well, now just one hand, intent on finding every spot that made her gasp with pleasure or writhe with delight. And he did find them…the inside of her elbow, the hollow at the base of her throat, the sides of her torso.

"Hold onto the headboard," he directed her, curling her fingers around the wrought iron. "Do you want me to tie you up?"

Once again, she melted inside at his words, that he'd asked such a wicked thing with such matter-of-fact consideration. Her eyes got very moist as she gazed up at him in the pale light from the snow outside. She so hesitated to admit it, but..."I do," she whispered.

He smiled at her, the corners of his eyes crinkling, and rolled off the bed, returning a moment later with a length of silky rope. As he bound her wrists to the bed, she said, "You had this here?"

"Yeah."

She bit her lip, questions backing up in her brain, unbelievably turned on by the knowledge that he had rope in his bedroom.

"I told you before." He gave one last tug on the rope. "I like it too."

Her eyelids grew almost too heavy to hold open, her entire body dissolving with lust. "Yay," she said, and he grinned.

He bent and kissed her mouth and then resumed his exploration of her body, making her shiver and shake and give soft little cries. He kissed and stroked his way down her legs, licking the inside of her knee, and sensation cascaded over her nerve endings. She loved the feeling of being stretched on a rack of bliss, helpless and at his mercy. She let go, let herself float as he took possession of her with gentle, yet firm touches.

Her clit throbbed as his hands and mouth neared it, aching for his touch, but he played longer, stroking her inner thighs, kneeling between her legs and lifting them. "Still love these shoes." He kissed the top of one foot, then the other. Holding both ankles, he pushed her legs up and back and his hand found her pussy. She could feel the cream slipping out from between her folds, and he immediately found it too, fingers gliding up and down there. "Mmm. Sweet, Nicole. I loved how you tasted. I want to do that again."

"No," she cried.

He paused and peered around her raised legs, one eyebrow raised. "Pardon?"

"I just…I liked that, I did, and I want it too, but it's not fair. You wouldn't let me taste you. You said you wanted to fuck me. And that's what I want too. Fuck me, Logan."

He gazed at her for a moment without smiling. Clearly he wanted to be in charge of this. Her heart thudded against her ribs, heat sweeping over her body in steady waves. "Well," he said. "Good thing you're tied up then."

And he dropped down between her thighs and buried his face there.

She gave another soft cry, her wrists pulling at the ropes. But it was so erotic, so gratifying that he wanted her like that, and the sensation of his lips suckling at her swollen flesh, his tongue rubbing over her, was exquisite. He spread her cream all over, all the way back to her rear opening, and she gasped.

He lifted his head to look up at her, his eyes gleaming, shiny lips curved into a questioning smile. "Hmm. You like that too, baby?"

She bit her lip and gave a tiny nod.

"Awesome." He bent his head again and nipped at the tendon of her inner thigh. "Me too. Can't wait for that. Can't wait to fuck your ass. But not this time."

Her pussy spasmed and creamed even more. How much more could she take? She was so aroused, so overloaded with sensation, intoxicated with it, she wondered if she could stand it.

But she did. Her head thrashed on the pillow as he ate at her, licking up her slit, all the way down to her anus, then rubbing there with his fingertips as his tongue dragged back up. Sensation sparkled and spread from his touch at her back entrance. He tongued her clit from side to side, then sucked on it, and she jerked up at the ecstatic sensation.

"Jesus, Nicole." He kissed her clit. "Love how responsive you are."

"Uh-huh…" That insistent ache behind her clit intensified and spread through her pelvis.

"Okay." He drew back. "Let's turn you over."

Logan flipped her onto her stomach, mindful of her bound wrists. He couldn't keep her like that for too long, but he wanted to play with her this way too. Christ, she made him hard! He was aching to bury his cock inside her hot, wet body. She was melting, the cream literally melting out of her, and the way her body quivered and trembled, the little noises she made as he touched her, set him on fucking fire.

Her ass was perfection, round and firm, filling his palms. He curved his palms around her flesh and squeezed, gentle at first, then a little harder, bringing a gasp from her lips. He rubbed, and then laid a firm tap on one cheek. He was pretty sure that was the spot. "There?"

"Oh god."

He smiled. "Good." And he laid another smack there, then on the other cheek. It was such a turn on to be with a woman who wanted this, who didn't freak out at the things he liked to do. Ah, sometimes they let him tie them up, but he could tell they weren't really into it.

Nicole was into it.

He gave her a few more little spanks, just hard enough to pinken her skin, and then he thrust his hand between her thighs, and holy hell, she was dripping. "Mmm." He reached for her with both hands and hoisted her hips up, parting her thighs, revealing all her pink and pretty girl parts to him. He licked his lips, her taste lingering on them, and flames built in his balls, her sweetness a powerful aphrodisiac. He'd never tasted anything as delectable. He bent down for more of that.

"Logan," she gasped. "What are you doing?"

"Just tasting you again." He rubbed his face over her ass cheeks, nipped her soft flesh, then pressed his mouth to her pussy. He inhaled her scent and kissed her there, then opened his mouth and licked. His hands held her ass cheeks, his thumbs playing at her opening. Her legs began to quiver and he clasped her hips tighter. "Christ, you're incredible. You taste so fucking sweet. I could do this forever."

She made another whimpery noise, her hair spread out around her head, hiding her face. He reached up and stroked a hand down the length of her back, admiring the smooth graceful curve, then slid his hand back up and into her hair, fisting a handful of it. She moaned. So damn beautiful.

He tugged a little, lifting her head. "I'm going to fuck you like this."

"Yes."

He had to release her to grab a condom from the table and quickly glove up. Then he gripped the base of his cock and directed the head to her pussy, sliding it up and down and around in her abundant lubrication, over the bump of her clit, and she trembled again.

"Your pussy is wet. And so pretty." He stroked her more, torturing both of them, his balls aching, his cock throbbing. He took pride in his ability to control himself, and this time he'd wanted to draw things out as long as he could, but damn, his blood was rushing through his body, his head was starting to spin and all he wanted to was to feel the sweet clasp of her pussy on his dick. "Ah, to hell with stamina," he groaned. She made another noise that might have been a choked little laugh. "I can't hold back any more, I have to be inside you."

"Do it. *Please.*"

He pressed against her tight entrance, gritting his teeth. His body buzzed, pressure building. He felt the rush of liquid heat around his dick as he eased in, still working for slow and easy, but *fuck*, he was crazed for her. She tightened around him and he paused, his heart pounding, breathing fast. He tugged her hair again and thrust further inside, the clasp of her body so hot around him. He pulsed there for a moment, catching his breath, fighting back the orgasm that was gathering force deep inside him.

He slid out and then in again on a long, lush glide, in and out. He watched, mesmerized by the visual of his cock parting the swollen folds and disappearing into her body. Christ, that was hot. Her pussy flexed around him and his head went back, jaw clenched, eyes squeezed shut. He groaned and his fingers tightened on her hips.

"*Câlisse,*" she moaned. "That's so good. So deep. God, Logan, I feel you so deep inside me."

"Good." He liked that. A lot. He gave a harder thrust. And again.

"I love it like this. Love the..." She gasped. "Deeper angle...oh..."

She fucked him back, pushing her hips back at him and pleasure poured over him, unbearably sweet, agonizingly hot. His skin itched and that pressure built again, tingling at the base of his spine. Once more, he resisted the urge to come, slowing it down, pumping into her body with long deep strokes that made her groan and muffle her wails in the pillow.

Unbelievable. This was fucking amazing, the sizzling connection between them, the way they seemed so in synch, equally hungry and hot for each other, his need to dominate perfectly matched to her need to submit. And yet she was strong, physically and mentally. Their bodies fit perfectly, her long limbs and lean muscles a good match for his brawn, her pussy the perfect receptacle for his cock. He groaned. Better than perfect.

Much as he loved the view this way, he wanted to see her beautiful face when she came, so he slowly pulled out.

"Oh, what?" she cried.

"Ssh. Just gonna turn you back over."

"Oh." She sighed as he reached up to untie her hands and then roll her to her back.

Kneeling between her thighs, he ran his hands down one of her arms to her wrist and rubbed there. "Hands okay?" He moved to the other wrist and she flexed her fingers.

"Yes." He loved the breathy catch in her voice.

"Good." He lifted one hand and kissed her knuckles, then the other, his eyes fastened on hers, all dreamy and soft. He released one hand to find his cock and push inside her again, his eyes nearly rolling back in his head at the sweetness of it, and then he clasped both her hands again and pressed them to the bed on either side of her head. He leaned over her, still focused on her eyes, and she held his gaze so steadily, her lips parted.

Once more he slid in and out of her, rocking his hips against hers, using his thighs and his gluts, and then he lowered himself even more and kissed her mouth, deep, wet, tongue-tangling kisses. He rubbed his face against hers. "Nicole," he murmured, breathing in the scent of her skin. He released her hands and slid his arm around her head, into her silky hair, kissed the side of her neck. Her hands gripped his back, her legs wrapped around him like they had that day in the loft, and he fucking loved it, loved everything about it, loved her beneath him, around him, holding him. "Oh yeah. God yeah."

Her soft sounds of pleasure filled his ears, her body strong and responsive beneath him. He breathed in her scent, his body tightening, heated sensation building inside him, tingling over his nerve endings. He opened his mouth to taste her skin, licking the side of her neck, sucking gently there, and she gave another soft cry. The flames built higher inside him, taking over everything, incinerating his control and then the pleasure fragmented inside him. Electricity raced over his nerve endings and he buried his face against her, pulsing inside her. Her pussy contracted around him hard and he groaned, spasms still wrenching his body again and again. Finally, his harsh, heavy breathing finally slowing, his head finally clearing a little, he lifted back up onto his elbows, his lower body still cradled by hers, their bodies still joined together, and looked down into her face. His hands held her head, thumbs moving some damp strands of hair off her cheeks, and he gazed down into her beautiful eyes. "Wow."

CHAPTER TWELVE

Nicole quietly opened the door and stepped out into the hall. And came face to face with Taylor.

They stood there, staring at each other in the dark. Taylor's eyes shifted to the door of Logan's room, then back to Nicole's face.

"Holy shit," she breathed and grabbed Nicole's arm. She started down the hall toward the kitchen, dragging Nicole with her.

Oh-oh. How the hell was she going to explain this?

"What are you doing up so early?" Nicole asked when Taylor flipped on the kitchen light. She'd glanced at the clock beside Logan's bed when she'd climbed out to go back to her own room and it was only six-thirty.

"I have a headache." Taylor opened a cupboard and grabbed a bottle of painkillers. "I shouldn't have drank that red wine last night, it always gives me a headache."

Nicole leaned against the counter, rubbing her upper arms below the sleeves of the big T-shirt she'd grabbed from a chair in Logan's room. "Great, *you* have a hangover. *I* have a bangover." Her thighs and hips ached, her skin was abraded and she'd hardly slept at all.

Taylor sent her an amused glance as she tossed pills into her mouth. "Lucky you. Okay, *what* is going on?"

Nicole looked at the floor. "Um…"

"Were you there with him all night?" Taylor gulped down some water.

Nicole sighed. "Yes."

When Taylor was silent, Nicole met her eyes. "Another hockey player?" Taylor said gently.

"I know." Nicole closed her eyes and tipped her head back. "I know, Tay. I didn't intend for it to happen. But he's...hard to resist."

"I thought something was going on last night between you two. Serious sparks."

"Yes. Dammit." She shook her head. "He asked me out a couple of times, but I said no. I was going out with Paul. I tried to resist."

"Mmmhmm."

"I'm not getting involved with him," she continued. "It's just...you know."

"Sex."

"Yeah."

"Good sex?"

"Oh sweet mother of god, yes." A wave of heat swept over her.

Taylor grinned. "Well, that's good at least. But geez, Nic, you said no more hockey players."

"I know. I *know*. But I trust him, that he won't say anything about this to anyone."

"So it's okay as long as no one knows about it?"

"Aargh!" Nicole clenched her teeth. "That's not what I meant." Or was it? "I just meant, he's not like Cody. He's a good guy."

"Yeah. I think he is."

But Taylor was looking at her in a way that made Nicole squirm. "What?"

"Nothing."

"I can handle this."

"Don't get all defensive."

"I'm not. Okay, I am. I know I shouldn't have slept with him. But that's all it is."

"It won't happen again?"

"Um. Well. I'm not planning on it..." But wow, after what had happened between them, she wanted to do it again. She wanted to explore more with him. If he'd gotten inside her head like that and knew what she wanted in one night, she got hot and shivery thinking about all the places they could go.

"Oh god," Taylor said.

"It'll just be between me and him. So don't say anything to anyone. Not even Fedor. Okay?"

Taylor pursed her lips. "Fedor will see what's going on."

"No. He won't. There won't be anything to see."

"Okay. If you say so. I'm going back to bed. Maybe this ibuprofen will kick in and I can get a few more hours of sleep."

That had been Nicole's plan too, to climb into the bed in her own guest room and get some sleep before they tried to dig her car out. Because she hadn't gotten much sleep in Logan's room. Now she wished she could bolt right out of there and get home. She bit her lip and glanced out the sliding doors from the great room onto the deck. A snow drift obscured almost half the door. Great.

She followed Taylor down the hall and let herself quietly into her own room. The bed sat there, still perfectly made up. Glumly, she slid in between cold sheets, still wearing Logan's T-shirt. She curled up and tucked the covers around her neck, wishing for the warmth of Logan's big body beside her.

God. The things he'd done to her. The things he'd said to her. He was incredible, so generous and patient. He'd made her feel so feminine and sexy. He didn't see her as a tomboy buddy like so many other men did. He saw her as a woman and treated her as a woman, but not in a demeaning way. Everything he did and said spoke of respect and consideration and giving her pleasure. He was different.

It still didn't excuse her from succumbing to the temptation when she'd vowed she would never again get involved with a hockey player. She shouldn't have done it. She knew that. She had gotten defensive with Taylor when Taylor really hadn't even judged her or criticized her. Which she totally should have. She should have given her a smack and told her to smarten up.

She huddled under the covers, her body warming the bed a little. She took in a deep breath and let it out slowly, willing her muscles to relax. Maybe nothing more would happen between her and Logan. That made her sad. Already she felt a tingle down low inside her, a desire for more of what they'd just shared. And she knew if Logan wanted more, she was going to be helpless to resist it.

"It's an *optional* practice," Fedor said in the morning. "We don't have to go."

"There's no such thing as an optional practice," Logan said. "Move your ass and help me shovel my Jeep out. It's four wheel drive, we won't have any problem getting to the arena." He looked at Nicole, sitting at the kitchen counter with both hands wrapped around a big cup of coffee. His skin tingled just looking at her, remembering last night. But she was acting all cool and stand-offish. "I'll drop you off at home on my way, if you want. We'll have to dig your car out later. Until they plow the streets, you're not going anywhere in that Mustang."

"But how will I get my car?"

"I'll come back and get you later."

She sighed. "I hate to put you to that trouble."

He shrugged. "It's no trouble. I just gotta get to the arena for practice, though."

"You could stay here," Taylor told Nicole. "Until they get back."

"I need to go home. Silvia was there alone all night." She set down her mug on the counter. "Okay. Let's roll."

He watched her pull on those fur-lined boots, tucking her skinny jeans inside them, the same jeans and turtleneck she'd worn yesterday before she'd changed into that little black dress and sexy as fuck heels. His cock stirred at the memory of doing her in those heels. Hawt.

With Fedor in the back seat, their talk was mostly about the weather, specifically the shit load of snow that had fallen in the last day.

"This will be putting a crimp in people's Black Friday shopping plans," Nicole said, looking out the side window.

"Were you planning to shop?"

"Nah. I don't have a lot of Christmas shopping to do. I can't buy anything for my dad. My mom gets expensive perfume or bath oil stuff. I usually buy Julien clothes. Other than that, it's Taylor and a few other friends."

"Huh. I have to buy for my parents, all three brothers and now Remi and I guess Kyla, and holy crap, I guess for the baby if he or she shows up before Christmas. I think the baby's due in, like, two weeks."

"Uncle Logan," Fedor said from the back seat.

Logan grinned. "Yeah." He wasn't all that excited about babies, but he did like kids. One day Jase's little rugrat would be running around and calling him Uncle Logan. That'd be fun.

He pulled up in front of Nicole's townhouse condo and they all climbed out, Nicole to go in, Fedor to move up front and Logan to…make sure Nicole got to her door safely. Okay, it was only a few feet and it was broad daylight, the sun now out, all blinding brilliance reflecting off the abundant white snow, the air sharp and cold and blue.

He got the distinct feeling Nicole would not want him to kiss her in front of Fedor, so he didn't, but stood beside her as she let herself in. "Give me your car keys."

She blinked at him. "Why?"

He shrugged and held out his hand, waggling his fingers. "I'll make sure it starts and that we can get it out."

With a faint crease between her eyebrows, she handed over the keys. "Okay."

"I'll call you or text you later. And let you know what time I'll be back to get you. Maybe we can have dinner together."

She gazed up at him. "I don't know, Logan…"

He shifted just a little closer, wishing he could touch her. "You don't have another date with whatshisname, do you?" he growled.

"No, but…"

"You know you're driving me nuts," he muttered. "We just spent basically the whole night having the hottest sex of my life and now you're pushing me away again. What is it…" He stopped and drew a breath. "Can't talk now. Gotta get to the arena. But we *will* talk later." He gave her a stern look and she pressed her pretty lips together and nodded.

He trudged back to the Jeep through the snow and jumped back in.

"What's the deal with you two?" Fedor immediately asked.

Logan wrapped his gloved hands around the steering wheel. "I have no fucking clue."

"You like her."

"Yeah." But he didn't feel like talking about whatever was going on between them, so he changed the subject and they talked about other stuff until they got to the arena. He changed into shorts and a T-shirt and climbed on one of the bikes to warm up.

It was an optional practice, but what he'd said to Fedor was what he believed—no practice was really optional, especially when the team was still struggling to find its groove. So he was glad to see that most of the guys had showed up, despite the weather. But practices could still be fun, and he figured the guys who'd made the effort deserved to be rewarded for that, so he joked and fooled around a little on the ice to get everyone relaxed and laughing with him as they stretched. After spending time with some of them yesterday at Taylor and Fedor's, he was feeling more comfortable with the team, getting to know the guys on a personal level that helped him connect with them on a professional level too. There were a few jokes about blow jobs and what a lucky bastard Danny was. Then they got down to some hard work. All his focus was on the drills they practiced, on being the best he could be, on working his body and perfecting his skills.

As usual, he was the last one off the ice before heading into the dressing room with the other guys. After showering and dressing, he hung around a while longer, relaxing on one of the couches arranged in the seating area, drinking a bottle of water and talking to a few of the players who hadn't been at Fedor's the day before. Scott moved in and out between his office and the dressing room.

When Cody Burrell sat down on the couch, Logan's gut tightened. He'd never be able to look at that asshole without thinking about Nicole and what he'd done to her with that stupid remark. Which reminded him he had to go back to her place to get her, and although she confused him, it made him happy that he'd get to see her again.

He drove Fedor home first and the two of them shoveled the driveway and dug out Nicole's car.

"I should just drive her car over there," he said to Fedor.

"Then how will you get home?"

Logan resisted the urge to grin. If things went his way, he wouldn't be coming back. Not for a while, anyway. But once again, he kept that to himself.

"I could follow you, I guess," Fedor said.

No, that didn't work. "That's okay. I'll figure it out when I get there."

Fedor shrugged. "Whatever."

Logan climbed into Nicole's car and started it. Luckily it hadn't been that cold—if it snowed that much, it couldn't be *that* cold—so it started with no problem. He let it run for a few minutes to warm up the engine, then drove to her place. He'd said he'd call her, but showing up at her place might work better.

When she opened the door, he smiled and dangled her keys. "Your vehicle is returned to you, ma'am."

Wide-eyed, she took the keys. "You drove it here?"

"Yup." And without waiting for her invitation, he stepped into her condo. A wriggling, tail-wagging dog greeted him. Oh yeah. Silvia. "Hey, pooch." He extended a hand for the dog to sniff. "She's not much of a guard dog."

Nicole gave a little laugh. "No, she's not, but luckily that's not why I have her." She shut the door against the frigid air outside. "So how are you going to get back to Fedor's place?"

He straightened and moved in closer to her. Now that they were alone he could do what he'd wanted to all morning. He slid an arm around her waist, pulled her up against him and kissed her. Hard. "I have no idea," he murmured, then kissed her again. This time her mouth softened beneath his, then opened to him, and he deepened the kiss and slid his tongue inside before drawing back. "I guess I'm stranded here."

CHAPTER THIRTEEN

Nicole sighed. "Oh, Logan."

"What's wrong, babe?" He nuzzled her hair.

"You're making me all stupid."

He laughed and pulled back, arms still around her. "You're far from stupid, Nicole."

She shook her head. "Oh yeah, I am."

"Come on. Let's sit down. Tell me what's wrong."

He took off his hat and jacket and dropped them onto a chair in her living room, looking around. "Nice place."

Silvia popped up onto the couch and sat, head tilted to one side, watching him with interest. She liked men.

"Thanks. Not as nice as yours." He was a multi-millionaire hockey player, and although she'd grown up surrounded by that kind of wealth and privilege, now she lived a pretty ordinary life.

"Bah." He sat on the couch on the opposite end of the dog and patted the cushion beside him. "C'mere."

She sat beside him, nerves fluttering in her stomach and lust curling way down low inside.

"Okay," he began. "It's happened twice now. We had sex at the loft and then you turned me down when I asked you out. We had sex last night and when I offered again to take you out for dinner, you turned me down. I might get some kind of complex from all the mixed messages."

She couldn't help but smile. Damn, he just put it all out there.

"Sorry."

He searched her eyes with his. "So you want to have sex with me, but you don't want to date me. Is that it?"

Emotion closed up her throat and she just stared back at him for long seconds. "Well," she finally said. "Yes. That's about it."

His eyes flickered first with hurt, then disappointment. He pursed his lips as he regarded her thoughtfully. "Okay. Thanks for being honest."

"What's wrong with that? Isn't that what most guys want? Sex and no commitment. No strings."

"Huh. Yeah, I guess some guys do. And me. Sure. I'm just a guy. As if I'm going to turn down sex with a hot girl."

"You don't look happy about it."

One corner of his mouth lifted. "Surprisingly, I'm kind of annoyed."

"Annoyed?"

"Yeah." He shook his head. "Why won't you go out with me?"

"Because you're a hockey player."

He choked. "Christ. What the hell does that have to do with anything?"

She so did not want to do this. "Look. I've dated hockey players in the past."

"Cody Burrell." He said the name as if he was spitting something foul tasting out of his mouth.

"Yes. But not just him. I've had relationships with other guys. Hockey players. It was never something I aimed for, it was just...those were the guys I met. They were guys I liked, guys I had things in common with."

"Who? I can Google it and find out in two seconds."

She sighed. "Go ahead, if you want. Do we have to talk about our past relationships? I don't want to know every girl you've ever dated." She dropped her gaze, though, because she'd already been on Google and already knew that.

"Bullshit. But fine, never mind that. I'm not interested in talking about them, either. Just tell me what happened...what went wrong? I know what Cody did to you, but what about the others?"

"They didn't do anything to me. That's not it. They were good guys. Mark and I were together for a year. It just…wasn't working. Do I have to spell it out?"

"Ah." He smiled and sat back into the cushions. "I think I'm getting the picture." He shook his head. "Some guys are tough and aggressive on the ice. Not so much in bed, huh?"

Her cheeks heated. "You could put it that way."

He nodded slowly. "Okay. What about Cody?"

She rolled her eyes. "Do we have to talk about him?"

"Yeah."

"He's a jerk." She lifted one shoulder. "Yes, he's into kinky stuff. But he's just kind of…cruel."

"Fuck me." He jerked upright. "Did he hurt you?"

"If you mean physically, no. I didn't let things get that far. But it was close."

"That's why you broke up with him."

"Yes. And then he had to go and say what he did and tell the entire world I'm a hockey whore."

"He never said that."

"Oh please. You know that's what he was implying. Anyway, after that I vowed I'd never get involved with another hockey player. I nearly had to quit my job over that whole thing. In fact, I'm still not sure if I did the right thing by staying, because look what happened." She waved a hand back and forth between them.

"Yeah. Look at that." The corners of his mouth turned down. "I guess I understand that. But you know, you can date whoever you want."

"It's just messy," she said. "Things are awkward around Cody. Well, the entire team, really, now. I know it will pass, but right now…" She sighed. "I'm sorry. You don't want or need that either, Logan. If people found out we were dating, they'd be talking all kinds of shit about me. Maybe both of us."

He narrowed his eyes. "I'm a big boy. I can decide what I want or don't want to do."

"I didn't mean it like that. I just meant…I'm trying to keep myself out of trouble and I don't want you getting into crap because of associating with me."

"Fuck! You've got to be kidding me."

She studied him, her top teeth sunk into her bottom lip. Color washed up into his face and his eyes flashed.

"Listen. You are not a whore or a slut or even a puck bunny." He leaned forward. "You're a beautiful, smart, strong woman. I'm...I'm...hell, Nicole, I...want to be with you."

His words made her heart go soft and warm in her chest and her eyes got hot. She blinked rapidly a few times. She wanted to be with him too. So much. Her mouth went soft and pouty and she pressed her lips together as her heart beat faster. When he reached for her and pulled her up against him, she was a goner.

He slid his hands into her hair and kissed her, so gently and respectfully, and she gave in to it, kissed him back, holding onto his big shoulders. Her heart expanded so much she couldn't breathe in, and heat washed over her body. "Logan." She murmured his name against his mouth. "I want to be with you too."

"Perfect." His hands moved over her body and he shifted her on the couch, lifting her legs across him, then turning her into the cushions of the back of the couch and kissing her again. He cupped her face with one hand, slid the other up under the hooded sweatshirt she wore to find her breast. His tongue slid into her mouth and she licked him back, heat exploding between them once more.

Then he lifted his mouth from her and rubbed his stubbled face on her jaw. "But first," he said, his voice velvet soft. "We have to have another talk."

She almost groaned. "More talking?"

"We need to talk about limits."

"Oh." She fought her way back through a cloud of lust to try to focus on what he was saying.

"How much are you into, sweetheart?"

She knew what he was talking about. "Not a lot. I just like..."

"Tell me what you don't like."

She peered up at him through her eyelashes. "I don't like knives."

"That's it?"

She smiled. "No. Seriously, I'm not into a lot of things. I'm not into a master-slave thing, no collar, no leash, no humiliation. No way in hell are you peeing on me and if you like to wear pantyhose, I don't want to know about it."

He burst out laughing and pulled her head to his chest. "Oh Christ, Nicole. You kill me."

Warmth filled her. "What about you?"

"Hmm. I don't like to wear pantyhose. But ladies' panties, on the other hand..."

Her head snapped up. "Seriously?"

"No." He laughed again. "Not into cross dressing in any way. Water sports don't appeal to me. I'm pretty open-minded about anything else."

"What about pain?"

"Inflicting it or receiving it?"

She lifted her head and met his eyes. "Inflicting it."

He held her gaze steadily, reassuringly. "I like to give pleasure. If a little pain turns you on, I'm into it. But I'm not a sadist."

She nodded. Swallowed. "Okay."

"I'm big and strong and aggressive." He held her gaze. "I like to use my body. I play a physical sport for a living. I can dish out body checks on the ice. But I never do it with the aim of hurting anyone and I will never hurt you, Nicole."

She nodded. "I know."

She was strong and physical too. She'd also been an aggressive athlete, but when it came to the bedroom, that wasn't her. And she was so, so grateful that he got that. She'd met too many guys who expected her to be the dominant one.

"Mostly I like to tie women up. I like to suspend them. Have you ever tried that?"

Her pussy squeezed and heat rippled through her. She loved to be restrained. But she'd never tried that. "No," she whispered. "But I think I'd like to."

"It doesn't scare you?"

There were times she'd been in this position and she *had* been scared. Now she realized that what she'd been seeking all along wasn't just size or strength or control or even just domination—it was trust. It was choice. It was power. *Her* power.

Because even as he held her down and did what he wanted to her body, or hung her up and did what he wanted to her body, she knew she had a choice. And even as he held her down and did what he wanted to her body, he was doing it for her.

"No," she said. "I trust you."

He brushed his knuckles over her cheek. "Thank you for trusting me."

She did trust him. She'd already realized that the first time they'd had sex. And that trust was what made this different than with anyone else.

"I'm going to take control," he told her. "But you always have the right to say no."

Again she nodded.

With firm but gentle hands, he moved her away from him, then pushed her to the floor at his feet. He positioned her between his legs and her heart picked up speed, blood rushing through her veins in heated pulses. Her eyelids drooped and she stared at the bulge behind his fly. Her mouth literally watered. She knew what was inside those jeans and licked her lips.

Then he paused. "Uh...I feel like we're being watched." He jerked his chin toward Silvia, now lying on the couch with her chin on her paws.

Nicole laughed. "She's just a dog. Ignore her."

As if sensing Logan's discomfort, Silvia rose up, leaped down to the floor and stretched, first backward, then forward, then trotted over to a small dog bed in the kitchen.

"Better?" she murmured.

He smiled. "Yeah."

His fingers undid the button of his jeans, then slowly parted the fabric as he inched the zipper down. She watched expectantly, fascinated, there on her knees between his big thighs. His hand disappeared into his pants and he pulled his cock free. Her body continued to pulse with every heartbeat and her lips parted as she studied him.

"Look at you," he said hoarsely. "That is so fucking sexy. Licking your lips, like you're dying to suck me."

She slid her bottom lip between her teeth and lifted her gaze to his face. His cheekbones wore a flush of color, his eyes were dark and heavy-lidded. "I am."

He groaned and his hands lifted to her head. His fingers threaded through her hair, playing with it a little, which sent sensation cascading down over her body in delicious waves. Then his grip tightened, still gentle but firm, and he drew her closer to his throbbing cock. She parted his jeans more and tugged them a little lower on his hips and he lifted to help her with that. Seeing him sitting there, T-shirt pushed up on his ripped abs, the thick patch of rough hair at his groin revealed by his open jeans and his cock rearing up, made her pussy clench and ache. The sight was decadent. Erotic.

She curled her fingers around the base of his shaft and he moaned again, his fingertips on her skull inching her closer.

She took in the masculine beauty of his cock, amazingly thick, the head so smooth with a pronounced ridge around the crown, his flesh flushed with arousal. She traced over a vein with a fingertip, then rubbed her thumb over the damp head and he sucked in a breath. And then her mouth was there, and she rubbed the tip over her lips. Mmm. She put out her tongue to taste him, breathing in his scent at the same time, his singular scent of male arousal. His body twitched as her tongue swiped over him, and she swirled it around and around tenderly.

"Oh yeah, baby." His fingers tightened a little in her hair. "That's so good. Lick me...open up and suck me."

She shivered at the erotic pleasure in his voice, but didn't immediately obey. Instead she studied his cock with her tongue, exploring the ridges and veins, the smooth and weeping tip, then licked all up and down the shaft over the bulging veins and velvety skin, getting him nice and wet. Then she opened her mouth and took him in, letting the wet flesh glide over her lips and deep inside.

"Holy fuck," he gasped. "Oh yeah."

She tightened her lips on him and slid them up and down, loving the weight of him on her tongue, the salty taste of him filling her mouth. When she sucked hard, but let him pop out of her mouth, he moaned in protest. She lost herself in all the sensation, the smell of him, the taste of him, his groans of pleasure filling her head. She loved the velvety texture of his skin, the throbbing hardness beneath. The praise he gave her filled her heart, his pleasure filled her soul. She loved giving this to him, but had to admit that she loved it for herself too, the ache between her thighs intensifying.

"Your mouth is so hot," he moaned. "Hot and greedy. I love it."

She worked the fingers of her other hand inside his jeans to find his balls, curved her fingers around them and gently squeezed. Firm, drawn up tight, the skin there baby soft, they filled her palm deliciously.

"Yeah, yeah, that's good." His hips lifted off the couch to thrust into her mouth, gently but insistently, and she relaxed her throat to try to take him deeper. "Feels so good, Nic."

She slid her mouth all the way up his shaft, letting her teeth delicately scrape over the ridge of flesh at the crown, and he jerked against her mouth and hands. She rubbed her tongue there, teasing him, then sucked him deep again, picking up the rhythm of his body, his hands on her head, his hips pushing up toward her. He filled her mouth, her throat, and she fought not to gag, but then her throat closed up. She lifted off him and gasped for breath.

"Sorry," he murmured. "But goddamn, that felt good when your throat closed around me like that."

She smiled and brushed the smooth head over her lips again, then swallowed him again, as deep as she could. Her fingers played over the skin of his balls and she opened her eyes to look up at him over the wide length of his body. His head was back, his eyes closed, his beautiful mouth open just a little. God, he was gorgeous. Pleasure rushed through her, along with satisfaction and knowledge that even though he said he was taking control, even though he'd gently pushed her down to her knees in front of him, even though he held her head...she was doing this because she loved it.

She felt as if she'd finally found her place—not between his legs, she thought with some amusement—but with a man who understood the whole power exchange thing, who understood that he could only have the power she gave him, a man to whom she *wanted* to give power.

The whole dilemma of who he was and why they shouldn't be doing this nudged her, but she pushed it away. Another low groan of pleasure warmed her and she relished his enjoyment of what she did to him. She flicked her tongue over the head of his cock, swirled it around as she slid up and down his shaft, then nipped at him gently again with her teeth. She loved how his body twitched, his fingers hard on her head.

She looked up at him again just as he opened his eyes and the blaze of heat in them seared her, set her on fire. Her lips stretched around his girth, her tongue on his shaft, her fingers cupping his heavy testicles, she burned for him. Ached for him. Wanted to give him his ultimate pleasure. She paused in her movements, her teeth closed so carefully around him, and their eyes met.

Something drew out between them, warm and dense, and her movements slowed as emotion rocked through her. She didn't know what that emotion was, but it rocked her. A lot.

"Love that," he whispered, and one hand released its grip on her head to filter through her hair. "Suck me. All the way. Suck me dry."

His words made another flame leap inside her.

Yes. She wanted to give that to him. He palmed the back of her head and drew her closer and her blood rushed again hotly through her veins. She tasted the fluid that leaked into her mouth and picked up the rhythm of her movements on him.

His flesh slid over her tongue, heavy and hard and delicious. She let him slide out of her mouth, lifted his cock up and licked from root to tip, then closed her lips over him again and sucked hard. The soft noise he made sounded almost like pain.

Once again she let him pop from her mouth, kissed the tip, then explored again with her tongue until he growled and tugged her hair. "Suck me," he ordered. A thrill ran through her and she kept her eyes fastened on his as she again disobeyed him. Excitement built inside her as his expression tightened and then he removed her hand from the base of his shaft. She blinked.

He reached for her head again and held it with both hands and thrust up into her mouth again. Her insides turned to liquid as she realized that indeed he had taken control now and was fucking her mouth. His cock swelled even more in her mouth and she knew he liked this, taking over like this. And she liked it too. More flames built in her womb as she gazed back at him, surrendering to him.

"That's it," he rumbled. "Take it. All of it."

She couldn't take all of it. Her eyes widened and a flicker of panic filled her.

"It's okay, baby." He met her eyes. "Won't hurt you. It's okay. Relax." She sucked in a long breath through her nose and gave a tiny nod. He wouldn't hurt her. "Lift your chin."

She did so and this time his cock slid deeper, bumping the back of her throat, withdrawing before she reacted. Her pussy pulsed and heated with liquid warmth. He filled her mouth again, each time deeper. She willed herself not to gag, dying to have more of him, all of him.

He grunted his pleasure, his face taut. "Yeah. Just. Like. That."

Her eyelids drooped and her jaw ached, but she was still hungry for him and she sucked as hard as she could on his rigid length. God, she couldn't believe how excited she was by this. Her chin was bumping her own hand where she still cupped his balls, she was that close to taking all of him. Once again she looked up at him and caught the wonder on his face.

"You love it, don't you," he whispered. "Wow, Nicole. So hungry for it. Christ, that makes me hot. Gonna...not gonna last..." Her eyes grew wet, but she rubbed her tongue over him again, sucked harder, let him fuck her mouth. Her throat squeezed around him and she made a soft sound in her chest as his cock swelled even more and he shouted. His balls tightened and heat filled her mouth as he came. She kept sucking even as his body went tight and still, his hands tangled in her hair, his cock pulsing in her mouth.

He groaned, said, "Fuuuuck," and then relinquished his tight grasp on her. She slowly let him slide out of her mouth, her jaw throbbing a little, then she reached for him again and held him as she tenderly licked the crown where he still leaked semen. "Christ, Nicole."

She sat back on her heels, licked her lips and gazed up at him. His chest rose and fell with rapid breaths. They stared at each other for a long moment.

CHAPTER FOURTEEN

He touched her hair, let the silky strands fall through his fingers, caressed the side of her neck, her face. Holy hell. She'd completely blown his mind. What the fuck? He dragged air into his straining lungs, his blood still thundering through his veins.

Her eyes were wet and he brushed his fingertips beneath them. "I'm sorry," he whispered. "Did I hurt you?"

"No." Her voice rasped a little. "I liked it."

"Sure?" He rubbed his fingers over her red, swollen lips. He fucking loved seeing her like that, but Jesus, he had to make sure he hadn't gone too far, been too aggressive. That was who he was and he was pretty sure she liked it, but he was a big guy and it would be easy to get carried away. Especially since she made him nuts for her. It was weird, how he wanted to look after her, to protect her, to reassure her that one asshole didn't mean the whole world thought less of her, but he also found himself wanting to just pound into her and take everything she gave him.

"Yes." She held his gaze, smiling a little. "Oh yes." She bit her lip.

"Oh yeah," he said, answering her unspoken question. "Me too. Oh hell, yeah."

Her smile deepened, her cheeks flushed pink and he reached for her and hauled her up onto him. They sprawled on the couch and he wrapped his arms around her and kissed her sexy mouth.

She gasped against his lips. "You're squeezing me."

"Sorry." Damn. "You've got me all excited."

"Oh god, me too." Now she kissed him and wriggled her body against his, half-sitting, half-lying on the couch. He slipped his hand between them and between her legs and felt the damp heat there through her panties and the black yoga pants she wore.

"Mmmm. Holy crap, Nicole. Doing that made you that hot?"

She moaned her affirmation. His dick came back to life. Already! Jesus.

"Maybe we'd be more comfortable in your bed," he said.

"Yes. That would be good." She pushed off him and stood, her hair a tangled mess around her shoulders. She tugged the hem of her sweatshirt down over her firm abs. He grinned. It was a Minneapolis Caribou sweatshirt. Big and bulky, it should not have looked so sexy.

He grabbed his jeans and hiked them up under his ass, then stood to follow her down a short hall to her bedroom. Late afternoon sun shone in the window. Not even dinner time and they were going to bed. He liked it.

Silvia appeared in the door. Shit. He shook his head. He wasn't used to having an audience. But like Nicole had said, she was just a dog. He watched the animal pad over to another dog bed in the corner of the bedroom.

"She likes to be with me," Nicole said in a husky voice.

He looked around. Her room wasn't all girly and flowery, but then neither was she. The walls were a deep taupe color, the duvet on the bed a sage green and the bed itself was black wrought iron. He eyed the headboard with interest.

She didn't play coy. She stripped the sweatshirt off over her head, then pushed the loose cotton pants down over her hips, leaving her in white bikini panties and a sexy little white bra. Again, nothing particularly frilly or feminine, but there was no doubt about her femininity. He kicked off his jeans, reached down to tug off his socks, then pulled off his own shirt. Now they were both down to their underwear and that was good enough. He reached for her, anxious to feel her skin under his palms. Pulling her hips up flush against his, he tilted his head and went in for another kiss. She sank into it, sank into him, her arms draped over his shoulders, and he licked into her mouth. God, she was sweet, her taste in his mouth, her scent in his nose, the feel of her naked skin against his driving him crazy. Once again, heat flooded to his groin and he slid his arms around her.

She made soft little sounds in her throat and he loved it. He kissed her deeper, found the snap of her bra in the middle of her back and undid it. They were pressed so close together, the lingerie didn't move, so he shifted away from her, still kissing her, and slid the straps down her arms.

Oh yeah. There were those lush breasts. He filled his palm with one of them, the nipple tightening, and more blood rushed to his groin, his cock thickening rapidly. She moved against him, her hands running over his shoulders, squeezing his biceps, then sliding back up the sides of his neck. His skin tingled everywhere. With one arm wrapped securely around her, he bent her back a little, dipped his head and found that perfect breast with his mouth. He plumped it up with his free hand and took the nipple between his lips, sucking on it, letting his tongue rub over it. More incredible sweetness and once again she responded so beautifully, holding onto him, gasping with pleasure, her body twitching. He sucked and tugged at the tender tip of her breast with lips and teeth for a long time, feeling her excitement grow even as his own body vibrated with need.

"Love your breasts." He drew back to blow gently on the now swollen tip. He shifted her in his arms to give attention to the other breast, drawing on her nipple, squeezing the soft flesh so gently with his hand.

"I thought we were going to bed," she gasped, one hand in his hair.

"Oh yeah. Right. Got distracted."

He released her and she turned and yanked back the covers, then climbed in. She was still wearing her panties, but that was okay, it was kinda hot actually, and he liked removing them from her. He still had that pair he'd kept. He had no idea why. He'd had the weird idea after she'd turned down his dinner invitation that maybe he deserved some kind of memento of the hot sex they'd had in the empty loft.

He got rid of his own underwear, remembering at the last minute to grab a condom from the pocket of his jeans, now crumpled on the floor. He only had one, goddammit, but maybe she had some for later. Later, heh. He smiled.

"What's so funny?" she asked, lying in the bed watching him. He slid in beside her, the sheets cool against his overheated skin, but there, ah...there was her body, soft and warm, and he pulled her up against him and wrapped himself around her, arms and legs, all of him.

"Nothing. I'm just happy."

"Oh. Happy to see me? I'm sure there's a bad joke about a hockey stick there somewhere."

He laughed and rolled with her, tucking her under him, and kissed her. He let her feel the weight of his body pressing her into the mattress, sucked on her tongue, nipped at her lips and kissed her breathless before he moved off her.

"I don't have my rope with me," he said. "So you're just going to have to hold onto your headboard." He flipped her over onto her stomach and directed her hands to the wrought iron posts. He curled her fingers around them, then lifted her hips.

"I like it like that," she gasped.

"You know it. Me too, baby. Higher." He nudged her hips up. "I want to see your pretty pussy."

Her moan lit flames inside him. He set his hands on her ass and paused for a moment, breathing fast, heart galloping. He just had to admire that view for a moment, the smooth curves of her small buttocks, the dip of her lower back, the grooves of muscle running up each side of her spine. He stroked over one cheek, enjoying the feel of soft skin, firm flesh. He shaped his palm to her buttock and gave a gentle squeeze. "Nice ass."

She made a choked little sound.

He parted her cheeks, studied the perfect little star of her asshole, and his cock swelled and jerked. His gaze moved down to her pussy, as wet as he'd expected, shiny and pink. Her clit protruded from the soft folds, deeper pink and erect, and need for her rose up inside him, hot and powerful. He slipped his fingers into her folds. "So fucking wet. Wow, Nicole. You're just dripping."

He swept up some of her cream on his fingertips and returned to her anus to rub around it. She jerked in his hands. "Stay still." He gave one cheek a sharp tap, and now he knew exactly where she liked it. She moaned. He popped her ass a few more times, relishing her sounds of pleasure, the way her skin turned pink, the way she thrust her ass back at him as if she was begging for more. "Oh yeah," he muttered. "You want it."

"I do," she cried, though her voice was muffled by the pillow. "I do. Please."

He played there longer, knowing what he was doing to those sensitive nerve endings, and then he slipped his index finger into her back entrance. She cried out.

"Yeah." He groaned, moving it in and out, then swirling it around. "Do you like that, Nicole?"

"Oh god."

"Do you?"

"Yes!"

"Good." His cock ached to push inside that tight passage. She wriggled her ass. "Easy." He stroked her more there, playing in the silky heat, her response making his skin burn and his heart thump. Then he withdrew and gave her pussy a little tap with the flat of his hand. She jolted. Another wave of heat rushed through his body, centering in his aching balls.

He put on the condom as fast as he could, then kneed her legs farther apart from behind. He reached for his dick and found her pussy entrance, pushed in slowly, inch by inch. He groaned in pleasure at the feel of her body clasping around him, so tight, so hot. His fingers dug into her hips and he watched his cock disappearing into her, then sliding back out, the visual adding another layer of excitement on the sensation pouring over him. Her cream coated his shaft, the thin layer of latex shiny with it. Christ, what he wouldn't give to be bare inside her. The thought made more heat explode inside him, sizzling up his spine. Even his scalp and the soles of his feet were hot. Pressure gathered inside him, a burning ache, and he moved faster, hammering into her, sensation building.

She cried out and he stretched out over her, rocking his hips into her, breathing in the scent of her hair. "Like that?" he muttered in her ear. "Like it hard like that?"

"Yes. God yes. Fuck me, Logan." Her hips lifted against his and he went back up onto his knees, bodies slapping together, the sound of flesh against flesh erotic, his balls grinding to her body with each thrust. Sweat built on his forehead and his chest.

He grasped her ass in both hands, parted her cheeks to see her anus again and once more slipped his finger in there. He loved her soft cry.

His consciousness narrowed to a tiny point of light, his balls tightening, skin buzzing as pleasure rolled through him in wave after wave. He was dimly aware that Nicole had let go of the headboard with one hand and had slipped it down between her legs. "Aw, baby," he groaned. "Yeah, touch yourself, make yourself come. Wanna feel that."

"You make me come," she gasped. "It's you inside me, touching me like that, in my ass, my pussy, so deep, oh my god, Logan…" And with a soft wail she clamped around him, her pussy and her anal passage contracting hard and rhythmically, and he felt a rush of liquid heat around him.

He let it rush over him, sensation exploding through his nerves, blazing down his spine and shooting out his cock in a blinding surge of ecstasy. "Aw fuck!" He held her hips with bruising pressure, pressing inside her, his body pulsing tightly.

Long moments later, he gasped in a ragged breath of air and once more stretched out over her. She straightened her legs slowly and his softening cock slipped a little, but stayed inside her. His damp chest pressed to her back, he kissed her shoulder, her ear, rubbed his face on her hair. "God, Nicole. I think a freight train just hit me. I can't believe what you do to me."

"Um. I think you were doing it to *me*."

He half groaned, half chuckled. That wasn't what he meant, but he wasn't sure if he could really explain it. His chest felt hot and tight. There was something special between them, something he'd never felt with another woman, and for a moment he got all sappy, the idea that maybe he'd found someone, *the one* he wanted to spend his life with, floating through his still foggy brain. Whoa.

"I'm hungry." He heard her soft snort and regretfully withdrew from her clinging body. "I need to get rid of this condom."

"Bathroom right there." She waved a languid hand, not moving any other part of her.

He found the small attached bath, a little surprised to see female clutter on the counter. Not a lot of make-up, but scented lotions and creams and hair stuff. She did have a girly side. He smiled as he soaped up his hands with pretty smelling liquid.

He sat on the side of the bed and rubbed her back. She sighed sleepily.

"You gonna make me food?" He bit back a smile, waiting for her response.

"Order pizza."

He grinned. "Great idea." He found his cell phone and she told him where to call. Then he climbed back into bed with her. Her limp body told him she was asleep. He smiled and snuggled her in his arms. They hadn't had much sleep last night. Several rounds of energetic sex had lasted most of the night. He'd then gone to practice and busted his ass. He could use some sleep too. So he closed his eyes and drifted off, enjoying the sensation of a woman in his arms, soft sheets that smelled like her wrapped around them.

They woke up with a start when the doorbell rang, and Silvia leaped up, barking ferociously. She dashed out of the room, sounding like a Rottweiler, barking and growling. Christ, it was the pizza. He hopped out of bed, dug for his wallet and headed for the door.

"Logan. Put on some pants, for god's sake." Nicole was out of bed too, grabbing a robe.

"Uh. Yeah." He shook his head and grabbed his jeans, hopping into them sans underwear as he walked down the hall.

"I'll grab Silvia." She scooped up the dog and disappeared back into the bedroom while he paid the guy, and when she came out and he took in her long bare legs beneath the short silky robe she'd put on, he was kind of glad she had, or the delivery guy would've gotten an eyeful. She looked like a freakin' supermodel, all tall and lean, nipples clearly visible through the silk robe, with bedroom hair that could've taken a stylist hours to achieve and full pouty lips that didn't come from any kind of surgery. Gorgeous.

"I'm hungry too. Bring it in the kitchen."

Her kitchen was tiny, but efficient. He set the big cardboard box on the counter while she got two plates out of a cupboard. Silvia sat and stared at the pizza. Amused, Logan opened the fridge and peered inside, wondering if there might be a beer. Dammit, no, but he shrugged and pulled out two bottles of water. He held one up to her and she took it.

"Thanks."

Before they opened the box, he grabbed her around the waist and pulled her in for a smoochy kiss. She smiled at him. "What's that for?"

"Because you're so sexy in that robe. I think you have the best legs I've ever seen."

"Riiiiight."

"Seriously."

"I seem to recall that you also like my ass. And my boobs." She slid a piece of cheesy pizza onto her plate.

"True that." He shrugged. "You've got a hot body, what can I say."

Her gaze dropped and her cheeks pinkened. "I do not."

"Hey." Did she really believe that? He lifted her chin with his fingers. "You absolutely do."

She gave him a crooked smile, but he saw the pleasure in her eyes. "Thanks."

"Why is her name Silvia?" He looked at the dog sitting expectantly at their feet.

"Because she's a silver Schnauzer."

"She's not silver. She's black and white."

"It's called silver. And insulting my dog is not going to make me like you."

He grinned. "I'm not insulting her. I'm just saying. She's black and white. But she's cute."

They talked as they ate, about the dinner last night and how much fun it had been, about the practice earlier and the game tomorrow. Then his cell phone rang. He slid it closer from where he'd set it on the counter and glanced at it.

"My parents." He looked at Nicole. "Okay if I answer?"

"Of course!"

He thumbed the talk button. "Hey."

"Hi, Logan."

"Mom. How're you?"

"Good. Just got home. I thought I'd let you know what I got done while I was at your place in California." She filled him in on the details, then said, "Have you found a place there yet?"

"Yeah. I can move in on December fifteenth."

"Oh, that's great. I think your furniture and things can be there for that."

"Thanks for doing all that, Mom."

Her voice warmed. "You're welcome. I'm happy to help. I know this was pretty disruptive for you, having to pick up and move across the country with no notice."

"Yeah." But he was feeling more and more comfortable with his new life. He glanced at Nicole. Especially around her.

"How are things going?"

"Good."

They talked a little about how things were going with the team and then Mom said, "Your dad and I are going to come for the Chicago game."

"I wondered if you might." That game was about ten days away, and since his brother Jase would be in town, he'd thought his parents might drive down for the game. "Hopefully we won't have any more bad weather. Did you get this storm?"

"Not as much as you did, I think. I heard there was a lot of snow there. Jase says they fly in the day before, so we'll come then too and we can all have dinner together."

"Sounds great. Um…maybe I'll bring someone." He eyed Nicole. She blinked at him as she sank her teeth into her piece of pizza.

After a beat of surprised silence, he could almost feel his mom's excitement. "Really? Someone, like who? A girl?"

"Yeah."

"You didn't waste any time in a new city," she teased, her voice warm. "What's her name?"

"Nicole." He didn't bother telling his mom her last name. She'd find out soon enough who she was. Nicole's eyebrows pinched together at hearing her name. He smiled at her.

"Is she nice? Well, that's silly, of course she is. Oh, Logan, you never introduce us to girls you're seeing. She must be special."

"Well, I think so. But you know, it's early."

Nicole frowned.

"Now I'm really excited about seeing you! Here, your dad wants to talk to you." She handed over the phone and he talked to his dad for a bit, then hung up.

"What was that about?" Nicole asked immediately. "Were you talking about me?"

"Yeah."

She gave him an unhappy look. "To your parents? Why?"

"They're coming to town to see the Chicago game. My brother Jase will be here and they're going to take us out for dinner and watch the game."

"Oookay." She tipped her head. "You're not thinking I'm going to have dinner with you and your parents, are you?"

"Um. Yeah." He stared at her. "I was."

"Are you crazy? I can't do that!"

CHAPTER FIFTEEN

A faint red haze floated in front of Nicole's eyes as she glared at Logan.

"Uh...why not?" He just stared back at her.

"Did you not hear anything I said earlier?" She sighed with vexation. "*Câlisse*, Logan."

"What does that mean, exactly?" He eyed her.

"What? *Câlisse*? It's a swear word. If you translate it, it means 'chalice'."

"Oooh. Bad word."

"Okay, it doesn't translate well, but it is a curse. Don't distract me. Why on earth did you tell your parents about me? I don't want anyone to know about this!"

His mouth fell open a little, but damn him, he still looked so beautiful sitting there bare-chested with all those powerful muscles bulging and rippling, his stubbled jaw and messed hair reminding her of all the things they'd just done in bed, her skin abraded everywhere he'd kissed her.

"I heard what you said," he replied, his words clipped. "Did you hear what *I* said?"

She stared at him. What had he said? That had been...hours ago.

"I said, you can date whoever you want to. Forget about fucking Cody Burrell."

"I forgot about fucking him the minute I dumped him."

He didn't even smile at her joke. In fact, his eyes narrowed.

"Sorry." She sighed and flipped her hair back. "Okay, yes, we have something between us. Something hot. We're...we like the same things. I think."

He arched an eyebrow.

"But that doesn't change what happened. Logan, seriously." She looked at him beseechingly. "Think what people will say if they find out about us."

"I don't give a shit what people say."

She stared at him in mounting frustration. "Well, I do."

"Why?"

She blinked. "What do you mean, why?"

"Why should you care?"

"I...I..." She didn't know how to express that. "Do you have any idea how humiliating that was? When Cody said that?"

He pressed his lips together, his eyebrows slanted down. "Well, I know it was, but dammit, Nicole..." He gave her a look. "When I was a kid, there were a couple of stupid kids who were bullying me."

She started. "Bullying *you*?"

"Yeah. I was only about nine or ten. I wasn't always this big." He gave a crooked smile. "They were jerks. But when they called me names and said I was stupid, or when they said Jase was stupid, I'd get mad and sometimes I didn't react appropriately. Anyway, my mom tried to help me deal with it without getting into fights. When they said I was a stupid baby, she'd ask me if I believed that. I'd say no. Then she'd say, well then, it doesn't matter what they say if it's not true and you know it."

Her heart squeezed so hard at that she couldn't breathe, the image of him as a little boy being picked on making everything else disappear for a moment. *Stupid?* He had a degree in frickin' economics, for god's sake. She let out a long breath. "But here's the difference," she said slowly. "You weren't stupid. So it wasn't true. But what Cody implied *was* true. And I don't want to be that girl."

"So what are you saying?"

She rubbed her forehead. What *was* she saying? How had this all got started? Oh yeah. Dinner with his parents. As if! "I can't have dinner with you and your parents. And you shouldn't have told them about us."

"So you're still saying I'm good enough to fuck, but not to date."

"No! This isn't about you! It's about me." Her bottom lip quivered just a little and she sank her teeth into it.

"Okay. But still. You'll fuck me, but not date me."

"As long as no one knows about it."

He sat there for a long moment, their pizza forgotten. She *hated* the look on his face, imagining him as a little boy being called hurtful names, imagining his face looking just like that. Her insides writhed like snakes in a pit and her skin itched.

Then he slammed a hand down on the counter and she jumped. "For fuck's sake," he shouted. "I'm not sneaking around so we can be fuck buddies."

Pressure built behind her cheekbones and her eyes stung. She swallowed through an aching throat. "Okay," she said quietly. "Then just go."

He slowly moved his head from side to side. Her heart thudded in her chest and her palms went damp as they sat there for long, stretched out moments. Then he scowled. "I don't have a fucking car here."

Oh god. "You want me to drive you back to Fedor's?"

"Nah. I'll just call him." He grabbed his cell phone and slid off the stool. She heard him talking as he walked down the hall and into her bedroom. She stared hard at the piece of pizza on her plate. He must be getting dressed.

And yeah, he reappeared a few minutes later, now fully dressed. His face set in grim lines, he slid on his jacket, pulled his knit cap onto his head and wrapped his scarf around him. "He's on his way," he said shortly, shoving his feet into his boots. "I'll meet him outside."

"It's cold out. And dark now."

"Whatever." He paused at the door, his back to her, his big shoulders hunched. Then he glanced over his shoulder at her and said, "Bye, Nicole."

Less than an hour later, Taylor phoned. "Okay, what's going on?"

"What do you mean?" Nicole lay stretched out on her couch, feeling heavy and tired, staring sightlessly at the television, Silvia snuggled up against her hip.

"I mean you and Logan. He came back with Fedor, stormed into the house, grabbed a beer and slammed the door of his room. He hasn't come out since."

"Oh." *Tabarnac.* "I don't know."

"Bullshit. He was over there for a while. What happened?"

"Oh Taylor." She sighed. "He wants me to go out with him and I keep turning him down." She didn't mention the sex part.

"Wow. He seems pretty pissed about that."

"Yeah, he wasn't too happy when he left here. And I really like him too, but...you know."

"Yeah. I know." Taylor was silent for a moment. "What do you want me to say?"

"Huh?"

"You know. Do you want the 'stick to your vow and stay away from him' speech, or the 'forget about that stupid vow if you really like him' speech?"

Nicole gave a reluctant laugh. "You're a good friend, Taylor."

"I know."

"I'm sorry if I've made things awkward there for you. He'll only be living with you guys a couple more weeks, I think."

"Yeah. It's okay."

"Just another reason I shouldn't have gotten involved with him, right?"

"Well..."

"I know, I know." She sighed again. "Not going to happen again."

The next day was game day, so she headed in to work in the afternoon to make sure things like the game day copies of Faceoff were delivered and ready for distribution at the game, and to ensure the arrangements for food for the staff, media, refs and the team were in place. She got Ryan his list of shots the team and the NHL wanted from the game.

They'd run out of chicken fingers in the media room part way through the game, so she was on her cell phone to the commissary, walking along the concourse on her way there to deal with it. She paused to peek at the game. Midway through the second period, the Caribou were down four to one. Not good.

Her eyes immediately found Logan on the ice with uncanny instinct. As she watched, he turned over the puck to a Carolina player on the blue line and she cringed as one of their wingers fed it to their center who slammed it into the net past Burney, the Caribou goalie.

She bit her lip as the crowd collectively groaned. Five to one. Holy hell. She watched Logan take the next faceoff, losing to the Carolina center, and shook her head. He was definitely off tonight. Glumly, she made her way to the commissary to deal with the shortage of chicken fingers.

The entrance to the commissary was near the players' bench and as she walked by, she could hear Scott yelling at the players. Then she heard the word "turnover" and had a feeling he was yelling at Logan.

The vibe in the arena was pretty negative for the rest of the game, with a lot of the crowd leaving early to beat the traffic. She always disliked it when fans did that, feeling that even when the team was losing they deserved to be supported right to the end. Her work was done and she wasn't sure why she was still there herself, but hey, she considered herself a fan too, and even though the team was getting spanked, she stuck it out, watching the third period from the press box.

Well, they had been doing better lately, starting to come together better with the players who'd been called up to replace all the injured guys and with Logan added to the team, but you couldn't win every game. It just hurt to see the mistakes they were making and she had to acknowledge Logan's influence on the team. He was one of the hardest workers, had a way of encouraging the other players and motivating them, but tonight with him being off his game, the rest of the team was suffering too.

Why did she feel guilty about that? There was no way Logan's lousy game was because of her. Was it? *Merde.*

Practice the next morning was painful. They didn't usually practice on Sundays, and today they were at their practice facility because of a concert being held at the arena that night. The mood of the team was low, even though they all knew they had to put the loss behind them and get ready for the next game. Coach was pissed and Logan didn't blame him. It'd been ugly.

Yeah, he'd been distracted, but Christ, he was a professional and knew better than to let his personal life interfere with his game. Sometimes that was easier said than done. But hell, it wasn't like someone in his family was dying, he was just pissed at a girl who kept leading him on and then rejecting him.

He wanted to think that was done, but after he'd left her house on Friday evening, he'd been thinking a lot about it. She wouldn't go out with him, but she'd sleep with him. Was he nuts to turn that down? Probably. It made his gut ache, but hey, what was wrong with a little no-strings-attached sex? As long as he kept his mouth shut about it. Gah. As if he'd mouth off about something like that.

In the dressing room as they were getting their gear on, Logan spoke up. "Listen guys. Sorry about last night."

Stoner looked up at him. "Not your fault, man. We all played like crap."

"I know it's not all my fault," Logan acknowledged. "But some of it was. I was distracted by some shit last night. I shouldn't have let it interfere with my game. I let you guys down because of that. That turnover in the second was directly responsible for a goal."

"We'd already lost the game by that point," Burney said.

Logan sighed. "I know. But still. There were other things I screwed up and I'm sorry."

Coach stood there, arms folded across his chest, watching him with a frown. Logan met his eyes and shrugged. Coach gave a terse nod.

With singular focus, Logan put everything else out of his head, including Nicole, and gave the practice all he had in him. This was what he should have been doing last night, instead of feeling pissed at the world and consequently not paying enough attention to his game.

Afterward, he went and found Florian, the manager of the practice facility. He had an idea, something that had come to him because of practicing there, but he wasn't sure how hard it was going to be to set up. Fifteen minutes later, he grinned with satisfaction, although his gut tensed up a little thinking about how he was going to approach this.

Sunday night. He didn't know all that much about Nicole's schedule, but he knew she wasn't working and doubted if she was at a hip hop dance class. He smiled and shook his head at that. She was something else.

He drove to her place that evening without calling ahead, hoping she'd be home. She opened the door to him with a look of wary surprise on her face. "Hi."

"Hi." He paused, that clenching feeling in his stomach returning. "Can I come in for a minute?"

She let him walk in past her and closed the door.

He shoved his hands into the pockets of his leather jacket. "I must be nuts," he said, shaking his head. "But I thought about it and I guess fuck buddies is better than nothing."

She blinked at him and pursed her lips. "So this is a booty call?"

"No! I want to take you out somewhere."

Her eyes widened and her mouth flattened. "Logan…"

He held up a hand. "It's not what you think. Get your skates."

"My skates?" A crease appeared between her eyebrows.

"Yeah. You must have skates."

"I do. But…what…?"

"Just get them. Get some warm clothes on. I promise, nobody will know about this but you and me."

Still she hesitated. She sank her teeth into that plush bottom lip, making him want to do the same. "You're crazy."

"I know. I already said that." He gave her a crooked smile.

She blew out a breath. "Okay. Have a seat." She waved in the direction of her living room. When he sat on the couch, Silvia leaped up beside him. He let her sniff his hand, then rubbed her head. She moved closer. Yeah, she was kinda cute.

Nicole returned a short time later wearing a turtleneck sweater and jeans, pushing her arms into a puffy down jacket.

From her small closet in the foyer, she pulled out a scarf and mitts, and he grinned when he saw the Canadian Olympic team logo on them, the bright red mitts adorned with white maple leafs. "Nice."

"Thanks." She eyed him. "You played in the Olympics, didn't you."

"I sure did. Got the gold medal to prove it."

Their eyes met. She smiled slowly and he returned it. That connection between them was still there, pulsating slowly, drawing them together.

"I'm ready." She sounded a little breathless. Ha. Just wait.

"Let's go." He jingled his car keys and she locked the door behind them.

The night was clear and cold, the air sharp in his lungs when he inhaled. The snow crunched beneath their boots as they walked to his Jeep, their breath creating puffs of white. A far cry from California, but there were tradeoffs that weren't so bad.

"Where are we going?" She buckled her seatbelt.

"You'll see."

"Mr. Mysterious tonight."

He laughed.

"How was practice today?"

"Meh."

"That good, huh."

"I'm sure you saw the game. Or some of it."

"I did. You win some, you lose some."

"Hah. Time for more clichés. They caught us on an off night."

"Turnovers killed you."

He winced. "Ouch. We didn't get the big breaks today."

"You didn't get the job done."

"The best team won."

"You weren't mentally prepared."

"That one's true." He glanced at her. "*I* wasn't mentally prepared. I fully admitted that."

"Logan…"

"I'm not blaming you. But yes, I was distracted by what happened. That is in no way your fault. I'm the one who has to focus. I know how to do that."

"I'm sorry."

"Don't apologize."

"I'm not apologizing. I'm just…sorry."

He chuckled. "Okay. I get it."

He pulled into the parking lot of the practice facility. She looked at him questioningly.

"I arranged it with Florian. Nobody's here but us."

"Seriously?"

He laid a hand on his chest. "Serious as a concussion."

She laughed. "Don't even say that word."

"I know. Come on."

He led the way into the facility using the security pass he'd obtained. He put the lights on, the fluorescents taking a few minutes to come to life. "We can put our skates on over on the bench."

"It's been a while since I sat on a player's bench."

"I don't doubt it."

They laced up their skates and then Logan opened the gate and stepped onto the ice. The air in the big arena was chilly, but not as cold as outside. The only sound was the hum of the ventilation equipment. He held out a hand to Nicole as she too stepped onto the ice.

She took his hand and he gave her a tug, bringing her up against him. He looked down at her face, her blonde hair peeking out from beneath her knit hat, her cheeks pink, eyes sparkling. He wanted to kiss her. But not yet.

"Okay go," he said. "Show me what you've got."

She laughed and backed away from him. With easy, graceful strokes, she skated backwards, then pivoted on one blade to skate forward. She lifted her arms in the air and laughed. "I remember how to skate!"

"Was there any doubt?" He caught up to her easily, passing her and pivoting himself to face her and skate backwards. She grinned, put on some speed and darted around him. Laughing, they played a game of tag, picking up speed, flying around the ice. Damn, she was good. He knew she would be, but seeing her move on the ice made his chest swell. And sadly, turned him on. More than other girls he'd dated who wore short skirts or sexy designer dresses and heels and jewelry, seeing Nicole on skates, soaring over the ice, made him hot as hell.

"Want to shoot a puck around?" he asked her a while later.

"Yes!" She gazed back at him with so much joy in her face he almost went to his knees on the ice. He grabbed the sticks and puck he'd tucked away at the bench earlier and handed her one.

"Feels weird with these mitts." She laughed and pressed the blade of the stick on the ice to test its give and he watched her, a hot softness expanding in his chest. Then she caught the puck neatly and started skating, moving the puck from side to side with her stick. He shook his head and started after her. He took the puck away from her easily and she yelled at him. "Hey!"

He laughed and headed to the other end. She pursued him, and with a grin, he passed the puck to her lightly. They had no gear on, so he wasn't going all out, just playing around, like he had as a kid at the community center only two blocks from where he'd lived.

She flicked the puck into the empty net and pumped a fist, and he grinned. "Nice goal."

"It's easy when the net is empty." She rolled her eyes, but smiled and fished the puck out. She snapped it to him and he caught it on his blade with gentle ease. "Damn, you have skills," she said with a sigh.

"So do you, babe."

"I used to be better."

He forgot about the puck and let himself glide across the ice toward her, slowing to a halt right in front of her. Now he kissed her. Her cheeks and nose were cold but her lips were warm, clinging to his in a sexy smooch that had his groin tightening and his blood racing. She drew back and smiled. "Thank you. This was so much fun."

"I thought you might like it. Better than hip hop dancing?"

She laughed. "I haven't tried hip hop dancing yet. But I loved this." She swallowed, her eyes glowing as she gazed up at him.

"You're so beautiful." He reached out with a gloved hand to pull a strand of hair off her face. She dropped her gaze as she always did when he complimented her. He hated that. Once more, he lifted her chin with his fingers. "You're beautiful, Nicole."

"Thank you."

He wanted to say more, words springing to his lips that he had to restrain himself from saying. His feelings for her were growing. He was probably headed for trouble, getting involved with a woman who insisted they were no more than fuck buddies. But life was a risk and he had a feeling she was worth it.

CHAPTER SIXTEEN

He'd softened her up enough to let him spend the night with her. When she'd brought up the fact that Fedor and Taylor would know he hadn't been home, he offered to tell them he was with someone else. She hadn't really liked that idea, nor had she liked the idea of lying to her best friend. "Tell them," she'd said reluctantly. "I'll talk to Taylor about it. I trust them."

And they'd spent as much time as they could together since then, when she wasn't working, or he wasn't practicing, on the road or working with the charity he'd selected to get involved with in Minneapolis. It was all under the radar, and he really would have liked to take her out somewhere nice for dinner or do something in public like go to a movie or a bar, but there was nothing wrong with hanging out at her place, either, especially in her bedroom.

Speaking of hanging, he really had to get into his new place so he could set up that suspension bondage system. He was dying to try it out with Nicole. She got off on being bound, floating away on a beautiful, erotic high. Christ, it made him hard just thinking about it.

He was at her place when he got the call from Jase that Brianne had had the baby. A little girl. Both were doing fine. Jase sounded surprisingly steady and calm. Brianne hadn't wanted him there for the delivery, but he'd been to visit the baby. Logan felt more freaked out about it than Jase apparently did.

He talked to Nicole about it, kind of glad she was there to share that with. He was getting in deeper with her, really deep, but damn, he couldn't resist it and he just kept hoping if he was around enough, she might get used to the idea of them being a couple.

One morning, Coach called Logan into his office. Unsure what this was about, he was ready to man up and take what Coach dished out. They'd won the night before on the road, but it hadn't been pretty and they'd made some mistakes.

Coach closed the door. That was bad. "Have a seat."

Logan sat. Coach sat behind his desk, his laptop computer where he watched endless game videos sitting open on his desk. His office was a bit of a mess, with books, papers and DVDs everywhere, a big whiteboard on the wall with colored marker all over it where he planned out plays.

He smiled calmly at Coach.

"We got bad news about Ron today," Coach began. "Looks like he's out for the season." Their captain, Ron Jacoby, had been struggling with a series of injuries all season.

"Holy shit. Really?" That sucked. Logan rubbed the back of his neck. They'd juggled the lines and called up Chris Frame from their farm team, and he was working out pretty good, but hell, losing their captain for the basically the whole season was going to be rough.

"Yeah." Coach sighed. "We have to deal with it. And we are. But I needed to talk to you about something. I'm really happy with how you're working with the team. I know it wasn't easy."

Logan nodded. "Thanks. That game the other night…"

Coach interrupted him. "I know. You played like shit. It was a bad night."

"Yeah. I don't have an excuse, but…"

"I heard you in the dressing room. I heard you taking ownership. I heard the other guys stepping up and admitting their own mistakes. It's never one person's fault. You gotta play for each other."

"I know that," Logan murmured, watching Coach talk. Where was he going with this?"

"The thing is, you demonstrate a lot of leadership. Every day. Good or bad. I've heard you encouraging the guys and I've heard you holding them accountable when they don't work hard."

Logan just nodded.

"You make them want to play better," he said. "You lead by example. And when you have a bad night, you admit it and apologize for letting the others and move on."

"Uh...yeah."

"We want you to wear the C for the rest of the season."

Logan's eyes widened. Holy shit. "Me?"

"Yeah. You. Not just for this season. Indefinitely. You're a leader, Logan. You've been doing it unofficially ever since you got here. We want to make it official."

Holy shit. "Uh. Wow. Okay. Thanks."

Coach smiled. "We're still having our ups and downs. Consistency is going to be the key to making the playoffs. I'm confident we can do it, but we have a lot of hard work ahead of us."

"Yeah. We can do it." He felt it too. They had the talent. They had the guts. They were finding some chemistry. They weren't perfect, but nobody was. He wanted it, wanted to win, wanted to be the best. And suddenly he realized he hadn't felt that hunger for a while.

He left his coach's office. The news burned inside him, the need to tell someone compelling. And the person he wanted to tell was just through the tunnel in the office across the street.

Without thinking much, he nearly broke into a run, passing the silent Zambonis, the delivery trucks unloading supplies, the security office, the noise of the ventilation equipment a dull roar in his ears. He strode through the tunnel, up the elevator and emerged into the hockey club's offices. He remembered that first day when Nicole had showed him around, how attracted he'd been to her. Now, he was...more...so much more than attracted to her. She was important to him.

She sat behind her desk, tapping on her computer and looked up when he walked in. Her eyes flickered and her smile held warmth, but she reined it in and made it coolly professional for the sake of the others in the office. "Hello, Logan. What can we do for you?"

"I need to talk to you." He couldn't restrain the smile that broke free, excitement buzzing inside him.

"Um. Sure." She sat there, listening. Waiting.

"In private."

She blinked and her eyes shifted. "Um…"

She was all worried about the others overhearing this. He needed a reason to get her out of the office and alone for a few minutes. "Let's go get a coffee or something."

"I…"

"Go ahead, Nicole," Karla said. "You haven't had a coffee break yet."

She pressed her lips together. "I really need to finish archiving these photos…"

He gave her an intense look. "This will just take a few minutes."

She shot him a slitty-eyed look that normally would have made his nuts shrivel, but he was so giddy about what he had to tell her it was easy to disregard. She rose from her desk. "Fine."

They walked out of the office and down the hall. In front of the elevator doors, she said to him in a low and tight voice, "What are you doing, Logan?"

"I need to talk to you."

The elevator doors opened and a couple of guys got off. They were the owners of the team. They shot him a look. "Hey, Logan."

"Mr. Ehrlich, Mr. Thorley." He smiled.

The other people in the elevator rode down with them and got off at the street level. Then they were alone as the elevator continued its descent to the tunnel level.

"Okay, what is it?" She turned to him.

He didn't want to tell her there. Where the hell were they going to go for some privacy for a few minutes? He'd find somewhere. "Hold on."

They set off through along the corridor lined with painted concrete-blocks, the air chilly. The area was busy with staff unloading things, pushing dollies with cardboard boxes of merchandise into the storage area. They passed by Travis sharpening skates, sparks flying. Logan spied the door of the media room. Nobody would be in there now. He used his pass and opened the door. Sure enough, the room was dark. He flicked on the lights and let the heavy door lock behind them.

"*What* are you doing?" she cried with exasperation.

He grinned, grabbed her and hauled her up against him for a big kiss.

"Mmph." She shoved at him and tried to twist away. "Not here, for god's sake."

"Wait, listen."

"What has gotten into you?" She wrenched out of his arms and straightened her clothing, glaring at him.

"I have some news. Good news. I had to tell you."

"What?" she snapped, frowning.

"They're making me captain."

She still frowned. "Of the team?"

"No, captain of the fire department." He snorted. "Yes, captain of the team. Me!" He beamed at her.

She closed her eyes, sucked briefly on her bottom lip, then let out a breath. "Jesus, Logan. You had to drag me all the way over here to tell me that?"

His mouth fell open a little. Not the reaction he'd been expecting. She of all people should know what a huge deal this was.

"I work for the team," she said. "I would've found out."

His stomach bottomed out and his chest felt like a knife blade slowly turned in it. "I wanted to tell you myself," he said slowly.

"You should have waited until tonight! Not here, like this. Jesus, someone could have seen us."

He shook his head. "For Chrissakes, Nicole. That doesn't matter. People aren't going to jump to the conclusion that we're banging each other's brains out just because we talk or have coffee together or something."

"They might. I have to get back to work." She yanked open the door, then paused. "Congratulations."

"Don't say anything about it to anyone," he snapped as she walked out. "Nobody else knows yet." Her footsteps slowed, already out in the hall, and she started to look at him over her shoulder. Her mouth opened as if to say something. And then Cody Burrell walked out of the training room, through the door directly opposite the media room. His gaze fell on Nicole leaving the media room and then lifted to Logan standing there in the door watching her. His eyebrows lifted.

Nicole hesitated again, then kept walking, her spine stiff.

Cody met Logan's eyes. Shit.

Nicole nearly ran back to her office. Shit, shit, shit, of all people to have seen them together, it had to be Cody. *Tabarnac de câlisse!*

Along with fury and fear, though, guilt settled in her stomach, hard and heavy. Logan had wanted to share his good news with her. She hadn't realized he hadn't told anyone else yet, or that it wasn't public. He must have just found out. Jesus. She pressed a hand to her belly.

She was happy for him. She was. She let the bubble of joy expand inside her for a moment, trying to set aside everything else. He was going to be a great captain, and this was so good for him. She'd seen him fitting in with the team in the weeks he'd been there, how hard he'd worked, how he made the other guys want to work hard too. It hadn't been his choice to be there, but he'd made the best of it and this was such a great reward for all that.

Tears burned the corners of her eyes and she blinked them back as she hurried back to the office. She resumed her place at her desk and tried to focus on what she'd been doing before Logan had showed up. Thankfully, everyone else was busy and nobody said anything or asked any questions about what he'd wanted.

Worry made her jumpy and unfocused. What if Cody said something to Logan? Or to others? Oh my god, imagining the assholish things he could say hade her insides knotted up.

But maybe Logan was right. There was no way he'd assume she and Logan were sleeping together just because of seeing them like that. Although there had been a lot of tension between them at that moment. But still. God, she did *not* want to go through that again!

What had Logan been thinking, coming to see her like that! She'd been so stupid to get involved with him. He'd lulled her into thinking he could be trusted to keep this all discreet, but dammit, that had just been stupid doing that. Sure, he'd likely been excited about the news, but like she'd said, he could have waited to tell her.

It didn't take long for the news to get out and Breck was calling her into his office to discuss the communications plan for releasing the news to the media about the new team captain. She'd need to set up a press conference, arrange for new photos of Logan wearing his jersey with the C on it, update the website and a dozen other things. She was happy to be busy, even though her stomach still churned with nerves. Nerves about Cody. Anger at Logan.

Then some sort of commotion took place where Scott and Assistant Coach Brad Laasch came running in to talk to Matt, the closed door meeting going on the rest of the afternoon, even the two owners of the team heading in there at one point. What was going on? Then she shrugged. She'd find out if they needed her to do something.

Logan was supposed to come for dinner at her place that night. They'd fallen into this routine where he spent a lot of time at her place, since that night he'd taken her skating. How could she resist him after that? That had been the nicest thing anyone had ever done for her, and the way he'd looked at her when they'd been skating had made her feel so great, the admiration and affection and acceptance on his face completely melting away her defenses.

Taylor had been concerned about her spending so much time with Logan, but surprisingly hadn't tried to talk her out of it, nor had she made her feel guilty about breaking her own vow to herself. She beat herself up enough over that.

Anyway, she would let him know how pissed she was about him taking a chance like that. And find out if Cody had said anything. She nibbled on her bottom lip as she worked on the media release at her computer.

But Logan didn't come to her place that evening. She broiled a couple of salmon fillets, steamed some broccoli and cooked rice, but she sat there and ate it alone when he still hadn't shown up by seven o'clock. She pulled out her phone as she considered calling him. Instead she texted him. "Still coming over tonight?"

But he never replied.

"What the fuck were you thinking?"

Once again, Logan sat in Coach's office, and this time it wasn't such a pleasant experience. His knuckles still throbbed and he rubbed them discreetly. He eyed his coach. "I apologize," he said stiffly. "I lost my temper."

"We just fucking made you captain! You can't go around punching out your own players!"

Logan gritted his teeth. "I know. I'm sorry."

"Fuck me." Coach ran a hand through his thinning hair. He covered his eyes. "Tell me what happened."

"It doesn't matter. I was wrong to do that. If you want to take the C away, I'll understand."

Coach lowered his hand and stared at him. "Jesus Christ. You're not going to fucking tell me, are you?"

Logan narrowed his eyes. "I said I'm sorry."

"You can go now."

Logan felt like he'd been punched in the gut. Oh yeah, he *had* been. But more than just the physical blow, his insides now knotted so tightly he thought he might puke. He nodded and rose to his feet, then walked out of Coach's office.

Well, he'd been captain for about an hour and a half. Good thing he hadn't phoned his parents. Or Tag or Jase or Matt.

He couldn't regret what he'd done, much as he'd apologized to Coach for it. He'd apologize all over the place, because he knew he was supposed to. But he wasn't sorry he'd punched that asshole Burrell's face.

He left the arena. He didn't know where to go. He'd have his own place in a couple of days. He'd been waiting for that with so much anticipation, mostly because then he and Nicole wouldn't have to try to avoid Fedor and Taylor. He knew she hated that. At that moment, he wanted his own place so he'd have somewhere to go and be by himself and lick his wounds in private.

First Nicole had shut him down. Shut him out. Let him down. He'd been so pumped about being made captain. She'd been the first one he wanted to tell, the only one who mattered. And she'd fucking let him down. Her dismissal had been like a kick in the nuts.

Then that douchebag Burrell had seen them. Logan had been pissed at Nicole and somehow Burrell had sensed there was more to it than just business, but he'd waited to say anything, following Logan back into the player's lounge where some of the guys were hanging out, eating wings and watching TV. Logan had had the mistaken idea that he was going to be safer with others around, but when Cody had mouthed off about Nicole, red heat had exploded in his head and he'd mouthed off back at him. Then Cody'd nailed him in the gut and he'd retaliated by drifting the guy in the nose. Fucking broken it too, blood spattered all over the rug. Cody'd fought back, landing a couple of good blows, and the other guys had had to break it up, dragging them apart. He'd caught Fedor driving a fist into Burrell's stomach as he'd helped break up the fight. He smiled at that. Then Coach and Brad and Travis had come running in, and...well, he could kiss that C goodbye now.

Fuck. Who cared. He stopped at a red light, so tired he wanted to rest his head on the steering wheel. Guess he had nowhere else to go but back to Fedor's place. He really did not feel like facing one of his team mates at that moment. He let out a heartfelt sigh.

Tomorrow his parents and Jase would be in town for dinner. They were all excited about the baby. Mom was planning to fly to Chicago as soon as they got back to Winnipeg, all anxious to see her grand-daughter. Jase would be the hero yet again and he'd be the big loser, the guy who'd been made captain and blew it an hour later. The guy who'd found the perfect girl for him and was all excited for his parents to meet her, but she refused to meet them or even go on a date with him. And never mind the whole trade thing, which he understood was business, but still stung.

One free admission to the Pity Party. Yeah, that was him. Well, he could wallow in it for a day or so. Maybe. Maybe a week.

CHAPTER SEVENTEEN

Breck called Nicole into his office first thing the next morning. She hadn't slept and her head ached with a tightness that started at the base of her skull. Her heart ached too, over Logan and what had happened and the fact that she hadn't heard from him.

"Okay." Breck laid his hands on his desk. "We have a change in plans. Hold off on that media release and the press conference about Logan Heller being captain."

She rubbed her forehead, looking at Scott through tired eyes. "What do you mean?"

"There was an incident yesterday in the dressing room. A bit of a brawl broke out among some of the players."

"What?" She was really tired, but she wasn't getting this. "A fight in the dressing room? Our dressing room? Our players?"

"Yeah. Logan was there and involved in it. Apparently Cody Burrell instigated it by insulting a woman again."

Her stomach swooped and a flash of adrenaline heated her veins. *Merde!* He *had* said something! She squeezed her hands into fists briefly, then forced herself to relax, open her eyes and look at Breck. "Great. I gather it was me. We have to do this again?"

Breck actually grinned.

She gaped at him.

"I don't know who it was. None of the guys would repeat what he said or who it was about."

"And that's funny?"

"No, not funny. I actually think it's kind of sweet, these big, tough guys defending…uh, the woman. Protecting her, so to speak."

"It was me."

"I don't know. I'm guessing it might have been. But like I said, nobody will say."

She tried to wrap her head around all this. She knew it was her. Breck guessed it was her. But nobody was saying.

"We're trying to decide how to deal with this. Logan was involved."

"You mean they might not make him captain after all?" Her stomach swooped.

He sighed. "Your captain can't be brawling with his team mates in the dressing room."

"No. Of course not." She bit down on her bottom lip. Oh god, no. This was just horrible. And it was all her fault! "Does the media know about this?"

"We're trying to keep it quiet." He rolled his eyes. "Rumors get started pretty quickly, though."

"I won't say anything. Obviously."

"Logan's pretty tight-lipped about what went down, but we've talked to the others who were there and gotten a picture of what happened. Logan didn't start the fight. But he did participate. I guess he defended y…uh, the woman, called Cody some choice names and basically told him to shut the fuck up. Cody took a swing at him, Logan punched him and broke his nose."

Tabarnac de câlisse! She stared at him, wide-eyed. She closed her eyes, her blood roaring in her ears.

"The other guys broke Logan and Cody apart, Scott and Brad walked in and it was done."

"I'm sorry. I don't know why…I just…" She stumbled to a halt and rubbed her face. "I'm sorry, Breck."

Did he know about her and Logan? He hadn't said that. Should she say anything?

"Once again, this isn't your fault, Nicole. I don't know what Cody's problem is exactly."

"I feel like it's my fault."

"I can't say much more about it. They're still figuring out how to handle this. But we need to hold off on our communications for now."

She nodded. Her throat was too tight to speak, so she just gave Breck a tight smile and returned to her desk. A string of curses in French ran through her head. As if she was going to be able to concentrate on work for the rest of the day.

What was going to happen to Logan? He'd been defending her to that asshat.

Her heart swelled and ached in her chest. Even after she'd been so awful to him. He'd put his chance at being captain of the team at risk because of her. Once again, she could only beat herself up for having ever gotten involved with him. This was so bad for him! He'd been so excited about being captain. He deserved it. And now because of her, it was all screwed up.

She would totally understand if the team didn't want her working there. Her worst nightmare had come true. It had happened again. They'd said before it wasn't her fault, but sweet Jesus in the lap of Mary, she'd gone and gotten involved with another player when she'd vowed not to, when she knew how bad it could be, not just for her, but for everyone. The entire damn team.

At this point, nobody knew this was because of her. But word would get out. It wouldn't be hard for people to figure it out once they'd heard that the fight had been over a woman.

She could tell them the truth about her and Logan and wait for them to fire her. Or she could wait it out and hope the truth never came out. Or she could just save everybody the trouble and quit.

Once again, she had to face the very real, very heartbreaking possibility that it would be best for everybody if she left.

"What the hell is wrong with you?"

Logan lifted his head and looked at Jase. "Huh?"

"You're totally out of it. What's going on?"

They sat there in the swanky downtown restaurant with his parents. A bunch of other Chicago players were at a long table just across the restaurant, also having dinner the night before the game.

"Nothing."

"Is this because of Nicole?" his mom asked. "Why didn't she come for dinner too?"

"Who's Nicole?" Jase demanded.

"Nobody."

His mom made a sound. "When we talked on the phone, you sounded so happy. I was excited that you were seeing someone you actually wanted us to meet."

"Yeah, well, things didn't work out."

"Oh." He caught the concern on his mom's face. "Are you okay, Logan?"

"I'm fine."

They'd held off on the announcement about making him captain while they figured out how to handle this whole big fucking mess. So he couldn't tell his parents about that. And he couldn't introduce them to Nicole. *Loser.*

"What's happening with the baby?" he asked Jase, changing the subject. "Home from the hospital yet?"

"Yeah. Brianne took her home yesterday. I've talked to her, but haven't been over there."

"What the hell do you do about custody of a newborn?" Logan asked. Jase's face clouded. Shit. Maybe that had been kind of tactless.

"Obviously, Emily has to be with Brianne right now. She's breastfeeding her. I'll just visit sometimes..." He shrugged, the corners of his mouth drawn down. "We'll have to work out a custody arrangement later."

"Why did you name her Emily? Scott's little girl is named Emily."

"I didn't name her." Jase scowled. "Brianne insisted on that name."

"Huh. And how's Remi dealing with it all?"

"She's dealing. She's happy that the baby's here and she's fine. She loves babies." He sighed.

"When are you going to get married?" Mom leaned forward. "You and Remi should have a baby of your own."

Jase gave her a lopsided smile. "I'm trying to convince her of that. I didn't realize how much this was going to affect me. I'm really bummed about not seeing Emily much. But even though Remi loves babies and wants a family, she needs time for herself right now."

"That's kind of selfish," Logan said.

Jase's head whipped around to glare at him. "Selfish? Did you just call my fiancée selfish?"

"He didn't mean that." Mom reached for Jase's arm.

"I didn't mean to insult her," Logan said. "I just meant, she should be thinking of you."

"She spent her whole life thinking of others," Jase said hotly. "It's about time she put herself first. I'm not going to push my sad agenda on her if she's not ready for it."

Logan leaned back in his chair. He gave a dry laugh. Jase was defending the woman he loved. His gut cramped at the thought of how he'd tried to defend Nicole and what that had gotten him. Fucking nothing, that's what, and she didn't even give a shit.

Jase scowled. "What's so funny?"

"Nothing. Just ignore me. I'm in a bad mood."

"Yeah. I'll say." Jase shot him a black look.

"You're certainly not yourself." Mom's eyebrows pinched together. "You're usually so carefree and relaxed. You seem...tense."

"Sorry, Mom. You guys drove all the way here to see us and I'm being a jerk."

"You're not a jerk." She studied him with scary maternal perceptiveness. "But something's really wrong. Were things really serious with this Nicole?"

He looked down at the fork he was playing with. "For me. Not for her."

"I'm sorry."

As usual, Dad sat there and took it all in without saying much. That was him. But now he said, "Anything we can do, son?"

Logan shook his head, forcing a smile. "Nah. I'm good."

He got the conversation steered back to something nice and safe, something they all liked to talk about—hockey.

The next day Coach once again called Logan into his office. He was wearing out a path in and out of here. But this time the news was good. Somewhat.

"Okay, here's what's going to happen. We talked to the other players involved in the incident the other day and I think we have a good sense of what happened." He eyed Logan sharply. "Everyone was pretty unanimous in saying that you didn't start the fight with Cody."

Logan pressed his lips together, gave a short nod and held Coach's gaze steadily. "No, sir. I didn't."

"They confirmed you were defending a woman."

"Yes."

"Nobody will say who it was."

Logan let out a long slow breath, but said nothing.

"You know that was completely inappropriate behavior."

"Yes, sir."

"Cody won't dress for the game tonight," Coach said grimly. "And we're putting him on waivers."

Logan gripped the armrests of the chair he sat in and kept his face neutral. "I'm sorry to hear that. He's a good player."

"Let me be frank here. We still want to make you captain. It'll be announced officially tomorrow. We held off while we figured out what to do about this mess. Cody has been a disruptive influence on the team. He has talent, no question, but he needs to deal with some anger management issues. He won't play for the team again."

Logan nodded. This actually made him very happy, but it didn't seem right to be happy about someone else's misfortune. Cody was an asshole, but Christ, he was shitting his career down the toilet with his bad behavior. That sucked big time.

"Thank you," he said instead. "I appreciate your fairness in this and I'll make sure your trust in me to lead the team is earned."

Coach smiled. "Damn right."

They talked about the game that night. "My parents are here," Logan mentioned as he left. "They came to watch my brother and me play."

Coach shook his head. "Who the hell do they cheer for when that happens?"

Logan's cocky answer at one time would have been, "Me." But he didn't feel so cocky at that moment. Even though he hadn't lost out on the opportunity to be captain, his self esteem had taken a bit of a bruising. "My mom always says she just wants us to both play well and she doesn't care who wins. My dad, though, was a big Chicago fan for years, so I have a feeling he's cheering for them. That's okay, though."

He took another deep breath as he left Coach's office and released it slowly. Okay. This was good. He hadn't completely blown everything. Hadn't lost everything. Just Nicole.

But that was a lot.

Nicole ran through the arena that evening carrying a laptop. Their graphic designer Tassi's laptop had died and she needed it to edit the images the photographers were taking and upload them to the cloud storage used by the NHL.

There was always something. Nicole had been running all day after that disturbing meeting with Breck. There'd been some kind of printing problem with the game day issue of Faceoff and she'd been on the phone with the printer half the morning. A season ticket holder had complained that one of the team photographers kept blocking his view and he hadn't seen a goal all season. She'd had to track down Ryan to help her deal with that, placating the season ticket holder, making sure he was satisfied—they paid big bucks for season tickets, of course they wanted to see every goal—while making sure the photographers were able to do their job. There were only so many places the photographers could stand and get prime game shots, and depending on which team was playing, sometimes there were a lot of photographers there. And now this issue with the computer.

She hadn't had a lot of time to sit and stew about what she should do, but at some point she was going to have to sit down and make a decision.

She dashed into the media room where Tassi was working, a memory flashing through her mind of Logan dragging her in there that day and the excitement on his face when he'd told her his news. She grimly pushed that away and helped Tassi plug in and boot up.

"Okay, good," Tassi said with relief. "I uploaded my test image and it worked fine, and then all of a sudden, nothing. I gotta get busy now. Ryan brought me his first period shots, over two hundred to go through."

"That's a lot."

"Tell me about it." But Tassi grinned. "Thanks, Nicole, you're a lifesaver."

"Okay!" Nicole smiled back and let out a long breath. "What's happening in the game?"

"It's tied at one. I watched the first period." Tassi didn't have much to do until after the first period, when the photographers brought her their images. "Logan got one goal and his brother got the Chicago goal. Isn't that funny?"

"Yeah." Nicole's heart bumped. "I guess I'll go watch a bit." She was finished with   everything that needed to be done and could stop and watch some of the game. She left the media room and squeezed through the big curtain closing off the opening in the stands, then made her way beneath the seats to stand by the glass at rink level, near the Caribou net. A Chicago player took a slap shot from the blue line and missed the net, banging it off the glass near where she stood. She jumped at the noise, even though she knew she was safe, and grinned at Ryan, who was seated on a small stool there with the lens of his camera in a hole in the glass. He'd jerked back too, not wanting to take a puck in his expensive camera lens.

She took in the shouts of the players calling to each other, the scrape of their skates on the ice, the smack of the puck on sticks, the roar of the crowd. She loved it. She so did not want to quit her job. She was still mulling that over, knowing that as long as Cody was there, things were always going to be awkward. And probably with Logan too, now. She sighed. She needed to do what was best for everyone, which might mean giving up the job she loved so much. Her heart squeezed at the thought.

She watched Logan barrel over the boards from the bench, the Caribou changing on the fly, recognizing his shape and the way he moved without even needing to see the number on his jersey.

Where were his parents? In the stands or in someone's suite? Ah well, didn't really matter. He'd tried to convince her to meet them and she'd kept putting him off and then, when they were here, it hadn't really mattered because he'd stopped returning her texts. And she didn't blame him. She'd been a bitch to him.

But this was better for both of them, in the long run. They shouldn't have started something, even though when they'd been together it had felt so right. It just shouldn't have happened and he didn't need all her baggage dragging him down with the team.

But she couldn't help remembering being with him. It wasn't just the sex, although that had been beyond hot. She'd never been that intimate with any other man, letting him see so much of what was inside her. No, the intimacy had extended outside the bedroom too, even though she'd refused to let him take her out places. They'd kind of jumped past that "dating" stage and had been comfortable hanging around her place, eating, talking, laughing, and yeah, having lots of hot sex. But the most intimate thing of all that they'd done had been when he'd taken her skating.

Her heart still turned over in her chest every time she thought about that. How he'd known that would make her happy. How he'd set it up, kept it private, how he'd not only watched her, but had skated with her, shot the puck with her, let her be totally herself in front of him without worries about being seen as an unfeminine jock.

She brushed her fingers over damp eyes even now, remembering that. God. She missed him.

Logan flew past her and she shrank back a bit, not wanting him to see her watching, but he was intent on the puck, focused on his game. A Chicago player charged up behind him and slammed him into the boards and Nicole winced. But Logan knew how to take a check and immediately resumed his fight for the puck. The whistle blew for a faceoff.

Logan took the faceoff in the defensive end, won it and snapped the puck over to Adam, who took off with it toward the Chicago net. He passed it back to Logan and she watched their play, like choreography, planned and rehearsed and awesomely beautiful. Just like she'd thought they would be together. Logan drove hard to the net with the puck and she went on to her tiptoes to try to see down at the other end. The crowd roared in anticipation of a goal, then groaned when Logan apparently failed to put the puck in the net. Then the whistle blew and all she could see was a crowd of players as a little skirmish happened down near the other net. The crowd hushed and the atmosphere in the arena changed in an instant from excitement to anxiety. Nicole felt it like goosebumps, her skin tingling. She craned her neck, still on her toes, trying to see what was going on. Murmurs ran through the crowd. She turned to people in the seats behind her. "What happened?"

"Not sure," the man said, standing, as was everyone else now. "It's Heller. He's down."

Her blood turned to ice water in her veins. "Logan? Or Jase?"

"*Our* Heller," the man said. "Logan. Shit. He's not moving."

CHAPTER EIGHTEEN

Joe, the head athletic therapist for the team, jumped onto the ice and ran toward the other end. *"Tabarnac de câlisse,"* Nicole breathed. "Sweet Jesus and Mary." Her heart crashed against her ribs and her hands started to shake. Panic filled her brain. What should she do? She wanted to run to the other end of the arena to get a better look, but by the time she got there, he'd probably be up and gone back to the bench. Hopefully. God. What if he didn't get up? What the hell had happened? There'd been so many injuries on the team and so much talk about concussions and brain injuries and...nausea churned in her stomach, rose up to her throat, and she lifted a shaking hand to her mouth. God, oh god, she had to do something.

She turned and pushed her way back to the lower level corridor, past security, past the media people, and she ran, her footsteps ringing off the concrete floor, echoing off the cinderblock walls. She dodged other Caribou staff, jogged past the Zambonis and around the bend, her breath coming in sharp, hard pants.

Mon ostie de saint-sacrament de câlisse de crisse! He had to be all right. The last time she'd seen him, he'd been looking at her with that pissed off hurt expression. He'd been so excited to tell her his news about being made captain. She'd only realized as she was walking away and he told her not to say anything because nobody else knew yet that he must have come to see her straight away after talking to Scott. He probably hadn't even called his parents or his brothers to tell them. He'd come to her first and she'd been a bitch to him.

She'd been more concerned with someone seeing them, knowing about them, than she had about what was happening with him. She'd let him down. And for nothing. Because it didn't matter who knew or what they said if something had happened to him. That was the last thing in the world that mattered. She had to have the chance to tell him that, to apologize, to tell him how proud she was of him and what he'd done since joining the team. She'd tell him she was leaving so he wouldn't be dragged into her crap again. She had to tell him.

She ducked into an entrance, pushed through the crowd that had accumulated there to watch the drama on the ice. "What's happening?" she panted, as she tried to squeeze past someone. "Is it Logan?"

"Yeah. He's moving. But not much. Christ, looks like he's in pain."

"Oh fuck." She said the words, then covered her mouth, earning a strange glance from the man who'd spoken. She swallowed the fear choking her. She shoved her way rudely past someone else to get to the glass. Joe knelt on the ice right beside Logan, who was on his back on the ice, writhing, one arm crossed over to hold the other. Oh no! A wave of pain washed over her as if she was the one injured.

Most other players had returned to the bench, but Jase Heller hovered not far away, gnawing on his mouth guard, which was hanging out of his mouth.

She peered over the boards, through the glass, trying to get a sense of what was happening. She gulped down more nausea, her heart in the throat. Logan was tough. He knew how to take a check, she'd just seen evidence of that. She had no idea what had happened, though. Had someone hit him? Tripped him? He'd been driving to the net, looking like he was going to score. What the fuck?

The net was off its mooring. Had he hit the net? *Sacrament!*

Hockey was such a dangerous sport! Why did she love it so much again? This was stupid! He should not be lying on the ice like that.

The murmurs of concern from the crowd swelled around them. Then Logan shifted on the ice. Joe gestured and a couple of other players came and helped him get to his feet. He was on his feet. That was good. But they were hustling him off the ice pretty fast and he was hunched over in agony, which told her this was serious. He wasn't going back to the bench.

The crowd started applauding, everyone still on their feet.

Wide eyed, she turned and shoved her way back the way she'd come, fighting for breath. She ran back toward players' bench and the dressing room, arriving there as they practically carried Logan off. "Oh god." She followed them into the dressing room.

"Hey," someone said to her. "You can't come in here."

"Oh yes I can." She ignored him and tried to follow Logan.

Someone grabbed her and stopped her. "Hey. Nicole." Travis, one of the assistant trainers.

"No. I need to see him."

"He's okay."

"He's *not* okay!" She struggled to get free.

"Stop, stop. Listen, you gotta let us look after him."

She knew that. She knew that. They knew what they were doing. But still...

"Stay here. Let me go see. I'll come right back and tell you what's happening."

She wanted to cry out of fear and frustration. "Fine." Hands clasped together, she watched Travis disappear into one of the training rooms. People were running in and out. Dr. Stewart, the team doctor, an orthopedic surgeon, came in. The game had resumed, judging from the distant sounds of a huge shudder of a body check into the glass and the cheer of the crowd.

"His parents are here," Travis reported to those inside the room where they'd taken Logan. And she heard her name too.

She turned around, and through the open door saw a couple standing there. That had to be Logan's dad, looking so much like him and his brothers, not quite as big, with graying dark hair. The tall, short-haired woman beside him looked tense, but amazingly calm.

Nicole let out a shuddery breath. She moved toward them. "Are you Mr. and Mrs. Heller?"

"Yes." They didn't even really look at her.

"I'm trying to find out what's happening. I'm Nicole Lambert. I...I..." She lost it then. She didn't know what to say.

She wasn't anyone to Logan. She couldn't call herself his girlfriend. What she wanted to say was, "I love him." But she just stood there, choked up, blinking at them.

"Nicole," Mrs. Heller murmured.

She swallowed. "I...I work for the Caribou. In Communications."

"Nicole Lambert."

"Yes." She bit her lip. Her eyes met Mrs. Heller's. She saw her own fear and anxiety reflected there, along with a small sympathetic smile. Mrs. Heller put out a hand and squeezed her arm.

"Nicole."

She looked up at hearing her name behind her. Travis poked his head out. "C'mere." She hustled across the carpet, tension vibrating through her body, with a glance at Logan's parents.

"Come in. He wants to see you."

"Oh god." He was dying. He had to be dying. That was why he wanted to see her. She covered her mouth with her hands, then gave her head a sharp shake and tried to school her expression into something that wasn't going to terrify him.

He was on his back on the examination table, bare-chested, his short hair damp, his face pale. "Hey," he said when he saw her. "What are you doing here?"

She wanted to fall on him and weep with relief and gratitude that he looked okay. She tried to speak, but couldn't get words through her thick throat. He reached his right hand out to her, his left arm at his side with a pillow between it and his body. She took his big hand with both hers. "I was worried. Jesus, Logan, you scared the crap out of me. Us. Your parents are here too."

"I know. How'd you know?"

She shook her head. "I don't know. It doesn't matter. Are you okay?"

"Dislocated my shoulder. They popped it back in. I'm good."

Joe snorted. "Riiiight."

Logan tried to roll his eyes, but he still looked a little weak and dazed. "They want me to get an x-ray. In case I broke something."

Her knees almost gave out at hearing this diagnosis. "Not your head? You didn't hit your head?"

"No. I guess I might have blacked out for a few seconds from the pain. That got everybody freaked out."

Now a tear did slip from her eye. "Oh god."

"Fuck me, that hurt," he added. "Jesus."

She rolled her lips in and held them pressed tightly together while her eyes overflowed.

"Hey. What's with the tears?"

"I love you."

The room went all still, all the people buzzing around them doing their jobs suddenly quiet. Logan's eyes went wide. Neither of them even looked at the others, though, just focused on each other, their gazes locked.

"Fuck, Nic," he breathed. "Now? You're doing this now? Really?"

She nodded. She knew what he meant—so many people around, everyone listening to them, watching her break down and cry, telling him she loved him. Everyone knowing.

"It doesn't matter." Her voice cracked. "I don't care. I just...god, Logan. I'm so sorry."

He gave her a weak smile. "Hey. It's okay. Don't cry now, I'm fine."

"We have to take him for an x-ray," Joe said. "The doctor reduced the shoulder already, but we need to check for fractures. Tomorrow he'll get an MRI. But I think he's gonna be okay."

She nodded and let go of his hand. "Do you want to see your mom and dad?"

"Eh...go tell them I'm okay. Let's get this over with. I guess I'm done for this game."

"You're done for a while, I'm afraid, dude," Joe said.

"Shit."

Nicole left the room and stumbled out into the hall where Mr. and Mrs. Heller waited with admirable patience. "He's okay," she said, and then blackness started closing in around the edges of her vision. She put out a hand against the wall, but it wasn't there.

"Hey now," Mr. Heller said, sounding very far away. Hands caught her as everything went dark and the floor hit her hard on the butt. "Put your head between your knees."

"Oh my god," she moaned, bending forward. "I am not a wuss. Seriously. I don't cry and faint over stupid little things."

She thought they might have laughed. A gentle hand rubbed her back, pushed hair off her now damp face. Her entire body sweating, she fought for air as her vision gradually cleared. "How embarrassing."

"It's okay." Mrs. Heller rubbed her back. "Is Logan really all right?"

"Yes. I'm just so...relieved. He dislocated his shoulder. They're just x-raying it."

"Oh."

Nicole heard the relief in her voice. "You're very calm about this." She peered up at Mrs. Heller.

"I've been through this a few times," she said dryly. Then she blew out a breath. "Okay. He's okay."

"I played hockey. I know how it goes. I don't freak out over every little bump and bruise. Usually."

"I played hockey too," Mrs. Heller said.

Nicole's head snapped up. "Really?"

"Really."

"Oh. Wow. Cool. So yeah, it was just, we kind of had a fight, and I was a bitch, and I never told him I loved him." A wave of heat scorched her cheeks. "I'm sorry. I don't even know you."

Mrs. Heller smiled. "I think he might feel the same about you."

Oh...

"Let's get you up off the floor," Mr. Heller said. "You're attracting a little attention."

Nicole looked up and saw familiar faces in the hall around them. Shit. There was Greg Barnes from ESPN and Jack Chambers from the Minneapolis Daily Mail and the new guy from Versus.

Well, *merde*. "Hey, guys."

Logan was pissed beyond belief at being injured, but he had to admit he was enjoying the attention from Nicole. She took him back to her place after the game, after he'd seen his folks and assured them he was okay. Semi okay. They'd given him some heavy duty painkillers and muscle relaxants that made him a little dopey. He was happy to be in Nicole's bed again, but sadly wasn't up for much besides sleeping.

"Wanna talk to you," he mumbled as she tucked him into bed. "I'm mad at you."

"I know. I'm mad at me too. But we can talk tomorrow. Here, take your meds."

"I love you, Nicole."

She kissed his mouth, rubbing her face against his. "I love you too. And I'm sorry."

"You should be."

She smiled and snuggled in against his uninjured right side, which was very, very nice, even if she was wearing flannel pajama pants and a long sleeved shirt instead of being naked.

She drove him to the hospital for the MRI the next day, since he'd left his Jeep at the arena and she didn't think he should be driving. He dismissed her concerns, but let her chauffeur him around. Apparently he'd been lucky and hadn't done serious damage. His rotator cuff looked intact, but he'd been warned there likely was some minor tearing. He was going to be damn sore and need to wear the sling for at least a few days and do some physical therapy. He was used to that. He wouldn't be playing for a while, though.

Then Nicole drove him to the arena for the practice, where he hung out for a while and talked to Coach while she went to the office.

"And once again, I guess you probably want to make someone else captain."

Coach sighed. "This is fucking bad timing. But we'll just keep Bobby and Adam alternating captain for the next while until you're back playing again."

Logan nodded. "Thanks. Sorry about this."

"Shit happens. Just need to get you well."

He managed to drive himself to Fedor's place to get some of his things, then went back to Nicole's condo and let himself in with the key she'd given him. He grinned at the ecstatic greeting he got from Silvia and bent to rub her little head. Alone in Nicole's place for the first time, he wandered around and snooped through her things, looking at pictures, books, her medicine cabinet, interested in everything about her.

She'd blown his mind last night, although he had to admit his mind had been more than a little woozy from pain and drugs. But Jesus, she'd blurted out the fact that she loved him in front of the whole training staff and god knew who else. He grinned. It sucked to be out of commission, but damn, there'd been one good thing that came of it.

His cell phone rang and he checked the call display. His parents. No, it was his mom, guaranteed, after meeting Nicole last night. "Hey, Mom."

"How'd you know it was me?"

He grinned. "Call display."

"But it could've been your dad."

"I had a feeling it was you."

"How are you, buddy?"

She used the old nickname she'd had for him when he was a kid. His smile went crooked. "I'm okay, Mom. Gonna be out for a while, though."

"I figured. Did you have that MRI?"

He filled her in on the details of his medical condition. "Are you home? You made good time."

"We left early this morning. The roads were fine all the way. Okay, so I gather that was *the* Nicole?"

"I wondered how long it was going to take you to ask. Yeah, that was her."

"You two made up?"

"Yeah. We haven't talked a whole lot. I was pretty drugged up last night. I'm at her place right now."

"I'm so happy for you," she said softly. "Not for your shoulder, of course. She seems pretty great, Logan."

"She is."

"She's Jacques Lambert's daughter, isn't she?"

"Yeah." He shrugged, then winced. "Not that that means anything."

"No? That wasn't part of the problems you were having?"

"No. God no. The problem we were having was Cody Burrell."

After a silent beat, she said, "Ooooh. I'd forgotten about that."

"Well, she hasn't." He grimaced. "It really fucked her up."

"Logan."

"Sorry, Mom. I mean, messed her up."

"Well. I guess I can understand that."

"He's gone."

"From the team?"

"Yup. He won't play for us again. You don't even know the shit...er stuff that happened recently." He told her about being made captain and the fight and now the injury. "But I'm still gonna be captain," he finished with pride. "Once I'm back on the ice."

"Oh, Logan! That's fantastic! Your dad will be thrilled! He's gone to work for a while, but I'll get him to call you."

"Okay, thanks, Mom."

"Well, just get your shoulder healed and it sounds like things will be looking up."

"I hope so. Are you going to Chicago?"

"No." He sensed the disappointment in her voice. "Jase said not to come. Brianne's being pretty protective of the baby, so I wouldn't get to see her much anyway."

"Is he getting the paternity test done?"

"It's done. He's supposed to call us as soon as he knows."

Logan nodded. "Let me know too. I hope..." He didn't know what to hope. "I hope it works out for the best for everyone." If Jase really wanted to be a dad, then he hoped Emily turned out to be his. But it wasn't going to be easy.

When he was done with the call, he lay down on Nicole's bed for a while, the pain and the meds seeming to have sucked some of the energy out of him. He awoke to Nicole sitting beside him on the side of the bed in the dark bedroom, gently touching his face and smiling at him. God, she was beautiful. He turned his head to kiss her hand.

"Hi," she said. "How're you feeling?"

"Horny."

She laughed. "Shut up. You are not."

"Now that you're here, I am."

"I meant, how's your shoulder."

He sighed. "It hurts. But I'm okay. Could you get me a drink of water?"

She shot him an amused look and he smiled innocently.

"Okay."

When she returned with the glass of water, she handed it to him and flicked on the lamp beside the bed. He drank thirstily and set the glass beside the lamp. Then with his uninjured arm, he tugged her down to the bed on top of him. She kissed his mouth, long and slow and sweet. Emotion swelled in his chest, even as his cock swelled against her lower body. She wriggled a little and murmured against his lips, "I don't want to hurt you."

"Hurt me, baby. Please."

She chuckled and kissed him again. "I'm serious, Captain Heller."

"Okay then, how about this. This time you get to top."

"Oooh. I like that." She kissed his jaw.

"I'll let you know if anything hurts. Have at it."

"Okay." She trailed kisses over his cheek, then the side of his neck, nibbling a little with her soft lips, making him shiver. She unzipped the hoodie he was wearing because that was all he could get into, and kissed her way down his bare chest.

"Keep going." His right hand came up to palm the back of her head. "Lower."

"Ahem." She lifted her head and gave him a stern look. "I believe that is called topping from the bottom. You said I could be in charge."

He smiled. "Sorry."

"No, you're not." She resumed her exploration of his upper body. "This is nice. I like having you at my mercy." She nibbled on one nipple and sensation zapped to his dick.

"You've always had me at your mercy, babe. From the minute we met." He sifted his fingers through her silky hair and closed his eyes at the sensation of her soft hands and her hot little mouth.

"That's the nicest thing you've ever said to me." She nuzzled the waistband of his sweats, pushing it lower on his belly. His dick thickened even more

"It's true." He groaned softly as she rubbed her face over his groin, then kissed him through his sweatpants. His cock twitched and she opened her mouth over his thick length and set her teeth onto him, biting him through the heavy cotton so gently. His hips jerked and he got even harder. Heat washed down through his body, under his skin, pooling at his groin where he ached for more.

Her hands slid up to his chest, rubbed over his nipples and more sparks cascaded over his body as she continued to nibble on him through sweatpants. Then her fingers teased down over his abs, which tightened, and slipped under the waistband and tugged. She moved lower on the bed, between his thighs, pulling his pants down over his hip bones. Now his entire body tightened with anticipation, his injured shoulder forgotten as blood rushed to his cock, and then he was free, her breath brushing over him, his dick surging upward, aching for her touch. He spread his legs and bent his knees.

She kissed the tip of his cock, then shocked him a little by nudging his thighs even farther apart, pushing his knees back and lifting his shaft out of the way so she could lick his balls.

"Jesus Christ!" he gasped. "Oh yeah, baby, that's good."

"Mmm." She made little sounds of enjoyment as she sucked gently on him, taking one testicle into his mouth, releasing it with a pop, then the other. Sensation sizzled over his skin, every nerve ending on alert, tingles running up his spine to the top of his head, which might be about to blow off. She licked lower then nipped at his ass cheek, making him jump.

"Whoa, babe. You really like this being in control thing."

"It's kind of fun." She directed the head of his cock back to her mouth. The fingers of her other hand played with his balls and her fingernails scraped over his inner thighs. His entire body was a mass of twitching, jumping nerves, heat cascading over him. Her tongue swirled magic around him, her fingers drove him crazy, his hips lifting to her mouth. And then she took him in and sucked and every sensation coalesced at the place her mouth touched, so hot and wet and insanely beautiful.

"Nicole," he moaned, still touching her hair. "God, Nicole. I love you so damn much."

She bobbed her head up and down, her mouth sliding wetly, the friction so exquisite, and pressure built inside him.

"Stop," he begged hoarsely. "I'm gonna come any minute. I want to be inside you."

"Aw." She pulled off him with a sexy slurp. "I like it when you come in my mouth."

"I do too, Christ, do I ever, but right now, please, I want to make you come too." He reached for her arm and tugged on it. "I want to see your face."

She smiled at him as she moved off the bed and took off her clothes, the grey tweed pants and blue sweater she'd worn to work that day, then the black lace bra and thong panties. She worked his sweatpants down his legs and all the way off, tossing them aside, and then she climbed back on top of him, straddling him.

"God, you're gorgeous." He reached for her breast with his good hand, cursing the damn sling that kept him from touching both her gorgeous tits. Her softness filled his palm, her little nipple a hard point against his skin. He loved the lush fullness, the sensitive peak. Watching her center herself over him, he gently pinched her nipple. "You ready, babe?" There hadn't exactly been a lot of foreplay.

"I'm so ready." Her eyes went heavy-lidded as she lowered herself onto him. Hot. Wet. Tight. God. "I don't want to use a condom. Is that okay?"

"You sure?" He knew she was on birth control and they'd talked about their sexual health.

"Yes." Her eyes closed, the look of bliss on her beautiful face so gratifying.

"Then hell yeah, it's okay. Christ, Nic, you feel so good like that."

"Oh yeah, you too." She lowered herself even farther, her pussy clasping him, warm and wet. Further still, until she was all the way down, her body flush against his, and he looked down to where they were joined, his darker pubic hair a contrast to her golden curls, the tiny patch she kept there. Her strong, slender thighs bracketed his hips, her breasts flushed and pink, her teeth sunk into her bottom lip, and she leaned forward and set her hands on his chest.

"Open your eyes, baby."

Her long eyelashes fluttered and a smile teased the corners of her mouth. "There you go again. Bossing me around, topping from the bottom. Maybe I have to tie you up and gag you."

"No gags." He frowned at her. "Ever."

"You're no fun." She sighed and straightened, raising her arms to lift her hair off the back of her neck. This vision damn near undid him. His lungs seized at seeing her like that, a goddess above him, her breasts lifting, her stomach muscles tightening, her pussy rippling around him. His gaze moved to her face, her mouth full and soft, her eyes big and dark in the lamplight, shining with love and devotion, respect and gratitude. It humbled him, yet made him feel powerful, and those same emotions rose in him. She loved him, *him*, even though he'd told her about his deepest fears, his worries about not being good enough. She was the only person he really let see past the jokes and carefree attitude to who he was inside. She trusted him enough to be so vulnerable herself, physically vulnerable when he tied her up, emotionally vulnerable when she let herself care too. She made him feel like a god.

She moved on him, one achingly sweet sensation after another building inside him. Pleasure expanded through his chest, swelling hot and soft.

He reached for her hip and then she bent forward again to find his mouth with hers and they kissed, long, slow, luscious kisses as she moved herself up and down on him in a slow rhythm, breasts rubbing against his chest in a teasing erotic caress. Her tongue rubbed against his, then licked over his bottom lip. He gave it up, gave up everything he had to her, lost in mindless sensation as they rocked together, her hands moving over his body, over his chest, so gently over his shoulders, her fingertips stroking the sides of his neck. She bit his neck softly, then her tongue glided over his skin, sending sparks shooting through his veins. He found her ass with his hand, pulled her harder against him, gave her a tiny tap there. Her breath rushed warmly over his skin as she sighed in his ear.

He lifted his hips into her heat, held on to her with one hand as her body went tight. She pressed her face against his neck and her pussy rippled around him, her soft cries delighting him, and then his own pleasure peaked and he poured himself into her in long, shuddering pulses.

She lay atop him for long moments, their hearts thudding in tandem, bodies pulsing. "I love you," she whispered. "And I'm so, so sorry."

He gave her ass cheek a little squeeze. "Nicole."

She slowly, carefully, straightened her legs behind her and lifted her head to look at him. "It doesn't matter who knows about us." She met his eyes, hers full of remorse and love. "When you got hurt, I realized it didn't matter. I don't care who knows. And I don't care what they say about me. I just want you to be okay and…happy."

"I am happy. Well, I'm pissed about being injured. Fuck."

"I know. I'm so sorry this happened."

"This isn't your fault. It was just a stupid freak accident thing."

"But I'm still sorry. And I never meant to hurt you that day. I just…was stupid. When I realized that nobody else knew and that you'd come straight to me, I felt like shit, but there was Cody standing there, looking at us with that smirky smirk smile and I was just…scared."

"He can't hurt you, Nicole. Everyone knows what he's like. And he's gone."

"I heard that today." She searched his eyes with hers. "Did you really break his nose?"

He grimaced. "Yeah."

"You did that for me."

"Yeah."

"My hero." She smooched his lips.

"Not really. It was stupid."

"Yeah, it was."

"Hey. I thought I was your hero."

She smiled. "You shouldn't have gotten yourself in trouble and risked losing out on being captain because of him. He's not worth it."

"He's not worth it. But *you* are."

Her lower lip pouted and her eyes went shiny. "Aw." She blinked. "So are you. Last night when you were lying on the ice, I realized you're worth it too. God, I'm sorry something like that had to happen to make me wise up. I'm an idiot."

"You were kind of driving me crazy, but I was getting to you." He rubbed his stubbly face on her cheek. "Wasn't I?"

"Maybe." She giggled a little as he tickled her.

"I had the one man advantage."

"Huh?" She gave him a bemused smile.

"*I* know what you really want."

"Hmm. That is true. I guess that does give you a one man advantage." She tipped her head. "I think you had me that night you took me skating. You made me feel so good about myself. You always do. I never..."

"What?" He ran his hand over her head, down her hair.

"What you said about the bullying was true."

He blinked, then remembered telling her about what his mom had said. "Okay."

"I thought it wasn't the same because you said if I knew it wasn't true, it didn't matter. But I *did* know it was true."

"It wasn't true, Nicole. You've never been a puck bunny."

"I know. But it felt uncomfortably close to being true. But the thing is, I grew up around hockey and hockey players. It's not as if I just hung around rinks looking to get lucky with hockey players. In fact, most of the time, those hockey players never even saw me as a girl."

"That's hard to believe."

"It's true. I was a tomboy. I played hockey myself. I was friends with those guys. We had stuff in common. And then I dated a few hockey players who actually saw me as a girl. So what? That doesn't give anyone the right to insult me."

"That's what I was trying to tell you."

"I guess I've never had tons of self confidence." She bent her head. "Growing up with a superstar hockey player for a dad and a supermodel mother, then my brother following in my dad's footsteps…I was never going to be as good as any of them. So it was really hurtful for someone to insult me like that in front of the whole world."

"You kept your chin up and you kept going. And you don't have to be a superstar athlete or model to be as good as anyone else. You're amazing. The hockey club loves you, obviously. You do great things there."

"I was going to quit."

His jaw slackened. "What?"

She nodded. "I talked to Breck today. I told him about us. I told him I'm in love with you." She lifted her chin. "I told him I'd quit so there were no more brawls in the dressing room or embarrassing incidents. And he told me…that Cody was gone."

"Aw, Nicole."

"He told me they don't want me to quit." Her eyes shone. "I don't feel like I'm all that important to the team, but they want me to stay. I guess I do contribute in my own small way."

"That's what being part of a team is. Contributing in your own way. We players get all the attention, but everyone behind the scenes is important too, like Travis who sharpens our skates and looks after all our equipment, like everyone who works in the office. Like you."

She kissed him again, her eyes all shiny. "That's why they want you to be captain. They did the right thing trading for you."

"Yeah. You know, it's turned out pretty good." He grinned and stroked his hand down the curve of her bare back. "And more than just meeting you. I was in a rut in California. I loved it there, but it wasn't till I got here and felt some pressure that I really felt that drive to push myself, to make sure I did good."

"I was worried about how much pressure it was going to be on you, on one man. And look at you, captain of the team. Another one man advantage."

He grinned and pulled her mouth back down to his.

Thank you so much for reading One Man Advantage! Make sure you're on my mailing list for news about my next releases. If you enjoyed One Man Advantage, please consider leaving a review at the retailer of your choice or at Goodreads to help other readers find my books. You can also contact me at info@kellyjamieson.com to tell me what you thought of it or ask me any questions!

And enjoy this sneak peek at
Heller Brothers Hockey, Book 4,
Hat Trick

"I think she's afraid of me," Jase said when Remi returned moments later, Jasmine gone.

Remi laughed as he pulled her into his arms. She was so little and soft, but he loved how she felt next to him.

"What? I can be a scary dude."

"Well." She smoothed a hand over his shoulder. "You are pretty big." She looked up at him through her eyelashes, her pretty turquoise eyes all shiny and sexy. "But *I'm* not afraid of you."

"No." He pulled her a little closer. "You never have been, have you?" The first few times they'd had sex, he'd been the one who was afraid—afraid of hurting her because she was small and he was big and he liked sex the way he played hockey—hard, fast and physical. But they'd discovered she liked sex that way too.

"And Kyle is coming around too," Jason added, bending to kiss her cheek and nuzzle her ear. She shivered.

"I can't believe she did that," she said. "I'm so sorry, Jase. I can't believe she thought she could take advantage of your money. God!" She closed her eyes. "She's so spoiled! And I'm the one who did that to her."

"There you go blaming yourself again. Seriously, Rem. It's not all your fault. She's young and yeah, maybe she had life a little too easy sometimes, but not everyone ends up ungrateful like that. Kyle's not like that. I've seen how he appreciates what you've done. I think it's just part of her personality."

She nodded, eyes still closed, mouth clamped shut.

"You know I'd do anything for your family," he continued in a low voice. "If they really needed something. Anything. I don't want you to think I'm being a cheap prick." For a moment, the idea of paying for a trip to Puerto Vallarta for Jasmine and Ethan as their Christmas present had entered his head, but he knew that wasn't the right thing to do.

She choked on a laugh. "God, no. I know you would, Jase. Thank you for backing me up with her. That's worth more than anything. I love you so much."

"Love you too, baby." His hands slid around her ass and pulled her closer to kiss her again. Her fingers played in his short hair. He made a rough sound as pleasure trickled down his spine. "Wanna go out for dinner?" he asked.

"I'd like to cook something here in this beautiful new kitchen. Let's just stay in. But we need to put the rest of this stuff away."

He gave her a lingering kiss then released her. They each went to work on a box.

"We need to make a trip to IKEA for you," she said.

"Or you could move in and bring all your stuff back here."

She smiled and shook her head at his persistent efforts to get her to move in with him. He grinned. He knew it would happen someday.

"Think how much harder it would have been for me to say no to her moving in with me if I was living here," she said. "I couldn't use the 'not enough room' excuse."

"True."

Remi lifted a set of four wineglasses out of a box and set them on the counter. "Oh. I bought some wine. It's in the fridge. Could you open it? I'll start dinner. We have some chicken breasts, and I'll see what else." She moved to the refrigerator.

As he helped Remi make dinner, they talked about their upcoming trip to Winnipeg, the big family Christmas his mom had planned since all four sons were living so close to home now. Three of them played in the NHL—Tag right there in Winnipeg, Logan in Minneapolis, a short one-hour flight away, and Jase here in Chicago, not that much farther. His youngest brother Matt was a student on a hockey scholarship at the University of North Dakota, only a two-hour drive away from Winnipeg in Grand Forks. Their schedules had all worked out that they could get together for a few days, so it would be a short trip, but it had been quite a few Christmases since the whole Heller family had all been together.

After dinner, they watched a movie, Remi snuggled in against him on the couch in front of the big television he'd moved in. As often happened, she started dozing off on his chest while they watched the movie, and when it ended, Jase gave her a gentle nudge. "Bed, hon."

She made the soft little sleep noises he found so cute, and sat up blinking and pushing her silky blonde hair off her face. "Sorry," she mumbled.

"Come on. You're staying here tonight." He clicked off the TV and the lamp, then picked her up and carried her up the stairs. She was such a little thing, it wasn't hard. It was still funny to him that he'd fallen so hard for a girl who wasn't even close to his type, which used to be tall girls with bigger chests, but fallen he had. Hard.

His bedroom had been Remi's parents' room at one time, which had freaked him out a little, but it was the only room in the house big enough for his king-size bed. He'd had the room completely redone and it looked nothing like it had before.

"There you go, babe," he said, setting her on her feet on the rug beside the bed. He flicked on the lamp, then reached for her. His fingers went to the button of her jeans. Biting her lip, she lifted the hem of the turtleneck sweater she wore and pulled it up and over her head. His gaze lowered to her breasts. "Nice. My favorite bra."

He loved black lace and so now Remi had an extensive wardrobe of black lace lingerie. Only whereas she used to buy things from Victoria's Secret, Jase like to shop at Agent Provocateur and other expensive Chicago boutiques. This one was sheer black lace with a tiny scalloped-edge trim, cut scandalously low so it almost showed her nipples. She used to wear maximum push-up styles, but he liked things sheer. When she'd complained about her less-than-generous cleavage, he'd told her he loved her cleavage, and he didn't want to feel padding, he wanted to feel *her*.

He picked her up and sat her on the side of the big bed, kneeling before her to work the skinny jeans off her legs. Then he smiled as she sat there in sheer bra and thong panties—and thick black socks. He gently lifted each foot and tugged the socks off too. She leaned back on her elbows on the bed, pushing out her sweet little tits in the sheer bra.

"Fuck, that's hot."

Her tongue swept over her bottom lip and he let out a groan. He rose up over her and bent forward to press kisses between her breasts. Her eyes closed and her head fell back as his tongue traced the scalloped edge of the lace bra. Then he licked her nipple through the sheer fabric. Her body twitched.

He kissed his way down her body, over her belly, to the sheer black triangle at the apex of her thighs. He pressed a kiss there too, then set his big hands on her thighs and pushed them gently apart. He stroked his hands up and down her thighs, and she quivered as he nuzzled her pussy through filmy fabric. He breathed in her scent, delicate and feminine and aroused. Christ, it almost made him feel drunk, filling his head.

"Mmm. So sweet," he murmured. "Just wanna feast on you, baby."

"Jase."

He kissed her thighs, his eyes drifting closed, rubbed his cheek against her leg, kissed all the way down to her knee. Lifting her leg, he licked behind her knee where he knew she was so sensitive. Her sharply indrawn breath was his reward and he smiled against her soft skin.

She gave up trying to watch and collapsed flat on the bed. He kissed the inside of one knee, then the other, taking his time licking and kissing his way back to the center of her.

"You smell so good," he murmured, again nuzzling her panties. "You must be wet."

She moaned.

He tugged the panties off and she pushed her feet into the edge of the mattress to lift her hips. She dragged her eyes open and lifted her chin to look at him. "Take your clothes off too."

He smiled. "Not yet."

Bending again, he set his hands on her thighs and held her legs as his mouth descended to her core. He pressed soft kisses to her folds, gentle suckling kisses, up and down, moving to her inner thighs and then even lower as he pushed her legs higher and nipped at her butt cheeks. She lifted her hips against his mouth. "Jase, oh god."

His tongue came out and licked then, teasing over her skin, then dipping deeper, parting her folds, seeking out the center where she was hot and liquid. The delicate spice taste of her arousal slid over his tongue. "Mmm. Taste so good, Remi. Wanna lick you all over."

"God, you're good at this," she moaned. Warmth expanded inside him, knowing he was giving her pleasure.

He licked all over her pussy, his face pressed there between her legs, and then his tongue circled her clit. She made a soft sound of need, her hands fisted in the bedspread. Pressure and need built inside him, but he kept teasing her. When he finally licked over her clit, her whole body jolted.

"There," he murmured. "Like that?"

"You know I do," she panted, pulsing against his mouth, her hips lifting involuntarily.

"I like it too." And then he drew back and touched her, his big fingertips sliding over her. "Wanna play with this pretty pussy all night." Once more she tried to lift her head to look. He met her eyes then dropped his gaze to focus on her sex, and slid a finger inside her. Her pussy flexed and clenched around it. "Touching you like this. Tasting you like this." And he swept his tongue over her swollen clit, making her entire body tremble again.

He made another sound of appreciation low in his throat and again closed his eyes.

"Jase," she gasped."I'm going to come."

"Good."

"Want you inside me. Stop. Stop." She reached for his head.

He lifted his head and smiled at her, then wiped a hand across his wet mouth. "Okay, babe." In seconds, he had his fly undone, his jeans shoved down and his cock out, and she stared in fascination. Her lips parted hungrily.

"Oh babe, when you look at me like that I want your lips around my cock." His cock was on fire, heat rushing through his body.

She dragged her tongue over bottom lip and Jase groaned. He stripped his long-sleeved tee over his head and tossed it to the floor.

"Now," he growled. He picked her up and hauled her farther onto the bed, still sideways, then came down over her. He spread his knees wider, nudging her thighs apart, fisted his cock and slid the head up and down her pussy. "Oh yeah. So wet, Rem." He pushed into her, stretching her, and her body arched to take him deep. When he was in, all the way in, their bodies joined so intimately, he paused. He held himself there, deep inside her, pulsing. He looked down at her and their eyes met.

A moment passed, a long, lovely moment of sweetness and love. Hot sensation swelled in his chest. She stretched out her arms and reached for him, and he bent over her to claim her mouth with his. He released his hold on her legs and she wrapped them around him as they kissed, and held onto his shoulders.

Her body tightened, pulsating around him. "Jase. Please. So close..." Her body strained against his, and still he didn't move, so close himself. His balls grew tight at the base of his cock, pressed against her softness, pressure building inside him, his blood pumping through his veins. The muscles of his shoulders and arms bunched.

He touched her face, kissed her mouth, her cheek, her ear. And then he pulled out slowly, in an exquisite and excruciating drag of wet flesh, and pushed back in just as slowly. She gave a soft wail and he captured her mouth again, and this time when he slid out and pushed back in, it was harder, then harder still, faster. He felt her orgasm, her pussy rippling around him and she clung to him as he drove into her, finding his own release. A bolt of electricity seared up his spine, making his head buzz, then sizzled back down to his balls and out of his dick in hard spasms. He gave a long, low growl and went still, his body taut.

"Fuck," he muttered against her ear. "Fuck, that's good."

"Mmm."

They didn't move for long moments, both of them panting, hearts thudding against each other. "God I love you, Remi. Love you so much."

In the morning, Jase got up and left for practice early and Remi slept in. She finally climbed out of bed feeling deliciously well-rested and went down to the kitchen. Wintry sunshine filled the room and she again smiled and sighed over how beautiful it was.

Which reminded her of the scene with Jasmine yesterday. Her smile disappeared as she made herself coffee. Hopefully Jasmine had gone home and had an adult conversation with Ethan. Remi'd never been fond of Ethan, always feeling like he'd used Jasmine's immaturity and insecurities as a way to control her, which had often hurt her, but attempts to talk to Jasmine about that had not gone over well.

The back door opened and Jase stepped into the kitchen from the mud room, his hair still damp, his face still flushed with the workout he'd just had. His smile beamed at her when he saw her. "Hey, baby."

"Hi."

She moved across the kitchen to hug him. His cheeks were cold and so were his hands when he deliberately slipped them under her sweater, making her squeal. He laughed and kissed her mouth.

"How was practice?"

"Good. Mmm. Coffee." He moved toward the coffeemaker on the counter.

He'd been awesome yesterday with Jasmine. He was always awesome.

He'd make a good dad.

Oh yeah—he *was* a dad. Of a baby with another woman. A heavy sigh escaped her.

"What's wrong?" he asked, looking up from the mug he'd just filled with coffee.

Sometimes she managed to forget about that, but when memory returned it was always accompanied by a sick feeling and a dip in her mood. She hated to bring it up.

"You should get the DNA test results soon. Maybe even today."

His eyes shadowed and his lips tightened. "Yeah."

He hadn't even wanted to do the paternity test. Thank god his family had pressured him into it. She'd so wanted him to get the test done, but hadn't wanted to push. It would be easy to come across as jealous and insecure. Oh wait...she *was* jealous and insecure. But she was working really hard at not being that girl.

She and Jase had started seeing each other soon after his breakup with Brianne, his ex-girlfriend, fallen in love, and their world had seemed pretty perfect until Brianne dropped the bomb about the pregnancy a couple of months later. She'd insisted he was the father, and it was possible, given the timing.

But it had almost ended things between them. It hurt like hell to think of him having a baby with another woman, and especially when all her life she'd wanted to be a mother. She loved kids, hence the teaching career. And Jase had struggled too with the idea of burdening her with another woman's child in their lives. But they were getting through it, knowing things wouldn't be easy.

There'd always been that doubt in Remi's mind, though—the possibility that Jase wasn't the father. At first, he hadn't even believed Brianne was pregnant. He'd thought she was just trying to get back together. But now there was a little baby girl named Emily, who Brianne was being pretty protective of, despite Jase's determination to do the right thing and be a good father to his child. He was so determined to do the right thing he hadn't even wanted to have the paternity test done.

"It'll be okay," she said to him with a determinedly reassuring smile. "Whatever happens. Right?"

He nodded and held her gaze reassuringly. "Right."

It wouldn't be easy to have Brianne in their lives, and there was no way to avoid that if Jase wanted his daughter in his life. In the months since they'd found out about the pregnancy, they'd come to accept that that was how their life would be.

And that was one reason she loved him so much. How could she love a man who would renege on fatherhood or try to deny his responsibility? Jase, a big kid who liked to have fun and played a game for a living, had grown up fast. Or maybe the truth was, he'd always had that solid, responsible core beneath the fun-loving exterior.

"I guess we need to get rid of all these boxes," she said, looking around the kitchen. "And we should hit the grocery store and pick up a few things this afternoon."

"Okay."

A few hours later they were back in the kitchen, putting away the groceries they'd bought when the doorbell rang. They looked at each other.

Jase shrugged and straightened. "I'll get it."

He returned a moment later holding an envelope. When she saw his face, her abdomen tightened.

"I had to sign for it," he said.

"Is it the results of the DNA test?"

"Yeah."

She moved toward him, skirting an empty box still sitting on the floor. "Do you want me to open it?"

"No. I'll do it." He ripped it open and pulled it out. She watched his face. His lips parted as his eyes scanned the paper. Again. And again.

Her heart thudded and she dragged damp palms over her jeans.

OTHER BOOKS BY KELLY JAMIESON

Heller Brothers Hockey
Breakaway
Faceoff
One Man Advantage
Hat Trick
Offside

Love Me
Friends With Benefits
Love Me More
2 Hot 2 Handle
Lost and Found
One Wicked Night
Sweet Deal
Hot Ride
Crazy Ever After
All I Want for Christmas
Sexpresso Night
Irish Sex Fairy
Conference Call
Rigger
You Really Got Me
How Sweet It Is

Power Series
Power Struggle
Taming Tara
Power Shift

Rule of Three Series
Rule of Three
Rhythm of Three
Reward of Three

San Amaro Singles
With Strings Attached
How to Love
Slammed

Windy City Kink
Sweet Obsession
All Messed Up
Playing Dirty

Three of Hearts

Loving Maddie from A to Z

ABOUT THE AUTHOR

Kelly Jamieson is a best-selling author of over thirty romance novels and novellas. Her writing has been described as "emotionally complex", "sweet and satisfying" and "blisteringly sexy". She likes coffee (black), wine (mostly white), shoes (high heels) and hockey!

Subscribe to her newsletter for updates about her new books and what's coming up, follow her on Twitter **@KellyJamieson** or on Facebook, visit her website at **www.kellyjamieson.com** or contact her at **info@kellyjamieson.com**